D1323174

WOMEN OF THE UNITED FEDERATION MARINES

CORPSMAN

Colonel Jonathan P. Brazee
USMCR (Ret)

Copyright © 2016 Jonathan Brazee

Semper Fi Press

A Semper Fi Press Book

Copyright © 2016 Jonathan Brazee

Illustration © 2016 Jessica TC Lee

ISBN-10: 1-945743-02-6
ISBN-13: 978-1-945743-02-3

Printed in the United States of America

All rights reserved. No part of this book may be used or reproduced by any means, graphic, electronic, or mechanical, including photocopying, recording, taping or by any information storage retrieval system without the written permission of the publisher except in the case of brief quotations embodied in critical articles and reviews.

This is a work of fiction. All of the characters, names, incidents, organizations, and dialogue in this novel are either the products of the author's imagination or are used fictitiously.

Acknowledgements:
I want to thank all those who took the time to pre-read this book, catching my mistakes in both content and typing. I'd like to thank Miljana Milovanovic and Kathy Pen for their editing and proofreading. Any remaining typos and inaccuracies are solely my fault. Another shout-out goes to my cover artist, Jessica Tung Chi Lee. I love her work, and I think she nailed this cover as well. You can see more of her work at:

http://www.jessicatcl.com/news.html.

Original Art by Jessica TC Lee

Cover Layout by Steven Novak

Dedicated to all Navy corpsman who have served with the Marines, and all corpsmen, medics, hospitallers, and stretcher-bearers, who have cared for their fellow soldiers, sailors, airmen, and Marines throughout history, from the Order of Nights of the Hospital of Saint John of Jerusalem to the present. You risked your lives to save your bothers in arms and have earned the exalted title of "Doc."

CFSS IMPERIAL STABIAE

Hospitalman Apprentice Liege Neves tried to hug the bulkhead of the small corridor leading into the grand concourse. The report of automatic weapons sounded from just ahead of her. She gripped her M99, her palms sweating, making the stock of her weapon slippery.

"Stick on my ass, Neves," Sergeant Vinter snarled at her.

We're going up there? Liege thought, wondering how they'd make it through the heavy firing unscathed.

This was a far cry from the basic fire and maneuver she'd been taught at FMTC.[1] There, they'd had wide open spaces with plenty of room to hit the deck and find something to get behind. Here on the Confederation of Free States cruise ship, there was nowhere to take cover. She could see kinetic rounds—large kinetic rounds—ricocheting off the bulkhead of the grand concourse, not three meters to her front.

Already, Second Fire Team, led by Corporal Wheng, was out in the concourse, exposed. Liege could follow the fight on her comms, but it was all too much to take in, and she was simply focusing on her squad leader.

This was not what Liege envisioned nine months ago when she enlisted. She was supposed to be in a hospital somewhere, learning her craft while working normal hours in a safe environment. She'd never planned on being with the Marines while they took back a cruise ship from pirates. Heck, she'd thought that space pirates were just Hollybolly fantasies. She'd never dreamed they existed in real life.

---

[1] Field Medical Training Course

But they did, and what was supposed to be a simple show-the-flag deployment for Sirie 3's Freedom Days celebration had switched to a live mission. Pirates had taken over the cruise ship, and as the *FS Mount Kester*, with the embarked Golf Company, was the closest military force, the ship and Marines had been diverted and given the snap mission.

The *Mount Kester* had demanded that the pirates surrender, of course, but as expected, the pirates had just laughed in response. They knew the penalty for piracy. The Confederation might not have capital punishment, but the Federation did, and the ship was taken in Federation space. Since they wouldn't surrender, and with civilian lives at stake (and with Bacchus Lines wanting to recover their boutique cruise ship without damage), it was up to Golf Company to board and root out the pirates.

So HA Neves found herself flat on the deck of a billion-credit luxury cruise ship while 20 or so pirates tried to take as many Marines with them to hell as they could. The thought that they might blow the ship in suicidal defiance was heavy on her mind as well.

"Corporal Wheng, on three, give us cover," Sergeant Vinter passed on the squad circuit. "First and Third, you're up. We need get to the lounge."

Liege focused on her small helmet display. She could see the ship's diagram, but it didn't make too much sense to her. She stopped trying to interpret it. She'd just follow the sergeant and leave it at that.

"Get ready, Neves," she said over her shoulder, then back on the circuit, "One. . .two. . .three!"

A sudden increase of fire from out in the concourse provided them cover as the other two fire teams rushed out, followed by Sergeant Vinter and Liege. Liege's mind was almost numb as she burst out of the side corridor and followed the sergeant to the left. Sparks glanced off the bulkhead less than a meter to her right. At least one of the pirates had not been forced to take cover from Second Team's volume of fire.

Liege's logic told her she should stop and get out of the line of fire, but her body didn't cooperate. Almost on autopilot, she followed the sergeant. First Team peeled off into a small alcove where a red plush velvet couch that reeked of luxury took up most of the space.

Why the hell am I noticing the furniture? she wondered.

She felt displaced, almost as if she was floating above her body and simply a spectator to the fight.

Third Team and Sergeant Vinter charged forward, firing their own weapons. Liege hadn't fired her M99 yet. It barely registered with her that she had it, but she also knew that if she fired now, she'd probably hit the sergeant.

"Fuck!" someone shouted as a Marine from Third stumbled.

Liege's heart leapt in her throat, but the Marine kept going, and there wasn't a call for a corpsman. The EVA suits they were wearing didn't have nearly the protection of the skins and bones they normally wore into combat. But unlike the skins, the EVA suits kept them alive in the vacuum of space, and if the pirates blew the ship, those not caught in the blast should be fine. It seemed a fair trade-off.

Of course, unless they had access to emergency hoods, the passengers wouldn't fare as well if the ship was breached.

Sergeant Vinter dodged to her right, and for a moment, Liege was alone in the charge, facing whatever pirates were before her. She posted her left leg forward and bolted to the right as well, diving for cover behind another large sofa. An instant later, rounds tore into the top of the couch, bits of fluff flying off it to flurry down around her like red snowflakes.

She'd landed on Vinter's legs, and the sergeant kicked her off to rise and fire out a string of darts. Liege could see the sergeant's mouth working, but as nothing was coming over the squad circuit, Liege knew she must be on the line with the lieutenant.

A vibration shook the deck under her as a low rumble reached them. For a moment, Liege thought the pirates had blown the ship. But as her suit sensors indicated a normal atmosphere, she realized she was just too wound up. Whatever had caused the vibration had probably been instigated by the Marines.

Liege knew that there wasn't a snowball's chance in hell that 20 pirates could stand up to a Marine rifle company, but that was the big picture. In her little universe, an unknown number of pirates were facing her squad of 13 Marines and one very raw, very nervous Navy corpsman.

Liege had been merely along for the ride up to now. She knew she had to do something. Looking down, she clicked her M99's selector off safe. Liege rolled off her back, and taking a deep breath, rose above the top of the couch and fired a wild volley in the general direction of the barricaded pirates. She doubted that she'd hit anyone, but at least she had contributed.

And she felt good about it. Some of her nervousness fled as she had pulled the trigger and felt the slight recoil of her rifle. She ducked back down out of the direct line of fire.

"Listen up. We've got help coming, but we need to fix the pirates in place. Keep up a steady stream of fire, but no heroics! Don't needlessly expose yourself!" Sergeant Vinter passed on the squad circuit.

Almost instantly after the sergeant finished, someone shouted out in pain. The EVA suits' displays were not nearly as sophisticated as the normal battle AIs, but the avatars of each Marine were the same. One of the bright blue avatars switched to the light blue of a wounded Marine. Lance Corporal Seth Hanoshi had been hit. It took a moment for Liege to figure out from her helmet display just where Seth was; he was not more than two meters from where she was lying.

Liege peered around the corner of the couch; Seth was writhing on the deck out in the corridor, exposed. He was clutching his left thigh, and from under his gauntleted hands, bright blood ran out in little rivulets along the polyweave of his suit. Liege expected to see his body stitched with more rounds being fired by the pirates.

She was moving before she knew what she was doing.

"Cover her!" Sergeant Vinter shouted over the net.

She scrambled on her hands and knees in the bulky EVA suit, reaching out to grab the ankle of Seth's outstretched wounded leg. She tried to pull him back, but her knees flailed and slipped on the slick deck. Expecting to be hit at any moment, she swung her legs around, and sitting on her butt, she placed the grip-sole bottoms of her feet on either side of Seth's leg. Pushing out, the traction of the grip-soles allowed her to inchworm back on her butt, pulling a screaming Seth with her.

With three pulls, she was behind the edge of the couch. Two more, and Seth was under cover as well.

Liege looked up at Sergeant Vinter for orders, but the sergeant was on the command circuit again, fighting the battle.

Seth was rolling back and forth in pain.

"Help me, Neves!"

There was blood, a lot of it. Too much. Liege could see that a round had taken out seven or eight centimeters of Seth's thigh, and the femoral artery had been severed. He could bleed out in a minute or less.

Liege felt nausea starting to take ahold of her, and she had to fight it back down. She had to act.

She'd done this before, just not with a real person. If she failed with Sick Sam, the nickname for the medical simulacrum at FTMC, it was merely a down-check, and she'd have another chance. If she failed here, Seth would die.

Just like with Sick Sam, she tried to convince herself. *No different.*

Liege slung her medpack around so she could access it. Pulling out the first pressure patch, a Number 2, she held it up to the damage on Seth's thigh before dropping it and pulling out a Number 4. She started to open it before realizing she had to clear the site. Unsealing the tool pocket, Liege grabbed the scissors and cut away the fabric of Seth's EVA. She blanched; the mangled flesh was more vivid than she expected. Unsealing the pressure patch, Liege positioned it over the damage, then pressed it home.

The patch molded itself to the open wound, and Seth screamed out in pain. Liege almost jumped back in panic. Sick Sam was programmed to react and even talk with the corpsmen-in-training, but he'd never screamed like that when pressure pack was applied.

The pressure patch was only a temporary measure, a field expedient version of an old-fashioned tourniquet. Liege was not done. Next came the nano-injection. Using the scissors, she cut open the fabric over the thigh on his right leg and slammed home the Series 2 injector.   Immediately, a cocktail of drugs and nanobots—mostly consisting of coagulatory, infection-fighting, and construction bots—would be starting to course through his body, rushing to close the major arterial damage while building and re-routing bypasses to get blood to Seth's lower leg. Liege could take the leg off if she needed to, sealing off the stump before putting Seth into stasis, but that would increase regen time.   Even ten years before, that would have been her standard of care. But with the latest research on BRC,[2] the Brick, regen was now avoided when it could be. Seth had suffered significant trauma, so he was probably in for a good long stint in regen, but that would be up to the medical officers. Liege was simply there to keep Seth alive until then.

She took an injector of Hemocaps and applied the needle into his carotid. The injector wouldn't make up for the volume of blood loss, but the artificial red blood cells, far more efficient at transporting oxygen than the real thing, would be a tremendous help in stabilizing the lance corporal.

"Do you need pain meds?" she asked Seth.

"Fuck yeah, Neves!"

She gave his vitals a quick read. He was shocky and in pain, but tolerating his condition quite well, given the circumstances. Still, he had lost quite a bit of blood. Considering that, she decided on the morphanimine.   It was not the most effective pain suppressant, but blood loss contraindicated more effective meds.

Rounds hit the couch again, sending another flurry of red flakes down on the two of them. She casually brushed them off Seth's exposed right thigh and gave him the injection.   Within seconds, Seth started to relax.

"How is he, Neves?" Sergeant Vinter asked on the P2P.

"He'll be fine. I don't think we need to ziplock him."

"OK, keep me informed."

Ziplocking a Marine was done when he or she was killed and there was hope for a resurrection, or when the Marines was still alive, but the damage was life-threatening. Stasis would give the Marine a much better chance of pulling through.   But a small

---

[2] BRC: Boosted Regeneration Cancer, known as the "Brick." Twenty percent of those who have undergone regen eventually develop the cancer.

percentage of patients put into stasis never came out, so it was avoided if not necessary. And after reading Seth's vitals, she thought he didn't need it.

"Are my balls OK?" Seth asked, his voice blurry from the meds, as he reached out and grabbed her hand.

"They're fine."

"No, check. I gotta make sure," he said, pulling her hand harder.

The round had hit a good 12 centimeters below his crotch, but Liege complied. The pressure patch was beginning to loosen, a sign that the nanobots were doing their job. Liege lifted up the cut edges of Seth's EVA suit, and looked at his testicles. They were covered in blood, but after a quick check, she could see they were untouched.

"No problem, Seth. Not even scratched," she said.

Seth's hand slacked as he mumbled, "Oh, thank Saint Elsie."

He started to drift off when an explosion erupted from the direction of the pirates. Liege lunged for her M99 and turned to face what she was sure would be a charge. A flurry of fire sounded, both from the pirates' kinetics and the more whisper-like Marine M99s.

"Cease fire," Sergeant Vinter passed to the squad.

The fight down the corridor continued for another ten or fifteen seconds before petering out.

"First Team, move forward. We've got friendlies there," the squad leader passed.

The team moved forward and clambered over the makeshift barricade, followed by the rest of the squad. Six Marines from Third Platoon were checking the bodies of four pirates. A hatch was hanging askew on one hinge. The Third Platoon Marines had obviously used it for egress, coming into the corridor behind the pirates and their barricade.

Liege took over. Two of the pirates were permanent KIAs, their heads destroyed. One KIA needed to be evaluated for a possible resurrection. Liege wasn't sure why as the penalty for piracy was death, but that wasn't up to her.

The final pirate was WIA. He was seriously gut-shot, and Liege didn't give him much hope. She started to move forward to examine him when Sergeant Vinter grabbed her arm. Liege was about to tell her that her duties required her to treat the pirate just as if he was a Marine, but that wasn't what the sergeant wanted. She took Liege's M99, much to the corpsman's chagrin. Liege knew better than to put a weapon within reach of an enemy.

The pirate said nothing, but he glared at Liege when she pulled his hand off his belly. It looked like he'd taken multiple darts that had simply torn him apart. There was nothing much Liege could do. She didn't even bother giving him a shot of nanobots—they wouldn't work in stasis.

The all-clear sounded. The ship had been re-taken.

Liege still had work to do, however. One of the Marines tagged the prisoner with his capture information while she pulled out a ziplock. With assistance, Liege got it around the pirate, and with him still glaring at her, she initiated stasis. Within moments, he was out.

"You need to report to Chief Sou," Sergeant Vinter told her. "He needs all corpsmen to the ship's atrium to take care of the passengers."

"What about Seth?" she asked.

"We'll get him back to *Mount Kester*," the sergeant said.

Liege could see the location of the atrium on her helmet display. She nodded, then stood up to go.

"Not alone," Sergeant Vinter said, grabbing her arm and stopping her. "We think the ship is secured, but there could be holdouts.

"Corporal Wheng, take your team and escort Doc to the atrium. Wait there until she's done."

Liege looked back for Corporal Wheng when what Sergeant Vinter had just said hit her.

Doc? Not just Neves?

She felt a rush of pride as she realized she'd been accepted by the Marines. No more "Neves," no more "HA." She was "Doc."

Book 1

Jonathan P. Brazee

NOVA ESPERANÇA

Chapter 1

Nine months earlier...

"Not even in your dreams, *palito*," Liege Neves said as she stepped around the outstretched hand of the beggar.

Normally, the destitute left gangrats alone, but here at the crowded Falebella Center, the emaciated young man with the yellow eyes of a dopa addict must have thought he would be immune to retribution.

He's right, though, Liege thought. *Smart guy for a d-head.*

That didn't mean she was going to swipe him a few credits, but she had to admire his audacity.

She almost skipped up the broad steps leading up to the planet's Federation administrative center. Her heart was pounding in her chest, but she wasn't sure why. She doubted that any of her *irmãs* were around to see her; the *Commando Meninas'* territory was broad, but they normally left the District alone.

More than a few of the oh-so-proper suits walking about their business in the plaza eyed her, disapproval turning down the corners of their mouths, but Liege let it slide off her back. She'd long ago built up an immunity to the disdain of positioned society— not that she had much contact with them. Except for the do-gooders who built their small oases in the *favelas*, suits stayed in suitland and left the favelas to the gangrats, the addicts, and the impoverished who tried to eke out a living.

Liege angled off to the Munchen Building where most of the second-tier Federation offices were located. There was a queue at security, and she joined it at the rear, patiently awaiting her turn.

Most of the people in front of her were suits, but there were a few drudges sprinkled among them. No other gangrats; not that Liege expected any. Screening was fairly quick—until Liege was up. She dumped her PA in the tray, then as the screening uniform looked with frank distaste, she pulled her cheek-stick out, brandishing the 12-centimeter chromalloy spike with a flourish before adding it to the tray.

"Female search!" he called out. "Ma'am, please step through the scanner, then stand on the yellow platform."

I bet it kills him to call me "ma'am, Liege thought, trying to keep back the smile that threatened to blossom over her face.

Liege stepped through the scanner and dutifully stood on the yellow circle to which a female uniform was pointing. She raised her arms as ordered, then stood stoically while getting patted down.

"Thank you, ma'am," the uniform said, pointing back to where her tray waited.

Her PA was there, but the cheek-stick was missing. Another uniform handed her a plastic disc on which was printed the number "202."

"You can pick your. . .the spike thing when you leave," he said.

Liege didn't argue. The cheek-stick was in fact more than a fashion statement. It could be an effective weapon in the right hands, and they were somewhat of a trademark of the *Commando Meninas,* the most powerful female gang on the planet.

She looked up at the directory to get her bearings. Room 1015 was off to her right, so trying to look as if she weren't out of place, she strode off with far more confidence than she suddenly felt. It had seemed like such a good idea when she'd discussed it with Leticia, but now, as she walked down the granite-clad hallway, she was having second thoughts. What was she, a daughter of the favelas, a gangrat, doing here? What kind of reception did she expect?

When she'd made her appointment, it had seemed so easy. She hand't had to give her real name, so there was no screening. She was merely taking advantage of the rights of every citizen. But getting an appointment was not the same as getting accepted. She took a quick glance at her colors.

Maybe I should have listened to Leticia, she thought. *I could have brought something more, well, drudge to change into. Too late now, I guess.*

She stepped in front of the glass doors to Room 1015, took a deep breath, and then pushed the doors open and strode in as if she belonged. Avó always told her to act like she owned the world. The thought of her grandfather made her pause, and she had to quickly brush away the small tear that had started to flow from the corner of her right eye.

One of the uniforms, a Marine, she thought he must have been, was walking by, and he asked, "May I help you?"

"I'm 34377," she said, having memorized her registration number. "I'm here for my 10:30 appointment."

Liege thought she saw the tiniest bit of relief in his eyes as he said, "OK, you're not mine. Navy or FCDC?"

"Navy."

"Down the passage, first door on your right," he said, pointing past the reception kiosk and down the hallway.

Liege thanked him and followed his instructions to the designated door. "Navy Recruiting" was written on the clear material of the door, so she knew it was the right place.

She waved the sensor to open it, and entered what looked to be an anteroom. Three men and two women were sitting on hard plastic seats. All looked up eagerly when she entered, but when they saw she wasn't a uniform, they went back to their conversations. One of the men, though, lingered his eyes on the long expanse of thigh visible between her knee-highs and the bottom edge of her mini. Somehow that calmed her churning emotions. They might be drudges or even suits, and they certainly considered themselves several rungs higher than gangrats, but human nature was human nature. She knew how to handle hormone-filled young men, and the fact that his eyes lingered helped her realize that they were all the same. Some might have been born with greater advantages, but people were just people when all was said and done.

"You here for an interview?" one of the women asked her.

No, I'm here to run the floor vac.

"Yes, I've got a 10:30 appointment."

"Hah! Be prepared to wait. Mine's at 9:30."

Liege checked the time: 10:15. She sighed and settled in for a long wait.

Liege sat in silence for five minutes before the girl with the 9:30 appointment tentatively leaned over and said, "I love your mini. It's preme. Where'd you get it? Ferrone's?"

Ferrone's? Liege thought. *Yeah, like I'm going to that hiso boutique.*

She looked at the young woman, who was still eagerly awaiting her answer. Liege knew that if she shopped at Ferrone's, the woman was definitely a suit. She knew the type—rich suits who wanted to appear uber-copacetic by accepting all classes as equals. Maybe the girl was serious or maybe she was just trying to project an image.

Liege was tempted to tell her to get spiked, but she figured they might be under surveillance, so she said, "No, at Jaya's," instead.

"Oh, Jayas? I've heard of that. It's pretty exclusive, huh?"

Jaya was Bird's aunt, and she made clothes for their sept. This suit had never heard of Jaya, so that was utter BS. But Liege guessed as there were only eight girls in the sept, it was pretty exclusive.

"Yes," she said, concentrating to avoid her gangrat patois, "it is exclusive at that."

"Oh really? You've got to get me an appointment. I'm Evangeline," she said, holding out a hand.

Liege was saved from having to shake it when Evangeline was called for her appointment.

"I'll talk with you after the interview," the girl said as she followed the uniform back into the inner offices.

Liege looked around at the others. None were paying her any attention, so she just settled back to wait.

Yes, it is exclusive at that, she repeated in her mind. *Does that sound too hiso?*

Liege could shift from the creole spoken in the favelas to the *Commando Meninas'* code-talk to proper Standard without a problem, but she knew if she went into her interview with a snooty super-hiso accent, that would scream fake, and that wouldn't stand her any good. She just needed to speak Standard like any drudge.

She was still silently practicing phrasing and tempo when another uniform opened the door and said, "34377, you're up."

He was looking at the only other girl in the reception area, and when Liege stood up, he seemed surprised. The uniform tried to keep a neutral expression on his face, but Liege caught the slight tightening around the eyes that was a true sign of his disdain.

Liege caught the reflection of herself on the plastiglass as she walked forward, hand out to shake. Her white broganboots were not elegant, but they were weapons when it got down to hand-to-hand. Her pink knee-highs reached to just above her knees, and well above that, her purple mini sparkled as the lights caught the embedded micro-crystals. The tight fitting purple and pink rib-top hugged her form, the vivid colors screaming for attention. With her cheek-spike gone, the next, and perhaps most obvious banner of her existence as a gangrat was the half-brush. The right side of her scalp was depilated close, the skin painted with purple and pink lightening bolts. The hair on the left side of her head, died in fluorescent pink, stuck straight out.

I look cute, she thought, even knowing that her appearance labeled her as a gangrat.

She knew her sister had been right; she should have changed. But she was a gangrat, and she couldn't hide it. Maybe it was better to go in proud than to try and be something that she wasn't.

It wasn't as if the detritus of Federation didn't join the military or FCDC—especially the FCDC. But the Federation recruiters were selective, and someone like her had to convince them that he or she could adjust and leave that kind of lowso life behind.

"I'm Petty Officer Russell," the uniform said after Liege followed him into a small office. "And you are?"

"Liege Neves," she said, handing over her ID.

He did a quick scan and studied the results.

"OK, I see you've finished secondary. Good for that, at least," he said, more to himself than to her.

Liege wanted to stand up and throat punch the guy and his condescending attitude. Most favela kids finished secondary, even if their options after schooling were limited. But of course, the reputation of the favelas was that of a lawless anarchy.

He closed his PA, then asked, "So why do you want to join the Navy?"

"To serve the Federation, sir," she immediately replied.

That was a complete lie, of course. Deep in the favelas, there wasn't much loyalty to the Federation. It wasn't a hotbed of rebellion, either. It was just that it didn't impact most of them.

Liege was joining the Navy for one reason only. She had to get out of the favelas, and bring Leticia and her Avó with her. His brain was deteriorating by the day, and there was not much they could do about it with Universal Health. All the med-techs did was to sedate him as he sunk into oblivion. The only way he could get real care would be as her dependent and with her in the service.

That was her prime motive, but it wasn't the only one. Liege might look like a stalwart warrior for the *Commando Meninas*, but frankly, she was a gangrat for protection, only. Being a gangrat kept the hollow-heads and freaks away from their apartment, and it kept a brother gangrat from claiming her as chattel. But Liege wanted more in life; she might exhibit disdain for the drudges, but she'd love to elevate herself to that level. She'd love to visit the galaxy, to see how others lived. She was claustrophobic in the favelas, and she had to get out of them and experience life. Joining the Navy was an escape.

If all she wanted was health care for Avó, she could join the FCDC, the haven for people like her. But in the FCDC, she could easily be assigned to Nova Esperança, and even as a trooper, the *Commando Meninas* could reach out and touch her—or her family—

for forsaking the gang. No, if she was going to renounce her colors, she had to get off-planet, and that meant the Navy.

She gave pat answers to the uniform; just as his questions were obviously rote. Liege doubted that he had any hopes for her, but as a citizen, she was afforded this opportunity, and he had to play the game.

When he got to the end, he paused for a moment, then Liege thought that for the first time, she saw the real person when he said, "You know, Miss, I applaud you for volunteering, but you must know that your chances are pretty slim. I think you'd have a much better chance with the FCDC, and I could go talk with them. FCDC pay is the same as the Navy's, and so if you're looking for a, well, better life, you can really make a change for yourself."

She knew he was being earnest, but Liege felt a spark of anger.

He doesn't know shit about me, and he thinks I'm not good enough?

Liege didn't have a hair-trigger temper. She rarely got angry, but she felt the need to act out—which would be the worst thing she could do. She'd be refused enlistment on psychological grounds.

So she swallowed her pride and said, "Thank you, sir, but I really want to be in the Navy. So if you please, I'd like to proceed."

The uniform's eyes slightly darkened, and he gave a shrug.

"It's your choice, Miss Neves. Well, let's do your screening. This is the first test. You must reach our minimums to proceed with the process. Not reaching the minimum scores will result in a failure and stop the enlistment process. Should you fail, you may re-take the test after 30 days have elapsed, but no more than 180 days. After 180 days, your rejection will become permanent.

"So, do you have any questions?"

"No, sir."

Liege followed the uniform out of his tiny office and down past all the other equally tiny offices to a secured door.

"Please scan yourself," he said.

Liege leaned forward to get her right eye scanned. She didn't have a record, as far as she knew, but she still felt apprehensive as the red light momentarily flared in her eye. There were rumors that the government knew more about its citizens than it let on, and Liege was in a gang, after all. But there were no warning sirens, no FCDC police rushing to ziptie her hands behind her.

"Please state your name and citizen number," the pleasant voice of the security scanner asked.

"Liege Anna Neves, NE38559453," she stated.

"Confirmed. Good luck with your application," the voice said again.

Liege had to smile. Programming the scanner to wish applicants good luck was a nice touch.

Her uniform lifted a card to the lock, and with a whisper, the door opened. Directly inside, a middle-aged lady looked up.

"Who do you have, Terry?" she asked the uniform.

"Liege Anna Neves, NE38559453," he said. "Initial screening."

The woman looked at her display, tapped on the keyboard, then said, "OK, I've got her now. See you in two."

The uniform left, leaving Liege alone with the woman.

"My name is Darby Kim. I'll be your proctor for the exam. The exam itself is in four parts, each in 30-minute modules. If you finish any module before the allotted 30 minutes, you will not be able to proceed to the next one until the full 30 minutes have expired.

"You will be locked in one of the cubicles. If you have a problem, you can reach me by hitting the green button on the wall. I cannot answer any questions, but I can render a decision on technical glitches."

Liege knew the woman must have recited the rules thousands of time. Her tone had that repetitive sound to it.

"If you need to use the restroom, I will escort you to it, but I must warn you that you will not be allotted any more time. So if you think you're going to need it, I suggest you use it now."

Liege started to say no, she didn't need it, but she wondered if this was some sort of test as well, to see if she was the type to prepare herself. Even if it weren't some sort of convoluted test, it would be a pretty good idea, so she said she would.

As soon as Liege returned, the woman continued as if she had never been interrupted, "If there is an emergency, the right light will flash and you may leave the cubicle. Leaving for any other reason will terminate your test and count as a failure.

"If you have a PA, please leave it with me. We do have block-checks in the cubicles, so if you take a PA inside, it will be fried."

Liege quickly took her PA out of her side pocket and handed it over. The woman put it in simple open drawer with T-003 printed on it.

"The test itself is self-explanatory. So with that said, do you have any questions for me?"

"No, ma'am."

"OK, then, follow me, please."

The woman led Liege to the back of the room where doors to cubicles lined the wall. She stopped at one with T-003 printed over the door.

"This is your cubicle. Your test will begin one minute after I close the door."

She held one hand out, indicating that Liege should enter.

"Good luck, Miss Neves," she said as Liege brushed past her to enter her cubicle.

"Thank you," she said, looking up to catch the proctor's eye.

The woman had a smile on her face, and Liege realized that the woman had never given her the evil eye or the look of disdain that drudges and suits gave her kind. Either she was so inured to the thousands and thousands of applicants wanting government jobs who must have passed through her testing center or she really didn't care about Liege's background. Liege hoped it was the latter.

She took a seat in the small space as the door closed behind her. She took a deep breath as the display in front of her started counting down her minute. As it reached zero, the display switched to a new screen with the heading "Primary Skills Level Test."

Come on, Liege! Get it done!

****

Two hours later, the display died, and after another minute, the door whooshed open.

"You're all done, Miss Neves," the proctor said as she looked at some sort of readout screen.

Liege was drained. The four tests were much more difficult than she'd expected. She'd been a good student, but she also realized that the schools in the favelas did not have the same resources as those in suitland or even drudgeland. She'd been so confident that the testing would be a breeze; now, she was not so sure.

"Uh, can I ask how I did?"

"Petty Officer Russell will do that. I'm just a proctor here."

Liege knew she had to be looking at her scores, so if the proctor didn't want to tell her, they must be bad, she reasoned. If they were good, then Liege thought the woman would be more than happy to tell her that.

If she wasn't accepted, she didn't know what she and Leticia would do. Possibly the FCDC would still take a look at her, but as far as she knew, the test was the same as for all government jobs.

The third module, titled "Cognizant Awareness," had really kicked her butt. She didn't even know what the title meant. She knew each word, but used together like that almost seemed redundant, and even after finishing the module, she still didn't know just what was being tested.

The woman gave her a small follow-me, telling her to go to the waiting room where her uniform would pick her up. Liege thanked her and walked out of the testing center, past where she knew the recruiter offices were, and into a mid-sized waiting room. All the faces of the others in the room looked up as she came in. Liege recognized some of them from the first anteroom, and Evangeline brightened when she came in, waving her over. Liege was tempted to ignore her, but with her suspicious mind thinking the room might be under surveillance, she smiled and walked over to take a seat.

"Wow, that was hard," Evangeline said, taking Liege's hand as if they were sisters. "I mean, like, I guessed on half of the questions."

Liege frankly didn't care how the woman had done, but she did feel a slight bit of relief at her words. If Evangeline was having problems, then Liege wasn't alone in that.

Evangeline was a talker, and Liege tuned out 90% of what the woman was saying while she brooded over her scores. The wait was killing her. But bit by bit, Liege was being drawn into the conversation. Liege might consider drudges and suits almost as separate species, but she couldn't help it if she was a social creature by nature. She started listening to more of what Evangeline was saying, and before long, she was giving her own opinion. Nothing about which they spoke was serious, and that was probably a good thing. It kept their minds off the testing. When they started discussing a vid-novel that had been making the rounds on the under-net, two others, a guy and a girl, scooted over to join them. What Umuyaya was going to do about his lecherous uncle was front and center, and Liege laughingly had to agree with Pop, the guy who had joined them.

The fact that they all were following an under-net vid-novel surprised Liege. Of course in the favelas, the under-net was popular, but the other three came from much higher positions of society, and they had access to the best that life could offer. Liege wouldn't have imagined that any of them would follow a poorly-crafted trash under-net vid-novel.

She was almost sorry when Evangeline was picked up by her uniform. Liege gave her new friend a thumbs up and mouthed "Good luck" as she left.

With Evangeline gone, some of the energy had left as well, but Liege, Pop, and Gert stayed close together and chatted. Finally, Gert addressed the elephant in the room and asked her about being a gangrat, but Liege didn't sense any disdain, only curiosity. So for the first time in her life, she spoke frankly with people her age who were not from the favelas. Pop seemed almost fascinated by some of what she told them, particularly when she described her beating in.

Liege was not one of those gangrats who held her colors paramount and considered her beating in on an almost religious level. For her, it had been something to endure in order to gain the protection of the gang, simple as that. But as she told the two about

21

how she had fought ten of her future sisters and gotten the living shit kicked out of her, she could almost see how alien that must have seemed to them.

She could also see how Pop reacted. Liege had always been good at reading others, and she knew he was attracted to her and somehow turned on by her describing the beating in. Pop was a good-looking young man, in a pretty-boy sort of way, and Liege had to admit that she was more than a bit interested. But even if neither of them was accepted (she into the Navy and he into the Inspector Corps), she knew nothing would ever—could ever—happen. She couldn't go over to suitland and just wander around, and he would be easy prey should he set foot into the favelas; but still, the thought intrigued her.

Those thoughts were interrupted when her uniform stuck his head into the waiting room and asked, "Miss Neves, if you could follow me?"

Both Pop and Gert wished her good luck as she stood and went out the door that her uniform was holding. She waited for him to take the lead and followed his bouncy jaunt back into the recruiters' room and into his small private office.

He sat down, and Liege could see that he was feeling quite full of himself.

Is that because he's going to send me back to the favelas? He's an "I told you so" kind of guy?

He looked at her for a moment, the smile he was obviously trying to suppress forcing its way out.

"Miss Neves, have you ever considered being a navigator?" he asked, the smile making a full appearance.

"A navigator? Like on a ship?" she asked.

Despite wanting to join the Navy, Liege wasn't really up too much on what the Navy actually did. But she'd seen enough flicks and holos to know that the navigators were the bald freaks with the contraption bolted to the backs of their skulls and who controlled the ships in bubble space. In the flicks, they tended to be portrayed as aloof and rather weird.

"Of course on a ship. They're the most important people on the ship. Without them, the ship goes nowhere. If you become a navigator, you'll be promoted to E5 right out of Level Three School, and you'll be in line for warrant officer."

He continued on telling her what a great deal it would be for her when she started making sense out of what he was saying.

"So I did OK on the testing?" she interrupted.

"OK?" he asked, pausing to take a breath. "Yes, Miss Neves, you can say that. You did OK. Now, that's only the preliminary testing, but based on that, if you want, we can start the Navigation Test Protocol. Of course, it looks like all NPSs—uh, that is Naval Positional Specialties—would be open to you. Navigation, propulsion, corpsman, whatever you want, but if you ask me, navigation is where it's at."

This was going too fast for her. Did she want to become a freak? For all she knew, once you had the nav thingy put in your skull, it was permanent.

The uniform was going on again about extra pay, the prestige, the ability to quickly gain rank, and the huge salaries that could be commanded from the civilian side after getting out of the Navy. That last one caught her attention. Liege was poor, dirt poor. She didn't feel there was any honor in being poor, and with money, she could give Avó the best care available.

And looking at the uniform—Petty Officer Russell, she reminded herself, not "uniform"—she realized that the petty officer no longer saw her as a gangrat. He saw beyond the colors, the hair, the wild expression of her life to date. He saw her as a commodity, one that the Navy wanted. She appreciated that. It felt good to know that beyond the NE38559453, beyond Leticia and Avó, the "real world" wanted her for something, too.

She held up her hand, palm out, and stopped him mid-sentence.

"If you think I should do that, sir, then I will. I'm ready to serve the best I can."

DUGGEN

Chapter 2

Hospitalman Recruit Liege Neves rushed down the corridor to Classroom 105. She was late, just having gotten off the commercial comms with Leticia. An E1's salary was more than she'd ever legally earned before, but it was not enough for more than short once-every-two-week calls back home. Those calls were important, though, enough so that she risked being late today, of all days, so as not to miss her call slot.

She'd have more money if she'd qualified for navigator training, of course. She'd passed all the written and verbal tests, but failed the physical. Two of her readings had come in below the required minimums to undergo the transformation. She still didn't know if she was sad about that or not. She'd have liked the increased rank and money, to be sure, but at least now, she was still Liege and not some half-cyborg creature.

With navigator out the window, she'd had all the other NPSs open to her, and she'd chosen to become a corpsman. It was one of the largest NPSs in the Navy, and the chances to specialize were pretty broad. Many of the sub-specialties were in high demand in the civilian side of the Federation, and she'd be able to bring Leticia and Avó with her wherever and whenever she went. All she had to do was keep her nose clean and do a good job in her first duty station, and she'd have her pick of specialties. It might take a bit longer than had she become a navigator, but her plan was still in place.

The hatch to Classroom 105 was still open, thank goodness, and she slipped in, grabbing a seat in the back row.

"Glad to see you could join us," Frank Ferrere whispered as she slid down beside him. "It's not like, you know, anything important's going on."

"Oh, really? Like what?" she asked innocently.

Frank just rolled his eyes. He and Liege had battled to be the class honor man, both falling just short. Frank was number three while Liege was number four. Out of 115 who had started Basic Fleet Corpsman School, BFCS, that wasn't bad, but not good enough. Only the top two graduates got their pick of duty stations. For the rest, they entered three choices, but the needs of the Navy took precedence.

For her first choice, Liege had chosen Naval Hospital *First Station*, in deep orbit around Earth herself. *First Station* was the headquarters of the Federation Navy, and the hospital there was the most prestigious naval hospital, if not the best. Her second choice was simply "naval hospital," leaving it to the Navy to choose which one. By being in a hospital, she figured she'd be able to observe all of the corpsman specialties and choose which one to pursue after her tour was up.

Her third choice was the *FS Admiral San Denee*, the newest dreadnaught in the fleet. If she was going to be in space, she wanted it to be on a ship that had more than the basics in health care. The *Admiral San Denee* had what was essentially a small hospital on board.

With her wide-open second choice, coupled with her high class standing, Liege was pretty sure she'd get one of her choices. Still, she was as nervous as the other HRs as they waited for Senior Chief.

The last seven months had been a sea change for Liege, but one to which she'd readily taken. Two weeks after being recruited, she'd said goodbye to Leticia and Avó and left Nova Esperança for Duggen and the 12-week long recruit training. Unlike most of the other recruits, she'd never felt homesick. Other than her sister and grandfather, she didn't miss anyone, even her irmãs. Boot camp had been easy, much easier than she'd expected. The DIs had tried to make it a personal hell, but for a daughter of the favelas, for a gangrat, it was a cake-walk. She learned to act concerned, but her most difficult task was to keep the smile off her face.

Out of 525 recruits in her class, 498 graduated, and Liege graduated number nine, and only 0.15 points out of honor grad. The BFCS A-School was on Duggen as well, so three days after graduation, Liege started learning the basics of being a corpsman. Now, on the last day of the class, as a newly minted HM-0000, or a "Quad-Zero," she was about to learn her fate for the next three years.

The division officer, Lieutenant Commander Parsons, and Master Chief Hospital Corpsman Meung entered the classroom as someone shouted out "Attention on Deck!"

The class rose en masse, along with their instructors, until the two worthies reached the stage and took their seats. The class sat back down and eagerly—or nervously—awaited their assignments.

HMCM Meung didn't waste time nor formalities. He stood at the podium and called out the honor graduate's name.

"HR Castro, the *FS Pronghorn*."

Liege knew that Sybil Castro was selecting a small mover, but she didn't know why. She could have any duty station, and she chose a ship too small for a medical officer. The corpsman running the sickbay would be an independent duty corpsman, probably an HM2 or HM1. When Liege applied to a specialist C-School, she wanted a medical officer's recommendation, not that of a mid-level enlisted corpsman.

"HR Sukarna, *FS Admiral San Denee*."

Well, hell. No way I'm getting the San Denee now, Liege thought.

Still, any hospital or dreadnaught would do.

"HR Ferrere," the master chief said as Liege felt Frank tense up. "Fleet Marine Force."

"Oh, man, it sucks to be you," Liege whispered.

Most corpsmen stayed with the Navy, but still, the Marines required large numbers of them. Liege knew that maybe 25% of the class would be assigned to the Marines, but she was surprised that Frank, at number three in the class, would be assigned to the Corps.

Now he had the 18-week, intensive Field Medical Traning Course on Tarawa staring him in the face.

Unless he asked for it? she wondered, looking at him.

She was on good terms with him, but she'd never asked him what he had requested. Quite a few corpsmen wanted to serve with the Marines, so maybe he was one of them.

Wondering about Frank, she almost missed her own assignment.

"HR Neves, Fleet Marine Force."

What?

Numb, Liege thought she must have misheard the master chief. She'd hadn't requested the Marines. Far from it. She felt the stirrings of panic rise within her.

Some of the instructors had related horror stories of the FMTC, of how it kicked their asses. True, HM2 Pagnotti had spoken of how serving with the Marines was the best thing that had happened to him, but some people liked to be tied up and pissed on, too, so just because one person liked it didn't mean Liege would. What he had described didn't sound very enjoyable, that was for sure.

Liege wanted to ask if her assignment was a mistake, but when seven of the next ten of them were assigned to the Marines as well, the reality of what had happened began to sink in.

"I guess it sucks to be you, too," Frank whispered. "See you on Tarawa."

TARAWA

Chapter 3

"You coming, Doc?" Jessie Wythe asked, poking his head through the hatch.

Liege looked up from the small field desk where she was entering bio-stats into her M-PA. It was a mindless, time-consuming task, one that Liege thought was ridiculous. In today's age of data integration, she didn't understand why her "Private Doc" couldn't simply take the data from the log net. But instead of making it simple and easy, she had to download each Marine's bio-stats onto a stylus and then upload them—after converting the data—into her M-PA.

"Sorry, Jessie. Chief wants this done before COB."

"It *is* COB, in case you didn't notice."

"Your COB, maybe, but I guess not mine. You guys go ahead. I'll meet you there."

"How late you going to be, you think?"

Liege scrolled down the log repeater for a moment and then told him, "At least an hour."

"An hour?" Wythe asked. "No big deal. I'll tell the rest to warm up at the E-Club. You come and get us, then we'll head to the Down 'N Out together."

"No, you don't have to do that."

"Bullshit, Doc. We're going to get the two newbies drunk, and you got to be there, too. 'Sides, I'm feeling peckish, and you know what that means. Iffen anyone gives me some lip, I'm gonna lay 'em out, and I'll need you to doc them up."

"Peckish?"

"Yeah, peckish. It means. . .hell, I'm not sure what it means. Killer said it, so I'll ask him."

"OK, Lance Corporal Peckish, you go ask Corporal Wheng what it means. But for now, let me get back and finish this. I'll meet you all at the E-Club."

She had to smile at Wythe's retreating back. He was a character, for sure. And he'd been very protective of her since the *Imperial Stabiae*—all the more so since the chief officially assigned her to Golf Company for the upcoming deployment. Like most of the battalion corpsmen, she was a member of H&S Company, but she was now attached to First Squad, Second Platoon, Golf Company, for the duration of the deployment.

She also knew that Wythe fancied her. Oh, he'd never said as much, but it wasn't hard to read him. Given other circumstances, she might even give him a rodeo to see how he bucked, but as a squad, he was family, and you didn't mess around with family. She knew enough not to give him an opening, and she knew he wouldn't press.

Gangrats back home usually didn't know how to accept a "no," which was a major reason she had blooded with the *Commando Meninas*. Liege was grateful to know that in the Marines, which was in many ways just a bigger, more powerful gang, "no" was understood.

She also liked the fact that so many Marines were prime beef on the hoof, and Liege was not a blushing schoolgirl. She had and would continue to socialize, but as far as romance, it wasn't going to happen within the squad—heck, not even within the battalion.

She shook off that train of thought and buckled down to get the biostats on her M-PA. Forty-five minutes later, she was able to log off. Closing the hatch to the tiny platoon office behind her, she took the ladder two steps at a time to the third deck, then ran down to her room. Fanny had already left, as she'd expected, so she stripped off her utilities, jumped into the shower, and scrubbed off the day's grime. Within a minute, she was out and dried and opening her locker.

Her turquoise camisole top and bright yellow snake-pants were on a hanger on the backside of the locker door. A piece of paper with "Wear this!" written on it was pinned to the hanger.

Leave it to Fanny, she thought, taking the outfit and holding it up to the mirror-screen.

With her red hair, which was finally reaching almost to her collar after being shaved at boot camp, and light skin, she wasn't sure the colors really complimented her, but she'd take her roomie's advice. Another minute—which had to be a record for her—and she was out the hatch and taking three steps at a time back down the ladder.

The Area 5 E-Club was only about 200 meters from the barracks, so she still beat the hour she'd told Wythe.

"Liege!" Fanny called out, standing up from a crowded table as Liege entered the club bar.

As her bunkie, Fanny was the only person to call her by name. To everyone else, she was "Doc." It had taken Liege awhile to get used to it, but "Doc" was a badge of honor, one she now wore proudly.

"Pull up a seat, Doc," Corporal Wheng said. "We've got two pitchers to finish off before we hit the ville."

Normally, the three corporals and the sergeant would be at the NCO Club, which was why they'd planned the welcome for the two newbies out in town. But with Liege late, they'd been fine with starting the drinking on base. Pitchers were much cheaper on base, too, so there was that benny.

Liege liked Wolfshead Red or Guinness. Neither of which was sold at the club, though, but, she wasn't going to turn down free beer, even if it was the Munchen piss-water most everyone else seemed to love.

She took the proffered stein and wormed her butt in between Fanny's and Victor's.

"Welcome, boots," she said, lifting the stein to the two newbies.

"Boots!" Wythe said, laughing. "You heard that!"

One of the two, PFC Korf, really was a boot. He looked like a gangly baby, and he smiled stupidly, holding his stein as if he'd never had a beer before. He had the puppy-dog attitude, just happy to be playing with the big kids.

The other newbie wasn't technically a boot. Lance Corporal Tamara Veal was a huge girl, maybe bigger than any other Marine at the table. She hunched uncomfortably at one end of the table, her stein clutched in her hands. She looked out-of-place and not too happy to be there.

Liege hadn't really had much contact with Veal since she'd arrived the day before, but she knew the lance corporal had been on the Marine track team before getting banished back to the grunts. Liege had expected to see some slender runner, but it was obvious that this girl hadn't been tearing up the marathon circuit.

With Veal and Korf, the squad was now T/O.[3]

The party was supposed to leave the E-Club and head out of town, but pitchers kept being bought, and they each had to be drained. After an hour-and-a-half, it became evident that the night out in the ville had been abandoned. Sergeant Vinter made her excuses right about then, and Corporal Acosta left soon thereafter. Both Corporals Wheng and Sativaa hung around, though, closing the club at 0100 with the non-rates.

Liege had a good conversation with Korf, and her initial impressions were confirmed. He was an eager puppy, wanting to please. Although the party was for both of the newbies, he must have bought at least a third of the pitchers.

Veal was a tougher nut to crack, but Liege pulled up a chair beside the big woman and shared a stein or two with her. She thought Veal somewhat reserved, but not in a snooty way. One-on-one with Liege, the lance corporal opened up about her career to date, which was entirely on the track team. By closing time, Liege had decided that she liked Veal—which wasn't surprising; Liege liked almost everyone.

Wythe and Williams wanted to take the party out in town as the E-Club closed, but with a 0600 PT[4] session in the morning, cooler heads prevailed.

---

[3] T/O: Table of Organization. "Being T/O" means that a unit has the full complement of personnel that it is supposed to have.

[4] PT: Physical Fitness

More than slightly tipsy, Liege and Fanny started to leave together to go back to the barracks. As they stepped off, Liege looked back to the table and saw Veal standing in the awkward manner of someone not quite knowing what to do.

She pulled Fanny to a halt and asked Veal, "Well, girl, you coming? We sisters have to stick together, you know?"

The lance corporal smiled with a hint of relief and joined them. With one arm linked in Fanny's, Liege hooked her other in Veal's, and the three squadmates stepped through the club's front hatch and into the night.

Chapter 4

"You have what?"

"I've got the Brick."

Liege stared at the lance corporal standing in front of her. Golf Company had been out in the field for the last two weeks on their work-ups, and this was her first day back assisting in the battalion sick call since then.

"Uh, according to your records, Lance Corporal Weisman, you've never been in regen, so how could you have BRC?"

"I don't know," he said. "I just know I have it."

"OK, wait a second while I talk to the chief."

Liege left the Marine standing there as she searched out Chief Sou—Chief Hospital Corpsman Soukianssian and the senior corpsman in the battalion.

"Uh, Chief?" she said when she tracked him down. "I've got a lance corporal who's telling me he has the Brick."

"Have you taken his vitals?"

"No, Chief. I mean why? He's never had regen, and he's 19 years old. He doesn't have the Brick."

"You know that and I know that, but does he?"

"We're eight days from our shake-down cruise, Chief. He's trying to scam out of that."

"Who is he?"

"Lance Corporal Weisman, from Fox."

"Bigeye, what can you tell me about Weisman, lance corporal, one each," the chief asked HM2 Fiorelli, one of the Fox Company corpsman who was going over some sort of list at an adjacent desk.

"Weisman? Good kid, bad story. He brought his honey-wa from Kunter or Dysktra 3 or someplace like that and set her up in the ville. Only this fine young lady is rather fond of the many strapping young Marines here. Rumor has it that she's had more than a few boyfriends since she's been here and she's only waiting until we deploy so she can shack up with some guy from 3/4. Weisman's been pretty stressed out, from what I hear."

"She's shacking up with other Marines? And they know she's with Weisman?" Liege asked, surprised at what Fiorelli had just said.

"That's the scuttlebutt."

"But they know Weisman's a Marine?"

"Geez, Neves, come on back down to reality," Doc Fiorelli said.

"But that's a Jody," Liege protested.

"And the military doesn't Jody each other, yeah, we know," Bigeye said, rolling his eyes as he looked up at the chief. "Most won't, but there will always be some assholes. You should see what happens after a fleet deployment from Station One. All those Quadrant widows and widowers go crazy looking for hook-ups."

Liege was shocked and more than a little embarrassed about her naiveté. She was single, and she'd been enjoying the attention and company of men outside of the battalion, but she'd also assumed that no Marine or sailor would Jody another. To hear that some would was a major let-down. She'd heard the term "Quadrant" or "Quad widow" of course, for women or men whose Navy spouses were off on deployment, but somehow she thought the Marines, at least, didn't play that game.

"So now we know what's up, don't we? Weisman's afraid his doe will find another stag, and he wants to be here to keep it from happening," the chief said. "It happened with your sergeant on the last deployment," he added to Liege.

"Sergeant Vinter? She's married?"

"Was married," the chief corrected.

"And her ex ran off with another Marine?"

"No, a civilian. Lots of civilians, including a Marine wife. Vinter came back and found out, and we thought she was going to kill him. But no, she just went to Div-Legal and filed for an immediate divorce."

Liege tried to imagine coming back from a deployment and finding out a husband or wife had gone wild. Sergeant Vinter was one tough SOB, but it still had to hurt.

"So what do I do with Weisman?" she asked the chief.

"Work him up."

"But he doesn't have the Brick."

"Probably not. But you're not the MO,[5] and neither am I. While you're keeping him busy, I'm going to give the chaplain a call and see what we can do.

"You say Wiesman's a good kid, Bigeye?" he asked Doc Fiorelli.

"Yeah, a good Marine. Just young and in a hard place."

"Doctor X'anto might want to get him to psyche to make sure his mind's on straight. We don't need him doing something stupid. Give First Sergeant Herrera a head's up, too. He needs to make sure someone keeps an eye on the young man until we embark."

"Weisman would be better off without the witch," Fiorelli said.

"You know that and I know that, but I doubt the kid agrees."

"That's because he's young," Fiorelli said.

Liege was young, too. She and Weisman were the same age, but she didn't think she could ever get so messed up about a guy that she'd lie just to get out of a deployment.

As she walked back to her station, Liege wondered how he'd even managed to support his girlfriend or whatever she was. Tarawa was not the cheapest place to live, especially near the bases, and being a lance corporal, he wouldn't have much money to spend on her. Liege had just received approval to make her Avó a dependent, and that had been a major goat-rope of bureaucracy. It was only after a medical exam back on Nova Esperança had found him 100% disabled and Liege could prove at least six months as his main source of financial support that it had been approved. But until her next promotion, she would not be authorized military housing, so for the time being, Avó and Leticia had to stay back in the favela.

---

[5] MO: Medical Officer

Liege felt more than a little guilt as she sat back down across from Weisman. He'd managed to bring his girlfriend to Tarawa, and despite the fact that with an authorized dependent she made more than the lance corporal, she hadn't thought it possible to bring Avó and Leticia to join her.

Lance Corporal Weisman looked nervously at Liege, wringing his hands. He had to know he wouldn't get away with this, at least the part about him claiming he had the Brick. Maybe the chief could get something going through the chaplain, but Liege doubted it. Like it or not, Weisman was most likely going to be with the battalion as they deployed. He'd have to rely on his fellow Marines to pull through.

"OK, Tad," she said, reading his first name off the display as she pulled out a scanner. "Let's see what's going on with you."

WYXY

Chapter 5

"We don't know what we're going to get. It could be all 500 hundred, or it could be none," Chief Sou told the gathered corpsmen.

Liege blanched at the thought. Over 500 Wyxy civilians were being held hostage by the SevRevs, and if "none" needed medical care, that would probably mean they'd been killed by the religious fanatics, as was usually the case.

"Don't join your team until you're released by your commanders. Fox, that might not be for a while for you. But Golf and Weapons, join your team as soon as you can."

Echo and Hotel were in blocking positions on the other side of the Rose Garden Farmers Market, and HM1 Knight had another triage team ready to go for any civilians who managed to escape to that side. But the bulk of the civilians, however many that might be, were expected to come their way. Golf was the support element for the assault, so the Golf and the three Weapons Company corpsmen might not have their own Marines to treat; as soon as they were free, they would augment the five H & S corpsmen and Doctor X'anto and provide the bulk of the triage for the aid station.

"OK, back to your Marines," Chief ordered.

HM2 Gnish, Second Platoon's senior corpsman, jerked his head in a follow-me motion, and Liege and Nica—HM Veronica Lester-Mrchenigian, Second Squad's corpsman—followed him back to where the platoon was in position. A newsie in a bright red fiesta top, tight "butt lifters," and an ancient helmet that was canted half off her head, with her camcorder operator in tow, saw them and rushed over.

"Justina Gunnersen, VDV Universal," she said, introducing herself. "So, are you here to rescue the civilians?"

No, we're here to shop for tomatoes, Liege thought. *Can't you tell by our snazzy uniforms and weapons?*

"Sorry, ma'am. We've got to get into position," Doc Gnish said, trying to brush by her.

The woman executed a deft little sidestep, blocking his way.

"Can you tell me your battle plans?" she persisted.

"You'll have to ask the PAO[6] about anything like that," Gnish said, trying to push around her again while Liege and Nica split off, abandoning him to face the newsie alone.

There had to be over a hundred newsies on the scene. Most had little or no armor protection. Liege thought that with the Marines in full battle rattle, and with the Farmer's Market only 600 meters away, they would have taken the hint, but there seemed to almost be a holiday air as various newsies jockeyed for interviews.

This entire operation was a huge dog-and-pony show. Oh, the mission was righteous. The SevRevs were truly evil incarnate, and the Wyxy hostages were in grave danger. But the SevRevs loved publicity, and by the time the battalion had been diverted to conduct the rescue mission, pretty much every major news organization in human space and more than a few minor ones had made it to the planet.

Even the location of the assembly area had been selected with a nod to the newsies. At only 600 meters from the market and lacking cover, it broke most rules of offensive operations. This might be Liege's first land battle, but even an E3 corpsman knew better than that.

Liege spotted Sergeant Vinter and took her place by the squad leader. They hadn't prepared improved positions; the entire squad was on the open ground at the edge of the assembly area.

"Chief says that—"

"I got the message. I'll release you as soon as I can," the sergeant said, interrupting her.

---

[6] PAO: Public Affairs Officer

Liege nodded and looked out over Fox Company, which was going to lead the assault. A tiny drone flew down low, hovering a meter away from her. She wanted to swat it away like she would a mosquito, but she tried to look serious, not knowing to where her image might be transmitted. Vinter, on the other hand, ripped out a huge burp, and the drone immediately took off for more civilized pastures.

A Wasp overflew the assembly area and buzzed the market. All the newsies and drones turned to capture the scene. A Wasp was a deadly looking fighter, but Liege knew it was just for show. No one expected the SevRevs to simply give up, and being buzzed by a Wasp was not going to change that.

The rest of the battalion headquarters moved into position. Liege knew the assault would kick off soon.

The small PsyOps team took center stage a 100 meters from Liege and Sergeant Vinter.

Speaking through a small, but incredibly powerful directional speaker, one team member said, "Inside the market; we are the United Federation Marines. You are trapped where you are. If you want to live, release the hostages. If you comply, you will not be harmed.

"If you do not release the hostages and resist us, you are inviting a certain destruction. It is up to you. Surrender and live or resist and die."

It might have been nice drama, but no one thought it would have any effect. The SevRevs welcomed the End of Days, and none of them expected to survive the upcoming fight. The announcement was more for the newsies and public consumption.

With the platoon in position, Staff Sergeant Abdálle shouted out, "Check your curtains!"

Liege toggled the deployment switch and was rewarded with a little puff of mist that seemed to disappear. The slowly blinking green light on her display let her know her curtain was employed.

The SevRevs had used super biologicals on Janson to kill Confederation troops, so each Marine and sailor had been outfitted for full NBC[7] protection. The curtains wouldn't do much against projectiles, but they would protect from chemical or biological attacks.

In front of Golf's line, Fox started crossing the LOD.[8] The assault was on.

Liege glanced back at the Alpha command.

The CO was moving away from a reporter and her camcorderman, trying to ignore the two as she went about monitoring Fox. A big Marine was trying to pull back the reporter, but the woman was nimble, dodging the Marine and pressing the CO.

Five meters to her right, Korf said "I wouldn't be doing that," as he watched the same thing.

Next to him, Tamara tried but failed to smother a laugh.

"Eyes front, you two. To your sector," Sergeant Vinter chastised them.

Liege snapped her eyes back to her sector as well. Fox was moving out over open ground, and the lead elements were close to half-way to the market. Liege checked her settings and confirmed the sights were set for 600 meters.

The M99 had an effective range of 900 meters, but for Liege, 600 meters was pushing it. Marksmanship was not her strongest suit.

Liege kept expecting fire to reach out from the market, but a sudden snap from her right made her jump. One of the snipers, who had taken position on top of a public toilet, had just fired and was cycling in another round. She fired once more before answering fire reached out from the market.

Despite herself, Liege ducked lower, hugging the dirt. It was the Fox Marines, though, who reacted. They immediately moved into a bounding overwatch, pouring fire into the market as they rushed forward.

To her right, the sniper continued to fire, her shots coming unbelievably quickly. Liege couldn't tell if either the sniper or the Fox Marines were killing SevRevs, but the volume going out was impressive.

---

[7] NBC: Nuclear, Biological, Chemical
[8] LOD: Line of Departure

Just as the lead elements from Fox approached the market, the entire building exploded in a huge fireball. A shockwave rolled over Liege a moment later.

"*Filha da puta!*" she exclaimed, rising up on her elbows to get a better look.

The closest Fox Marines had been knocked to the ground, but most looked to be struggling to stand back up. In front of them, an immense column of dense black smoke billowed high into the air.

Liege had never seen anything like this in her life, and her mouth hung open. She could imagine what had just happened to the hostages, and it made her sick to her stomach.

To her huge surprise, figures foundered out of the ruined market, stumbling towards the Fox Marines.

"We've got people coming out," Sergeant Vinter shouted. "Get ready."

As the support element, one of Golf's missions was to assist with the hostages. Third Platoon would create a corridor into which the hostages would be funneled, First Platoon would be the handling teams, and Second Platoon would provide immediate security.

"Remember, these are friendlies, but be on the alert," Sergeant Vinter reminded them.

Liege was assigned to the Green triage team, which would be back at the assembly area and conduct the initial assessment. Blue, with more of the senior corpsmen, would conduct the secondary assessment and start treatment, and Purple, made of Fox corpsmen, would go into the burning mess and do on-the-spot triage and life-saving measures.

For the moment, though, Liege was still a member of the squad. She took her place beside Sergeant Vinter, her M99 at the ready.

Within a few minutes, the first two hostages stumbled past, looking dirty and bedraggled. These were followed by more, and most of them showed signs of injury. Many needed help to walk.

These were the lucky ones. Others had collapsed along the way, unable to move, and even more would still be inside the market—hopefully alive. The corpsman in her wanted to rush to their aid, but she was supposed to remain with her squad. A SevRev could be hiding among the hostages, and if he attacked the Marines, she had to be ready to act.

"Doc!" Wythe called out.

Liege looked over to where Jessie was helping a man lower an injured woman to the ground. She hesitated for only a moment before slinging her weapon and rushing over to them.

The woman was badly burned and in shock, her breathing rapid and shallow. It was hard to tell with all the soot and tattered clothing, but it looked like she had third-degree burns over 20% of her body. She should make it, but she was in bad shape for the time being. Liege pulled out her injector, dialing in a Series 1. A skin injector wasn't going to work here, so she deployed the needle. Next, she knew she needed to get fluids into her.

Liege was supposed to be conducting triage, not treating patients. There still could be others who were hurt worse and needed treatment quicker. But there looked to be only 50 or so hostages who had gotten out of the market, and there were more than enough corpsmen to handle that few.

Wythe helped the other man to his feet and asked, "Are you hurt, too? Are you OK?"

"I've got information, sir. I need to talk to your commander. Lives are at stake!" the man said, his voice fraught with stress.

"Corporal Wheng!" Wythe called out. "This guy says he needs to talk to the commander."

The corporal was taking a small child from the arms of her mother, pointing out the way to the initial collection point.

He barely gave Wythe a glance over the crying toddler, but he said, "Take him, then," as he nodded to where the battalion commanding officer was standing with her staff.

Liege took out the saline. Over the centuries, there hadn't been much improvement on how to manage an IV. Liege held the rectangular package with one hand, thumbing the catch. The packet flipped open, a long tube falling free. With her right hand, she held the needle to the woman's forearm, right over the cephalic vein. Three quick presses activated the snake, and within moments, the needle wormed its way into the vein, and the saline began to flow.

She pulled out her field stand, extended it, and hung the pack, letting gravity power the flow of the saline.

"What the fuck?" Jessie Wythe shouted.

Liege looked up to see Tamara tackling the man who had helped bring up the woman. Jessie was knocked back, and as all three of them hit the ground, Tamara was grabbing at the man's hand.

"Veal! What the hell?" Wythe shouted, rolling away from her. "Are you bat-shit crazy?"

Tamara was big, but the man was at least 25 kg heavier than her, and he looked like a bull. He was jerking his arm, shaking Tamara as he rained punch after punch on her head with his free hand.

Liege took several steps toward them, her mind trying to make sense out of what she was seeing. All she knew was that someone was beating up her friend.

She started into a run, leaving the wounded woman behind, when the man's head jerked and blood poured out of the side of his head, drenching Tamara. Tamara still held onto the man when Sergeant Priest, the company police sergeant, leveled his old Piedmaster and blew away the hostage's neck and half of his face.

"Don't let go, Marine!" a voice called out.

Priest, Wythe, and Korf, were kneeling around Tamara, reaching out to keep her hands closed around the hostage's— although it was pretty clear now he hadn't been a hostage but was a SevRev—hand.

"We've got it now," the first sergeant said, standing over her. "Keep holding it, and we'll get someone here to disarm this guy."

Liege stepped up, giving Tamara the once over, but the blood covering her didn't seem to be hers.

"Hey, Korf, can you get off me?" Tamara asked weakly.

"Oh, shit, sorry," the PFC said, moving his knee from out of her side.

"Just don't let go. I'm a little woozy, I think."

By now a crowd had gathered. The first sergeant ziptied the three Marines' and the dead SevRev's hands together.

Liege stood there a moment longer, but no one other than the SevRev was hurt, and there wasn't anything she could do for him. She left the gathered Marines and went back to the woman. The IV pack was still flowing.

"Go report to the Chief," Sergeant Vinter told her.

"But my patient?"

"Is she stable?"

"Yeah, for now," Liege admitted.

"Well, you get back to wherever you're supposed to be, and we'll get her back to you."

Liege knew that made sense, so she started back to where Green team would be forming. The people around Tamara were being pushed back, and an EOD tech, in full disposal suit, stood over Tamara, Jessie, and Korf. Evidently things were pretty serious, but Liege had to let the EOD Marine take care of it. She had her own job to do now.

"Neves! Help Dingo," HM2 Dykstra, the Green Team leader, told her as she walked up to him.

Liege spent the next ten minutes helping HM3 Jim "Dingo" McAllister evaluate the wounded coming back to the triage station. She had hoped to have more work, but unless Fox pulled more survivors out of the wreckage, the butcher's bill was pretty high. Only 48 hostages had made it back to the collection point. Twelve of them were seriously hurt and being treated.

Liege kept listening for an explosion from over where the EOD tech was working. To her relief, there wasn't one.

The operation was being touted as a success, at least from what she could tell from the newsies who were hovering around. Only four Marines were WIA, none seriously. At least twenty SevRevs had been killed, either by Marines or by their own hands. And 62 hostages—48 escaping to the front and another 14 out the back—had been saved. And then there was Tamara's exploits, which had been captured by numerous camcorders.

With almost 500 dead hostages, though, it didn't feel like a victory to Liege. She was glad when the trucks came up to take them back to the stadium in town for the shuttle back up to the ship.

TARAWA

Chapter 6

"I see you've got a good start on things, Jessie," Liege said as she slid onto the bench seat.

Wythe lifted a half-empty stein in a salute and simply announced, "Doc!"

Liege took one of the unused steins on the table and filled it from the only one of the three pitchers that still had beer in it.

"So, where's the belle of the ball?" she asked.

"Veal? Don't know. She'll be coming soon, I'm guessing. Ask her bunkie."

"She wasn't in the room when I left, but she'll be here," Fanny said.

With the unexpected mission to Wyxy interrupting their shake-down cruise, their scheduled full deployment had been pushed back to let the battalion and the ship finish hitting their pre-deployment checks, so they were all back on Tarawa. Tempo was high, but the battalion had moved into their final admin stand-down, which meant the junior Marines had been cut loose after noon chow, and they had the evening free. When Tamara Veal had said she wanted to meet everyone at the Down 'N Out, it seemed like a good excuse to have one last party on Tarawa before shipping out.

Liege took a sip of the beer and made a grimace.

"What's this Munchen piss-water?" she asked. "Let me get something decent," she added, standing up.

"They're your credits," Wythe said. "But I'll drink whatever you bring back."

Liege bought three pitchers of Wolfshead Red and brought them back to the table. Wythe drained his stein, refilled it with the Red, and immediately drained half of it.

"Oh, I've got to hang out with you more, Doc. This is the good stuff!" he said. "But it sure runs through you. I've got to go pay the rent," he said, getting up to use the head.

Within the next ten minutes, the entire squad, minus Veal and Vinter, had arrived, and spirits were high. It was good to unwind like this, Liege thought as she sat back for a moment, just listening to the chatter.

"So what's the scuttlebutt about Crow?" Corporal Francewell Sativaa asked no one in particular.

"Hell of a shot, hot as a volcano, but rather a bitch, from what I hear," Tyrell Goodpastor said. "Why do you ask?"

"Veal invited her here, you know, to thank her for zeroing that SevRev."

Liege hadn't known that someone else would join them this evening. She felt a little disappointed. But Tamara had organized the party, so it was her call.

"You're right about her being hot," Vic Williams said. "She hits the gym late sometimes like me, when it's less crowded, and she's mighty fine to look at. Won't talk to anybody, though."

"And did little Vic try to pick up on the corporal? Get turned down?" Fanny asked as if talking to a baby.

"Not me," Vic said with conviction. "I like me a woman with a little personality, if you please."

"Oh, yeah, sure. Like that green-haired dancer on Left Out?" Killer Wheng shouted as most of the table erupted into laughter.

Vic mumbled something, his face turning bright red. Liege hadn't been with the squad the last time they were training on Left Out, so she had no idea what they were laughing about. But if the volume of the laughter was any indication, she sure wanted to know that story.

"What're you laughing about?" Wythe asked, returning from the head.

Corporal Wheng said, "Vic and the dancer on Left Out."

Wythe started laughing himself as he took his seat again. Since no one started to expound on the story, Liege cleared her throat to ask.

She wasn't about to find out anything as Fanny shouted out, "Hey, it's The Blonde Terror!"

Tamara Veal was making her way through the tables to join them, a sheepish smile on her face.

"Sit down, Veal. I've got a pitcher with your name on it!" Wythe said, waving a mostly full pitcher of beer.

Tamara wormed her way onto the bench seat against the wall.

"Took you long enough," Fanny said. "We've almost drunk all the beer Jessie here bought for you, and the next pitcher's on you."

"That true, Wythe? You buy this?"

"True that. I told you on the *Caracas* I was buying, didn't I? An' a Marine never goes back on his word, am I right?"

Doc understood Tamara's hesitance to believe that. Wythe was well-known for his credit-pinching—and mooching—ways. Besides, that particular pitcher was one of the Wolfhead Reds she'd bought.

Wythe poured her a stein, and Tamara took a slow, deep swallow, making a show of smacking her lips, and then said, "The skipper wanted to see me. Couldn't get out of that."

While the rest of them laughed, Wythe made a fist, put his nose in the hole made by his thumb and forefinger, and rotated it back and forth. Tamara rolled her eyes and gave Wythe a wicked punch to the arm.

"That's 'cause you're a bleeding hero," Fanny said, drawing out the "e" in hero.

"Eat me," Tamara said as the others laughed.

In the favelas, the smack talk that Marines seemed to love was there, but not to the same extent. It would be too easy to step over the line and instigate a *fuedo*.[9] Here in the Marines, though, it seemed to be simply part of the landscape.

---

[9] Fuedo: Portuguese for "feud."

"Eh, you'll get one, maybe a BC1," Vic said, reaching his stein over the table to clink with hers.

Tamara half stood, then leaned over to accept his clink.

"Hey, watch it. I don't need your boobs in my face when I'm drinking!" Wythe shouted out, spilling some of his beer.

Laughter and shouts of "Oh, you love it," and "That's as close as you're going to get to any," greeted his statement.

Tamara turned a bright shade of red.

She's embarrassed! Liege realized. *Maybe the smack talk's a little much for her.*

"This one's on me!" Tamara shouted, too loudly and obviously trying to change the subject. She grabbed the pitcher and asked, "What are we drinking? San Miguel?"

"You can't tell? What a lightweight!" Liege said. "That's Wolfshead Red, Tammy."

"That's Tamara, Doc. I'm not a freaking Tammy. But Wolfshead Red it is. What about Corporal Medicine Crow? Did she show up yet? I owe her more than I owe you guys."

"The Ice Bitch is coming?" Wythe asked.

Oh, someone else didn't know that the sniper was coming, Liege thought, relieved that she wasn't the only one left in the dark.

"The Ice Bitch?" Tamara repeated, confused.

"Yeah. Crow. Hot as snot on the outside, but cold as Hades on the inside."

He clinked his stein with Vic's in a toast.

"Well, she sure 'iced' that SevRev," Veal said, looking smug.

"Touché, Tammy," Liege said. "We girls have to stick up for each other. Wythe's just mad because he's like all the rest of the guys in the battalion, lusting after Corporal Crow when she won't give any of them the time of day."

"Tamara, Doc, Tamara. But if it's raging hormones talking, then I need to get the beer to cool these guys off."

The "Tammy" had slipped out naturally, but it took Liege slightly aback to get corrected like that. No one else seemed to have noticed as Veal made her way back to the bar.

"So what happened on Left Out?" Liege asked.

"You had to be there," Wythe said. "But you can ask 'Little Vickee' there and see if he'll man up."

Wythe drew out the "Vickee" in some sort of weird accent.

Liege shook her head, knowing she'd never get the story. The conversation drifted to Corporal Medicine Crow, and bets were made on whether she was a lesbian or not. Wythe and Goodpaster were firmly in the "likes girls" camp, while Wheng, Acosta, and Dolsch insisted that was just sour grapes because the sniper didn't date anyone in the battalion.

I don't date anyone here, either, Liege thought.

But she knew that was different. She didn't hide her socializing with men outside of the battalion. And looking over at the adjacent table, a rather good-looking Marine had caught her eye a few times and smiled an invitation. Maybe when this broke down, she'd go give him a look-see.

Veal came back with a pitcher, which was immediately passed around, and the talk ran the gamut from one topic to the other, and more than once, several topics were on the table at the same time. Before Liege knew it, it was midnight, and first two of them, followed five minutes later by three more, took their leave.

Liege looked over to where the Marine who'd had his eye on her was sitting, but he'd evidently lost patience, and the table was empty. She wasn't crushed, but she was a little disappointed. They'd be deployed for at least six months, and that meant no dating for the duration.

Oh, well, that just means time for one more beer.

"So Vic, or should I say 'Vickee,' you sure you won't tell me about Left Out?" she asked, leaning over the table.

She didn't think he'd give in that easy, but it could be a long six months, and given the time, she was confident she could break the guy.

Chapter 7

The squad milled about in the barracks commons, waiting for Tamara and Fanny. Tamara had insisted on no big send-off, but no one in the squad paid any attention to that. Tamara was family, and family didn't send off one of their own without acknowledgement. Tamara still had to check out with the CO, and Liege could see the lieutenant and the staff sergeant waiting outside, but inside the barracks was their territory. Some of the other Marines from the platoon were outside waiting as well, but they had ceded the commons to First Squad.

All heads swiveled as Tamara and Fanny came down the steps. Tamara carried her lone seabag, which seemed too small to represent all the Marine owned.

"Hey, I said no send-off," Tamara said, even if she looked pleased.

"You don't got no choice, Veal. You are one of us, even when you're out there on Malibu getting all trained up," Wythe said.

Sergeant Vinter nodded to Corporal Wheng who opened his cooler and took out twelve bottles of San Miguel, Tamara's brew of choice. Alcohol in the barracks was forbidden, but even if the staff sergeant and the lieutenant could see through the window at what they were doing, neither made a move.

As soon as everyone had their bottle, Sergeant Vinter raised hers and said, "To Lance Corporal Tamara Veal, who's going to be the baddest gladiator of them all. Ooh-rah!"

Everyone echoed the "ooh-rah" before tilting back their bottles.

"You're going in as a Fuzo," the sergeant continued, "and you'll always be part of the squad. So wherever your life takes you, know that we are with you in spirit."

Liege thought she saw a tear form in the corner of Tamara's eye.

"And kick some Klethos ass!" Wyth shouted, which was followed by more "ooh-rahs."

Liege felt conflicted. She knew being selected as a gladiator, from all the billions of humanity, was a great honor. But it was also a death sentence. Tamara could earn untold glory, but even if she survived the Klethos, she probably had fewer than five years before the Brick[10] claimed her. The modification her body would undergo was just too drastic to keep the Brick at bay. She liked Tamara and considered her a friend. As a human being, as a sailor, she felt pride at what Tamara was going to do, but as a friend, she mourned her sacrifice.

There was a knock on the hatch, and Liege turned to see the staff sergeant discreetly rapping on the glass, head down.

Sergeant Vinter saw it too, and taking her cue from him, said, "OK, everyone say your good-byes. Tamara needs to get to the CO and then off to her shuttle."

One-by-one, each Marine went up to Tamara and shook her hand, followed by a hug. Liege hung back, then as everyone else had said good-bye, stepped forward.

"I'm going to miss you, Tamara," she said.

"I'll miss you, too, Doc."

Liege didn't bother with the handshake; she leaned in and pulled the big Marine into a hug, squeezing as hard as she could.

"Kick some ass," Liege whispered.

"Tamara, you're running late," Sergeant Vinter said.

The two broke their hug, and Tamara looked around before saying, "After being on the track team, I want to say I'm glad I was finally a 'real' Marine, and that it was with you. I could never pick a better bunch of warriors to go into battle with. Semper fi."

There was one last shout of "ooh-rah" as Fanny picked up Tamara's seabag. She was going to make sure she accompanied Tamara all the way to the shuttle, Liege knew.

It took a few more moments to get Tamara through the front hatch, where she received a rousing welcome from the gathered Marines.

---

[10] Brick: Boosted Regeneration Cancer, or BRC.

"So much for no send-off," Vic said.

"Did you really think that was going to happen?" Tyrell asked.

Liege had intended to follow Tamara to the battalion CP, but it seemed as if the entire battalion—and more—had gathered. The honor of being selected was Tamara's, of course, but still, it was also a point of honor for the battalion as well. The Fuzos had a storied history, and this was just one more page added to it. There wasn't a Marine or sailor in the battalion who wanted to miss this.

Tamara, Fanny, the lieutenant, and the platoon sergeant were making their way down the sidewalk, Tamara reaching out to shake hands as she went, while more Marines closed in behind her.

There wasn't much more for Liege to do. She'd said her goodbyes, and the mass of people was just too much.

"Fair winds and following seas, irmãs," she whispered before turning back into the barracks.

FS JOSHUA HOPE-OF-LIFE

Chapter 8

Liege leaned back in her chair so she could look Greg in the eye.

"Regeneration? Why that?"

"Oh my sweet dear newbie," HM3 Gregory Knutsen said. "Regeneration. No deployments, just a nice hospital gig. And when you do your time, beaucoup credits. More than our good Doctor X'anto is making now."

Liege didn't think she was still a newbie, but she was more interested in what Greg had to say. She'd never considered putting in for regen training, but maybe she'd have to consider it.

It was only the second day of their deployment, and the Marines were pretty busy getting settled in, so the morning's sick call had been light. The ship had given the battalion medical team their own space. If there was anything serious, they could send a Marine to the ship's sickbay, but the initial assessment was the battalion corpsmen's to make.

With no customers, talk had gravitated to follow-on specialty training. Taking the training would increase a corpsman's service commitment, but that didn't matter to Liege. She wanted that training in order to make her commercially viable out in the real galaxy. And as an HM, an E3, one more promotion and she could bring her Avó and sister out to live with her.

Liege had been considering several specialties. Being an imaging technician paid well, and there was a huge demand for them. Respiratory therapy had caught her attention. It wasn't a huge field at the moment, but with more and more people suffering from environmental regression, the need was growing.

"You and your regen, Greg. Most of that is with the government, and those pay scales are locked," Bibi said.

"Au contraire, mon ami. You're out-of-date. There are tons of civilian opportunities. Hell, the Confeds are contracting out their military's medical services."

"So you're under Confed pay, not Federation. No difference."

"But working for GenMed, not the government. Civilian pay scales," Greg said, a bit of smugness seeping through into his voice.

Cal Zylanti looked his fellow corpsmen and frowned. Cal, the senior corpsman with Fox, was a diehard fleet Marine doc. He had orders to the Special Reconnaissance Corpsman Course waiting for his return from the deployment, and for him, happiness was serving with the Marines. Liege planned to do her duty on this tour, but she had no intention of staying on the green side. She needed the skills she could then parlay into a good job on the civilian side, and taking out bad guys wasn't high on the list for most civilian companies.

Still, the Fleet Marine Force Enlisted Warfare Specialist badge Cal wore on his blouse looked pretty cool, and Liege knew it would stand her in good stead whenever she finally decided what specialty she wanted.

Liege had already completed some of the requirements for the badge merely in her day-to-day performance of her duties, but she didn't know the entirety of them. This cruise was low-key, and not much was expected to be accomplished, so she wondered if she'd have time to earn the badge before getting back to Tarawa. She made a note to herself to find out what she had to do to qualify.

"So, regen tech. You really think there's a demand for them?" she asked Greg.

"I swear there is. One of my buddies, he's a tech now, and he's already got standing offers for when he gets out. And 120k is the starting salary."

Liege took a surprised breath. 120,000? Starting salary? That was more than five times her current salary. That would provide lots of care for her Avó.

She'd been leaning toward respiratory therapist, but starting salary for them was 90k. Regen therapist was pretty routine, from what little she knew, and might not be as exciting, but 120k was nothing to sneeze at.

"So, what is the training like for that?" she asked. "What's the extra commitment?"

With an interested audience, Greg's eyes lit up as he launched into his spiel. Liege listened with rapt attention. She was actually enjoying her tour with the Marines, but she had a family to take care of, and she had to think of what was best for them. Maybe being a regen tech was the right choice after all.

JERICHO

Chapter 9

"Keep it tight, Doc," Korf hissed.

Liege hurried to close the gap between Corporal Wheng and her. She'd been looking up, expecting to see an enemy sniper, and had lost track of her place in the column.

With Tamara leaving just before the deployment, there hadn't been a replacement for her, and instead of bird-dogging the sergeant, Liege had stepped into Tamara's billet. She'd had training for just such requirements back at FMTB, but she'd be foolish to believe that short training had made her as skilled in warfighting as even newbies like Lassi or Pablo.

At least it wasn't a real war, but more a show-of-force. The battalion had absorbed a few mortar rounds, but there hadn't been a clash with the locals. Liege didn't even know who they supported in this conflict. Both sides were Federation citizens.

As both sides were Federation, there wasn't an official enemy. The battalion had been sent in as a neutral force of peacekeepers. Everyone knew this really should have been an FCDC mission, and the FCDC had also been deployed, but the fact that the Marines had been sent in as well was telling in its own right. The Federation thought fighting might break out again.

There were 217 planets and stations and another 87 nations in the Federation, so it was probably inevitable that mini-wars would break out between and within Federation worlds. Mankind had warred since Homo habilis climbed out of the trees, and that hadn't been bred out of their DNA. This conflict had been over resource rights, with the northern continent's population revolting over what it saw as the western and eastern continent's control over its resources. When they shut down the mines, the government had sent militia to reopen them, and fighting had broken out. The militia was driven back, and a state of war was declared.

It wasn't so cut-and-dried, though. Svealand, the northern continent, was controlled by the Opal Party, which was the minority party on the planet as a whole. The People's Right Party, the PRP (which had members spread over half of the Federation) and the local Republic First Party were the major political powers in the two southern continents. All three parties were spread throughout Jericho, however, and between themselves, controlled more than three-quarters of the planetary parliament, with the remaining seats belonging to independents and minor parties. So when war broke out, 40% of Kaglsand were self-declared loyalists and almost 15% of the southlands supported the north.

One FCDC regiment had been sent to the planetary administrative center of San Martin, and a second regiment was at Nya Asgard, the largest city in Svealand. The Second Battalion, Third Marines, the "Fuzos," had been sent to Skagerrak Point, the 300,000-person city on the isthmus connecting Svealand with the eastern continent of Gran Chaco. Skagerrak Point, besides having a protected deep-water harbor, was the nexus for the roads and maglev lines between the two continents. Within the borders of Svealand, the population was pretty evenly divided between those supporting the north and those supporting the southlands. The war's worst fighting had been in the city, atrocities had been committed by both sides, and now the Marines had been plopped down right in the middle of it.

Liege knew that both sides claimed that the Marines were there to support them, so it was doubtful that they'd come under direct attack. Still, she felt her stress levels rise as she scanned the buildings for signs of aggression. The dark alleys of Barrio Blanca, a Tino neighborhood, weighed heavily on her heart. If the Tinos decided to hit them, they'd be able to inflict heavy casualties.

With the bulk of the Tinos supportive of the PRP, and the PRP being a Federation-wide party, logic would dictate that here in the barrio, the citizens would welcome the Marines. Logic was not a universal trait, however.

The favelas back at home looked far more hostile, but Liege understood them and their rules. The barrios here, though, were new territory, and Liege didn't feel comfortable in them at all. When the patrol emerged from the barrio and snaked back across Drottninggatan—which the Marines designated Route Gazelle—Liege felt a weight lift off her shoulders. The Svea who lived north of Gazelle might not wish the Marines well, but at least Liege felt the Marines could now see any threat that might be waiting for them.

Two hours later, the patrol returned to the battalion base camp, back in what had been the port's bonded cargo facility. It wasn't home, nor was it the *Josh*, but Liege felt much better and less exposed than she'd felt patrolling in Barrio Blanca.

They'd been on Jericho for only two days so far, and as far as Liege was concerned, that was already two days too many. She just hoped that the two sides could come to an agreement without it breaking down into a fight again, and that the Fuzos could re-embark and get on to its previously planned missions.

Chapter 10

The mission took a turn on the seventh day of the deployment. Liege was just getting chow when the QRF[11] was called out. She dropped her half-eaten burger and rushed out of the chow hall and down to the aid station.

Liege was attached to Golf Company, but her secondary billet was with the rest of the corpsmen in the battalion aid station. If she wasn't on a mission or training with her squad, she was to report to the station for both routine sick call as well as for any emergencies. If the QRF had been called out, she knew she might be needed.

Most of the corpsmen were pouring in while HM1 Anthony, the battalion's second-senior corpsman, manned the command net. Liege waited nervously, straining her ears to catch sounds of fighting. She thought she heard a single blast, but if she had, it was pretty far away.

She almost jumped when Anthony turned and shouted out, "We've got one Class 1 WIA inbound!"

A Class 1 was serious, life threatening. Liege felt her heart leap in her chest.

Dr. X'anto went into action, pulling his Trauma Team 1 into position while others scurried to be ready for the patient. With only one WIA, neither Liege nor any of the other company corpsmen would be needed, but she didn't want to leave. Couldn't leave. She felt a compulsion to stay.

When she'd worked on Seth, she'd almost been on auto-pilot. She'd reacted, and when trying to recall things later, her memory had been curiously muddled. With the civilians on *Wyxy*, she'd simply helped assess some of them and administer initial aid to the burned woman. Even the gut-shot pirate on the Confederation ship hadn't really affected her, and she'd simply ziplocked the man for

---

[11] QRF: Quick Reaction Force

someone else to treat. So in some ways, this was going to be her first opportunity to see an actual medical team in action, doing what all their training should have led to. She faded back to the rear bulkhead along with Nica and a few others, trying to stay out of the way but still able to observe. Gnish saw them, nodded his approval, before he slipped out.

It was almost ten minutes before the patient was carried in.

"It's First Sergeant D-Ski," Nica whispered.

Liege had been looking at the mangled remnants of the Marine's right leg and had not looked to his face. She sure did now.

First Sergeant Dzieduszycki was the very popular India Company first sergeant. Liege knew this would hit his Marines hard.

"He's had a Two," Doc Psythe, one of the India company corpsmen, said as they carried him in, indicating the Series 2 recipe of nano-bots. "And two Hemocaps."

Liege thought that a Series 1 would have been more appropriate given the first sergeant's injuries, but she wasn't about to second guess another corpsman.

"Motherfuckers hit us with two mortars, and the first sergeant got it when he was getting everyone else to hit the deck," Doc Psytle added as they put the first sergeant on the table.

"We've got it now," Dr. X'anto said. "You're contaminated, so you need to step back."

It looked like Psytle was going to argue, but with a shake of his head, Chief Sou squashed that. Pystle and the three Marines who'd brought in the first sergeant hesitated, then left the theater.

The prep team quickly stripped the first sergeant, who was shifting back and forth in and out of consciousness, then sprayed him down. Ellen Western-Roulade brought the irradiator down over the first sergeant, then stepped back as the doctor and his team stepped up. Between the spray and the irradiator, the first sergeant and the bed were as sterile as possible.

Liege stepped a little closer to be able to see. Bright bits of white bone were visible emerging from the scarlet mass of tissue that had been his lower leg. Her stomach churned, and she upchucked a tiny bit of vomit, the gastric acid burning her throat.

No one was looking at her, so she swallowed, forcing it back down. She might have to deal with similar trauma in the field, and she had to master her emotions.

Trauma Team 1 did a quick assessment. Both visual and scanner indicated that other than a few minor wounds, the leg was the only major injury. After receiving the report, Doctor X'anto stepped up to examine the first sergeant. It took him less than a minute to make up his mind. What was left of the leg had to be taken off at the knee at a minimum, and while he could do that in the aid station, there was no need with the better equipped medical facilities on the Joshua.

"How long before we can get him back up the ship?" the doctor asked Anthony.

"Shuttle is inbound now. ETA nine minutes."

"Then we just stabilize him and get him on up," Doctor X'anto said.

He pulled out a Number 6 pressure patch and molded it around what was left of the first sergeant's leg. If the patch had problems with the uneven surface and mangled bits, Liege couldn't see it.

"Are they going to put him in stasis?" Nica quietly asked Liege.

"I don't know," Liege answered, wondering the same thing.

Doctor X'anto gave First Sergeant D-ski another injection of something, but that was about it. The first sergeant was wrapped up in a blanket, and the examining table's legs were lowered to make it mobile. In a modern hospital, the table would have hover capabilities, but in a field facility like this, the less complicated the better.

Within a minute, two corpsmen, followed by Doctor X'anto, were taking the first sergeant out of the aid station and over to the LZ. In thirty minutes, the first sergeant would be on the ship and probably losing his leg. He had a pretty long regen in front of him.

Liege and Nica walked out of the aid station together. Liege considered going back to finish eating, but her appetite was gone, and the sour taste of gastric acid still filled her mouth.

The one thing that had hit her was that there hadn't been any magic cure just because the first sergeant made it back to the aid station. Doctor X'anto hadn't done anything more than what Liege could do out in the field.

The lesson in that hit Liege hard. Out there, it was up to her. She was the first, and probably the most important factor in saving her Marines. There wasn't some big brother who could take over for her. Her squad's life rested squarely on her shoulders.

It was a very heavy load.

Chapter 11

Liege trudged ahead, her stomach growling.

I should have eaten more for breakfast.

On the patrol the day before, Liege had gotten nauseous and had tossed her breakfast, much to her embarrassment, and she'd vowed not to let that happen again. Today's platoon-sized patrol had been planned for three hours—a simple escort of a Navy civil affairs officer to meet with a barrio president—so Liege had figured she could go light. But plans were just plans, and when the barrio president had suggested he call in the presidents of two other barrios, the Navy lieutenant commander had readily agreed. So the platoon had set up a perimeter and waited—and waited. Now, at 1840, they were finally heading back. Liege hoped that Staff Sergeant Abdálle had called back to Gunny Coventry, the battalion head cook, and asked him to hold hot chow for them. It wasn't like it would be difficult; just keep the fabricators warmed up and waiting for them. Knowing the platoon sergeant, though, he hadn't bothered. The guy lived for field rats, telling all who would listen that they made Marines "hard."

Liege was enjoying her tour, but sometimes, the inherent Marine need to prove they were tougher than anyone else in the galaxy got a little tiresome. Liege was not the baddest person around. She'd held her own in the *Commando Meninas*. They'd thought themselves to be mean bitches, but she knew now their little gang was kindergarten compared to the Marines. She was serving alongside the cream of the Federation military, and she was not ashamed to admit that she couldn't kick all of their asses—or maybe any of their asses. Save them, maybe, but not kick them.

The platoon, in a dual column, crossed Route Gazelle, leaving the closed-in warrens of Barrio Blanca and entering a more open Svea neighborhood. Liege knew that they were not here to take sides between the Tintos and the Svea; still, she couldn't help but feel some of the stress leave her as they started on the last leg for their camp.

Liege was trying to spot the fire team acting as route security a hundred or so meters down the boulevard when a crack caught her attention.

She turned around to spot what had made it when Corporal Wheng yelled, "Get down, Doc!"

It took her a moment to realize that all the rest of the Marines near her were rushing for cover. More cracks sounded out, and Liege belatedly got her legs beneath her and sprinted for the recessed doorway of a closed shop, pulling her legs in to attempt to keep them out of any line of fire.

Liege was serving as a rifleman, but her prime duty was still as the squad corpsman. She flipped her display to the squad's bios. All twelve avatars showed bright blue and healthy. She superimposed their positions for a moment to see where everyone was. They'd been hit just as First Squad was halfway across Route Gazelle. Liege and Korf were in the recessed doorway together. Corporal Wheng and Wythe were about five meters to the west of them. Third Team was across Gazelle, as was Sergeant Vinter, but First had retreated to the Barrio Blanca side of the road. All except Pablo Sukiyama, who was huddled against a tree in the narrow median. As Liege watched, several rounds hit the tree, sending splinters flying.

Pablo ducked lower, trying to get as small as possible. The tree was only about 20 centimeters in diameter, and Pablo was quite a bit wider than that.

"Do you see him?" Korf asked, peering around the edge of the doorway.

Liege got down flat, then nudged forward, barely getting past the edge as she looked to the west, trying to spot whomever was firing at them. She saw nothing.

She flipped on the command circuit, and orders were filling the airwaves. Marines were beginning to return fire, but from the traffic on the net, Liege gathered that the enemy was high above them in a well-fortified position. From below, the Marines couldn't get a decent shot.

Liege looked over at Pablo, knowing that if he was hit, it would be up to her to go get him. She flipped off the command circuit, trying to center her thoughts. The sergeant could still send her orders, but the general chatter ceased.

Just get up and run for it, she silently pleaded her fellow Marine. *Get some cover.*

That tree wouldn't protect him if the enemy gunman took him under fire again. She drew her legs under her, ready to dart out the moment she saw him hit. She was scared—really scared. She didn't need to look at her bioreadouts—she could feel her heart racing.

Five seconds. I can get to him in five seconds.

"Shit, they just cancelled the Wasp," Korf told her. "I guess they don't want to take down some svermin's building."

The battalion had one Wasp assigned to the deployment. A single fighter aircraft might not make much of a difference against a well-armed enemy, but here, it ruled the skies. It would have no problem zeroing the gunman.

The firing from the enemy above ceased, but Liege didn't notice. She was rocking forward, ready to go.

Korf let out a laugh and said, "Saint Gregory's ass! Scratch one svermin sniper."

"What?" Liege asked.

"That's why the Wasp was canc'ed. We had a guardian angel getting eyes on the asshole."

Liege was confused, and she turned to look at Korf for clarification.

"Guardian angel?"

"Shit, Doc, sometimes I forget that you're still a newbie. No offense," he quickly added. "Yeah. 'Guardian angel.' Our snipers. One of the teams had overwatch."

"Oh, like the Ice Bitch," Liege blurted out.

"Yeah, but not her. Wait," he said, and she could see him with the vacant face of someone listening to his comms. "Hornet-Eight. That's who did it. I think that's Sergeant Maud. 'Long Arm,' they call him."

"Long Arm?" Liege asked with a laugh, suddenly euphoric that she was not going to have to dash into fire to save Pablo, who was only now beginning to look around in confusion. "Is that because he can fire long distances, or because he has another arm that is overly long?"

Korf looked at her for a second, his brows furrowed, before he erupted into loud braying.

"Hell, Doc, I never thought of that. And who'd have thought our sweet little doc had her mind in the gutter. Wait until I tell Wythe."

Liege wasn't a shrinking violet, but she'd been attempting to present somewhat of a civilized front to the rest of them. She knew, though, that she could be as earthly as the saltiest dog. The *Commando Meninas* had quite a reputation for it. But the relief of no one getting hit and the enemy being zeroed had swept over her, releasing the inner Liege.

Sergeant Vinter got everyone back up to move out. Liege casually sauntered over to Pablo, making sure he was OK. It was a far easier walk than what she'd been ready to make.

Liege gave the sergeant a thumbs-up, although she probably already knew that. The squad leader's battle AI might not be as sophisticated, as Liege's as far as bioreadouts, but it was detailed enough to know that Pablo wasn't hurt.

As the platoon began to move out again, she heard Korf talking to himself.

"And is something else that long, Doc asks. Saint Gregory's ass! Ha!"

Chapter 12

Liege wiped the sweat from her brow. The heat wave outside was bad enough, but inside the old warehouses, it bordered on the unbearable. She didn't know why they just didn't turn on the air conditioners—certainly the warehouses had to have them.

She ran another quick download of core temperatures, ten minutes after she'd run the last one. There were the normal slight elevations, but nothing going into the danger range as of yet. She took a swallow of water, then considered telling the rest of the Marines to drink again. They were probably sick of her keeping on their asses to remain hydrated.

The platoon was on a search and seizure mission. Intel had indicated that this line of warehouses, outside of the bonded warehouses at the port, but within two klicks of the Marine camp, might be being used as a cache for weapons. First Platoon had been given the unenviable job of searching for the weapons.

It was almost fall in this hemisphere of Jericho, but the temperatures had been ungodly hot over the last few days. When the platoon had arrived at the complex, it had been a blistering 43 degrees. Inside the stifling warehouses, it was closer to 47 degrees—and without a hint of a breeze.

After two hours of searching, they hadn't found anything suspicious. Liege was beginning to wonder if some insurgent was out there watching them, laughing as they cooked while chasing some fake intel.

Liege was getting nauseous again, and she was determined not to puke. Her tender stomach was becoming somewhat of a joke among the squad, one she was determined to squash.

"Doc, come to me," Sergeant Vinter passed on the P2P.

"The sergeant needs me," Liege told Korf, who nodded as he opened up a crate.

Jonathan P. Brazee

She checked the squad leader's bios as she hurried over, but they read fine.

"What's up?" she asked as she met the sergeant by the open cargo bay door.

"Second Squad's got a medical situation," the sergeant said. "They need you."

"Doc Lester-Mrchenigian's there," Liege said automatically. "She's just as trained as I am."

"She's part of the problem."

Shit! Nica? I haven't heard any fighting! she thought, her heart jumping in her chest.

"What's going on? What's happened?"

"I'm not sure. But Sergeant Quincero's sending over a fire team. They should be here in a moment. You go over there and see what you need to do. When you're finished, call me and we'll send a team to get you."

Liege tried to remember the procedures to bring up Second Squad's bios on her AI. Due to privacy legislation, she only had access to those Marines under her care. She could touch-load any Marine's data, but to pull them off the net when they weren't co-located took authorization.

She tried two codes, then had to query her AI. That wasn't good. The fact that she'd had to query would be noted and sent to the chief.

No getting around it, she thought. *But I need to know what's happening.*

Within a few seconds, Second Squad's bios filled her display, and it was immediately clear what was wrong. Of the 13 Marines and one corpsman, nine had elevated body temps. Three were over 40 degrees, with Nica 41.3. Temperatures like that could be fatal.

Liege rushed to the open cargo door, looking around to the right to the warehouse being searched by Second Squad. No one was in sight.

"I'm going, Sergeant," she yelled back at her squad leader.

"Wait!" Sergeant Vinter yelled, but Liege was already dashing out into the sun. For a moment, the air brushing past her was welcomed, but as she ran, she started to gasp as her body temp

68

rose. Two Marines came out of the warehouse and headed her way, and Liege crossed the baked areas between the two buildings, dodging into the shade alongside Second Squad's building.

"This way," Corporal Reverent Son shouted when he spied her, waving his arm as if to speed her up.

Liege slowed to a quick walk, breathing heavily, the hot air making her dizzy. She reached the corporal and PFC Jessep Warren and let them guide her in.

Liege thought it was hot in their warehouse, but this one was even hotter at 48 degrees.

"All of you, drink, right now!" she passed on the platoon command circuit. Second Squad had their own net, but Liege didn't take the time to have her AI query and join that circuit.

"We are drinking, but we don't have much," the corporal said as Liege hurried to where two Marines and Nica were prone on the ground.

"What do you mean, you don't have much?" Liege asked and she knelt beside Nica. "Why not?"

During hot weather conditions, the inner layer of a Marine's skins had a membrane that wicked sweat via capillary cohesion to an osmosis reclamation module. Along with a urine reclamation unit, purified water was re-introduced both into the camelback as well as a tiny lattice of cooling tubes woven into the fabric. Simple body motion powered the heat exchange, keeping the water in the tubes five or six degrees below the ambient temperature.

"Well, uh, we kinda didn't activate the piss catchers," Corporal RS admitted.

"You what?" Liege asked, her attention riveted on the corporal.

The urine reclamation unit was woven into the material of the skins trousers. In high-temperature situations, a simple command from a Marine's combat AI activated it, and when a Marine felt the urge, he or she just let loose into the trousers and let the unit do the rest. This was such a situation, and Liege knew that the command had been passed.

"We, uh, most of us didn't activate them."

"Why the hell not?" Liege asked, getting angry.

"You know. The piss crystals."

When the urine was collected and run through the first reclamation step, solids in the urine were left behind. These small flakes could be a little hard, and some people didn't like the feel of them as they moved about.

"So you let a little itch overcome common sense? *Filha da puta!*"

Liege was about to explode at their stupidity, but she didn't have time for that now. She could see the squad gathered around three prone squadmates. She rushed up, shouldered several Marines aside, and started her assessment. It was obvious that all three were suffering from heat stroke. All were flushed with hot, dry skin. All three unconscious or semi-conscious. All three were panting with short, shallow breaths. She didn't need a formal scan. She knew she had to get the three back to the battalion aid station.

"Golf-Two-Actual, I need an immediate CASEVAC, Level 1, at my pos. Three pax," Liege passed back to the lieutenant.

"Is that a Level 1? Confirm."

"Roger. Level 1."

"Roger that. Sending that up now."

Liege wasn't surprised that the lieutenant had wanted to confirm. A Level 1 was for life and death situations. Either a Navy shuttle or the one of the two Storks would be dispatched, and with the current situation, that meant the Wasp had to fly cover. That could affect any contact elsewhere in the AO. As the platoon was not in contact, the request might have seemed odd to the lieutenant, but the call was hers to make.

And it was the right call. The three were victims, just as much as had they been combat WIAs. If their temperatures were not brought down and brought down quickly, they would die. It was as simple as that.

Liege ran a quick scan on each of the three and uploaded her readings to the aid station. She knew they would be ready for them—if the three could get there in time. If not, it was stasis and a hope that their brains were not too fried for a resurrection.

Liege had to give her three patients more time. She reached over to release the sealing seam on Nica's blouse.

"Get their clothes off," she said to the Marines standing over her.

Several of them knelt to follow her command. Sergeant Quincero took off Nica's boots, as Liege rolled her to her side to remove her blouse. Together, they pulled off her trou.

"Whatever water you have, pour it over them, starting at the head and going to their chests. Don't bother with their arms and legs."

Liege unhooked the drinking tube of her camelback and let the water pour first on Nica's face, then she trickled the stream over her chest. She had a liter and a half left, and all of it went over her fellow corpsman.

Liege ran her scan over Nica: 40.9 degrees. She was still too hot. She scanned Eddie and Beaver. Beaver was just below the magic temp of 40 at 39.8, but Eddie was still 40.2, his heart still racing at 220.

"Is that all the water you have?" she asked.

"Yeah, we're all dry."

"How soon for the CASEVAC?" she passed back to the lieutenant.

"ETA eight minutes. I'm trying to goose them."

Eight minutes? To fly two klicks? What the hell's wrong with them? Liege wondered as panic started to take hold of her.

Nica was panting while her pulse raced back and forth between 210 and 180. Her eyes were rolled back into her head, her skin dry and hot. It was almost as if the water Liege had poured on her had evaporated like drops on a hot frying pan.

"I want Doc Gnish here now!" she passed.

"He's on his way," the calm voice of the lieutenant reached her. "But you're there now. You've got this."

Liege ran through the options in her mind. She could give each of them a shot of Hemocaps, but there wasn't enough liquid volume in them to do much good in as far as cooling them. None of her injector recipes would help in this case either, except maybe to slow heart rates. But the heart rates were symptoms, not causes. She had to get them cooler.

Well, there was one thing that could help.

"Since you haven't been using your urine collectors, you all must have full bladders. All of you, piss on their blouses," she ordered.

"Doc?" Sergeant Quincero asked, obviously confused.

Several of the other Marines looked to Corporal Hineman, Corporal "Know."

He seemed to contemplate what Liege had said for a moment, then he nodded and said, "Ah, evaporation."

He hit his zipper seal, pulled out his penis, and started to piss on Beaver's blouse.

Liege wanted to roll her eyes, but she refrained. She knew that the rest of his squad thought the corporal was some sort of walking google, but she was the only medical expert here, and she shouldn't have had to get Hineman's approval.

"Try and get the entire thing wet," Liege said.

Within moments, the other Marines were emptying their bladders on the clothing.

"Isn't piss hot, though?" Sergeant Quincero asked.

"Not as hot as these three are," Liege answered, picking up one of the blouses and waving it in the air to cool it down. "And it will cool off pretty quick as it evaporates."

She took the wet skins and put them on the chests of the three, continually scanning their temps. Nica's was still hovering dangerously high, but Beaver's was dropping. He started mumbling and struggling to sit up.

Doc Gnish, accompanied by three Marines, rushed into the warehouse.

He gave a questioning look to Liege as he scanned Eddie.

"No water. I had them piss onto the blouses."

He nodded, then unhooked his camelback drinking tube, pouring some water onto Nica's forehead.

"Is there anything else you can do?" Liege asked him.

"No. You've done about as much as possible out here. They need to get back and into lavage."

As if on cue, the sound of a Stork landing told them it was time.

HM2 Gnish quickly took charge, assigning three Marines to each of the stricken. With him on their asses, they carried each of them outside. Liege followed in trace until they were loaded on the Stork, and the big bird lifted up and flared right to return to the camp. Nica and the two Marines would be in the aid station within three minutes, getting the treatment they needed to save their lives.

She'd been tempted to jump on the Stork herself, but it would have served no good. And with Nica gone, she had to remain with the platoon. This was still a war zone, and they could be in contact at any time.

"Uh, Doc, how're you going to report this?" Sergeant Quincero asked quietly as he came alongside her.

"What do you mean?"

"You know, about us not using the piss collectors."

He was shifting his weight from leg to leg, anxiously waiting for her response.

Liege was pretty upset with him. It was his job to keep his Marines safe, and letting them turn off the collectors could have killed Nica and Eddie. But it might not have been just the urine collectors. It was extremely hot in that warehouse, and they should never have been put in the position to work inside for two hours as they had done. Bypassing the collectors certainly contributed to the heat stroke, but it wasn't the only cause.

"I'm not sure, Sergeant, just what's going to be in my report just yet. I have to go over my treatment notes. But right now, you are standing down. All of you are to sit in the shade until we can get you back. Understand?"

"Yeah, Doc. Sure," he said, turning to relay her orders. "Oh, and thanks for saving them," he added.

Liege's righteous anger started to fade. She thought all three would recover in time, but this had been a stupid waste. The insurgents, both Svea and Tino were bad enough, but Marines didn't need to be put out of action because of stupidity up the chain of command.

Chapter 13

Liege flicked off her PA screen, leaned back in her rack, and stared at the overhead a mere meter in front of her face. She was bored. The battalion was getting mortared daily and patrols were being hit, but still, she was bored. The Navy, in their indubitable manner of making sure sailors were as comfortable as possible, had sent down four big ion-display screens and over 80,000 holo-shows, flicks, and documentaries, more than anyone could possibly watch in a lifetime of service. Some of the flicks were newly released; even Pinnacle Productions, a Confederation studio, had sent their latest releases to the Navy, including the blockbuster *Deepslayer 3*.

But Liege could only watch so many flicks, could only read so many books. It wasn't as if she had a surfeit of free time. If she wasn't with the squad out on patrol or manning checkpoints, she was conducting company sickcall or working in the battalion aid station. Still, with what limited free time she had, she was getting itchy to do something else.

Liege realized that part of her "itch" might be a lack of social interaction. She was comfortable with her squad, and she enjoyed spending time with them, but the Marines were her brothers and sisters, and Liege was still a party-girl at heart. But she was firm in her vow not to date within the battalion, so she was in the middle of a long social dry spell.

Most of the squads in the battalion had taken residence in empty shipping containers, with racks welded to the side in the back and a small common area in the front. Personal weapons were locked to each rack. The "Vineyard" (an admittedly weak attempt derived from Sergeant Vinter's name, but no one had come up with anything better), First Squad's squadbay, was probably no different from any other. Seabags hung on hooks on the bulkheads, while the over-riding smell of weapons cleaning gear seemed to defeat the small air filtration system that struggled to keep up. It was crowded, but it was better than the first two weeks when every squad just staked out a claim on a piece of concrete in one of the two warehouses taken over by the battalion. With the concerted effort of a Navy Seabee team, however, all of the rifle companies, along with Weapons, were in the containers, and within another few days, H&S would have theirs as well.

Liege sighed as she studied the pattern in the overhead, a pattern that was becoming very familiar to her.

"What, bored?" Vic asked as he rummaged in his seabag.

"No. Yeah. I guess so."

"Some of us are hitting the gym. Why don't you come along? Get some meat on you."

"No, that's OK. You go."

"OK, suit yourself," he said, pulling out a pair of weight gloves.

If there was one thing that Marines did no matter the circumstances, it was work out. Here they were in a semi-combat situation, living out of shipping containers in a port facility, and if they had any free time, they were in a gym they had managed to construct in a corner of small warehouse. The equipment was minimal, but ingenuity was rampant as they made do with what they could scrounge.

Liege rolled over on her side to watch Vic, Pablo, and Fanny get ready. She admired their discipline but thought they went overboard with the fitness thing. The Navy had minimum physical standards for corpsmen, even corpsmen serving with the Marines, but by definition, minimum was good enough, right?

She had to admit, though, that Vic looked pretty good. Very good. If he was in another battalion, she might be interested. Even Fanny was looking buff and pretty sexy in a fitness kind of way.

If you liked that type, she thought.

Liege held out her own arm, examining it.

OK, not so buff. But so what?

Fanny said something that Liege couldn't catch, then punched Pablo in the arm. All three of them laughed. And it hit her—for Marines, the gym wasn't just to keep fit. It was also part of the social fabric. All three of them were happy, laughing. They'd be able to forget Jericho for an hour as they did their thing, getting fit and relieving stress at the same time—and most of all, maybe, bonding.

"Hey, wait up!" she impulsively shouted out, sliding out of her top rack. "I'm coming, too."

All three turned to her with surprised looks on their faces before Fanny said, "Well, OK, girl. Come on."

Liege didn't have any weight gloves or other accessories, but the Marines worked out in their uniforms. She grabbed her M99 and joined the other three as they left the squadbay.

Liege looked around as they marched over to the gym, looking around to see if anyone had noticed that she was going to the gym, then feeling embarrassed that she cared. She told herself to just relax and go with the flow.

The gym was very Spartan. Makeshift free weights were plentiful, as were the ever-present Null G platforms. With the waist strap, the platforms were used in space to enable Marines and sailors to maintain a degree of fitness. Under gravity, the ribbon-plates functioned as stationary running platforms. There were at least 40 of the plates, all lined up in perfect formation, of course. Only three of the plates were free.

"I'm going to go for a run," she told the other three who were heading for the weights.

She took the free plate in the back row, surprised to see Doctor X'anto working up a sweat on the adjacent plate.

"Neves," he acknowledged as his legs churned.

Liege put her weapon beside the plate and gingerly stepped on. She'd played a bit with ribbon-plates before, and so the weird, almost slimy feel of the plate's surface wasn't a surprise. She carefully centered herself, and with hesitant baby steps, started a very slow jog. She felt as if she was going to fall at any moment, but the plate's surface adjusted to each stride, managing to give her a solid platform.

It felt as if she was running on a slightly giving surface, not the reality of her feet simply sliding over the plate.

Doctor X'anto looked out of the corner of his eyes, and Liege could read his opinion of her slow jog. She picked up the pace, her stride smoothing out. The ribbon-plates worked better the faster the person ran on them.

After only five minutes, Liege was breathing hard. She slowed down slightly, but that didn't do much good. After another two minutes, she came to a stop.

The doctor turned his head to look right at her, eyebrows raised.

"I just warmed up here," she gasped out. "I'm with my friends there hitting the weights."

She tried to retain her composure as she walked over to the weight area. All three of her squadmates were doing dumbbell lunges, so she grabbed two of the lighter-looking dumbbells and joined them.

"Keep you back straight, Liege," Fanny said in a low voice. "Like this."

Liege watched her for a moment as Fanny stood straight, dumbbells at her side, then lunged forward, right leg bent at the knee, left extended behind before using the right to thrust herself back upright. She nodded her understanding, then tried to copy her friend.

"Better. You don't want to hurt your back in here."

For the next hour, she followed along with the other three. If she didn't lift as much as any of them, they didn't seem to care nor look down upon her for that.

HM2 Cal Zylanti even came up, watched her do a rep on the piece of plastiboard that served as an incline bench, and then nodded his approval. Liege didn't know why that mattered to her, but it did.

"OK, children, if we're going to shower and get chow before our gate brief, we'd better vamoose," Vic said as Fanny finished her last bench press.

Is it that late already? Liege wondered, checking her PA.

She was tired, she might be a little stiff while on gate duty tonight, and she knew she would be sore in the morning, but she was happy.

Her boredom of the afternoon was a long-vanished memory.

Chapter 14

Liege stood behind the Marine in the PICS, wondering what it would be like to fight from inside one of the combat suits. She'd been in one at FMTB, and she'd even walked around in one for a few minutes, but that was merely an orientation. It had to be different to be locked inside one for a day or more at a time.

The addition of the PICS team to a routine checkpoint had been recent. The battalion had gone in light. Instead of five PICS platoons, the Fuzos only had two: Golf's Third Platoon and India's Second. The intent from on high was that the battalion was there to keep the peace, and having a "militaristic" footprint could send the wrong message.

To a man, the Marines and sailors in the battalion thought that was utter hyena shit. What was a Marine battalion but "militaristic?" That was what they were designed to be.

But with the increased level of violence, and with one Marine from Hotel KIA, the battalion commander had thrown that guidance out the window, and she'd gone as heavy as she could. Now, with the squad at Checkpoint 3, they had six PICS Marines reinforcing them. Checkpoint 3 was on the south side of Route Wildebeest just as it entered the city, and it was the major, well, the only north-south highway connecting Svealand and Gran Chaco. With almost all of the planet's armor in the southern and eastern continents, Wildebeest was the only avenue of approach for any significant armor force.

Not that the Marines expected any. The *Josh* would be able to spot any armored movement from up in orbit long before it could reach the city, but having the PICS Marines was probably more of a message. Still, the six should give anyone, not just an armored column, second thoughts about hitting them.

Liege wasn't even sure who was inside that monstrosity. She knew that Third Platoon's Third Squad, led by Sergeant diTora, was supporting them, but she couldn't tell who was in which PICS. She couldn't even pull up their bios on her display, which seemed asinine. Her combat AI couldn't interface with the PICS hub.

Whoever was inside the PICS, he or she hadn't moved in at least ten minutes. Liege wondered if the Marine was napping, or even if that was possible.

The PICS were very high-tech pieces of equipment, and their combat AIs had significant medical capabilities. A PICS platoon was only assigned one corpsman, unlike a rifle platoon's three, so Liege knew her chances of being assigned to a PICS platoon were minimal, especially considering her lack of combat experience. Still, the thought of running around like some super-hero had a significant amount of allure.

"You here with us, Doc?" Corporal Wheng asked.

Liege shook her head and came back to reality, embarrassed to be called out by the team leader. The fire team was in the on-deck position, ready to move into the checkpoint itself in another few minutes. But that didn't mean they could relax. Standing 20 meters back, they were supposed to be observing the big picture, looking for anything out of the ordinary that Third might miss.

And it wasn't as if Third was alone. There were both svermin and—

Svea and Tinos, or jericks, she reminded herself.

"Svermin" and "Arse-tins" were unauthorized nicknames for the two sides, and using the terms could now result in some unwelcomed extra duty.

There were both Svea and Tino police teams at the checkpoint. They'd both be taking potshots at each other after they'd got off duty, but for the moment, they were forced to play nice. Still, Liege thought they were barely tolerating each other's presence, even if they were nominally on the same police force.

Add the six PICS Marines and a sniper team on angel duty, and Liege thought the checkpoint was pretty secure. A long line of private hovers and trucks waited to be checked through into the city. Every 30 minutes, the northbound line would be blocked and southbound traffic would be allowed to pass through.

Liege focused back on the checkpoint. She looked over the waiting drivers, trying to spot something that would alert her, but not knowing what that might be. The drivers looked either resigned or peeved, and Liege could understand both emotions. Some of them might have driven 12 or more hours, and now, just a few kilometers from home, they had to sit and wait.

Each police team checked alternating vehicles, so two vehicles were being inspected at once. After the Svea police team waved through a red Hyundai Vortex, the corporal in charge of the team called the other five of them to the side of the road.

"What's going on, Corporal Olmstead?" Sergeant Vinter asked, walking over. "We've got a lot of vehicles to get through."

Corporal Wheng tilted his head at the other three in the fire team, indicating that they should follow him as he went to back up the squad leader.

"Nothing, Sergeant. I'm getting a recall back to the station is all. Another team will be out here in a few moments to take our place."

"So you should be waiting until they arrive. We can't slow down the inspections."

The Svea police corporal shrugged, saying, "You know orders, sergeant. It should only be a few minutes."

The Tino team stopped their inspection, looking at each other with concern.

"Keep inspecting, Olmstead," Sergeant Vinter said, steel in her voice.

"Sorry. We have to go," he said, motioning for the other five cops to follow him.

"Coyote-Three," the sergeant passed on one of the circuits, Liege listening from just off her shoulder. "We have a situation. The Svealander team has just abandoned their post. Can you please confirm why?"

"That's both teams, Sergeant," Wheng said.

Liege looked away from the sergeant. Sure enough, the Tino cops were quickly leaving as well. Not just the police. Several hovers from the rear of the line did three-point turns to get out of the way, and a large two-trailer truck was trying to slowly back up.

"This isn't good," Korf said to no one in particular.

Liege didn't need to be an experienced combat vet to know why. The mice were running away for a reason.

Corporal Sativaa started motioning for the rest of the hovers and trucks in line to back up. Liege's instincts were to find cover, but if something was about to go down, they couldn't leave the civilians just sitting there. She stepped up to join Third Fire Team in playing traffic cop.

One of the waiting trucks was a new Wiedner. The driver simply raised the hover, and using attitude jets on the front bumpers, spun the big rig around on a pivot as nicely as could be— but was stuck as the two-trailer GE didn't have the same capabilities. Liege walked over to the driver of the GE to help ground-guide him around when the shout of "incoming!" came over the squad circuit.

Liege spun around just in time to see three explosions: one hitting a PICS Marine, another hitting empty dirt, and one hitting the back of the Wiedner. Almost immediately, five PICS Marines returned fire, focusing on a point out of Liege's sight.

The PICS that was hit didn't come apart, nor did it even fall. It simply stood there silently. Liege rushed forward, only seeing the damage to the upper right thigh of the combat suit, almost at the juncture of the girdle assembly. It was a mass of molten metal and electronics covering a rough circle 25 centimeters in diameter.

"Cease fire, cease fire!" came over the net, but Liege was reaching up to touch-connect her PA to the PICS' transmitter. Liege might not be able to connect to a PICS' bioreadouts while on the move, but the universal peer-to-peer connection would let her PA act as a repeater.

To her relief, Corporal Jones was alive. She was unconscious, but her vitals were strong. Her PICS had shut down as it was designed.

Where is the stupid release? she wondered, scanning the back of the huge combat suit. *There!*

She reached up and hit the emergency molt. The suit went into the molting process with what looked to be solid pieces of the carapace splitting by layers until Jones's unconscious body was revealed. She started pulling Jones back and out to extract her when Korf stepped in to lend a hand. They pulled the Marine out and laid her on the deck.

Butterflies emerge from cocoons ready to spread their wings and fly. With Jones, it was like pulling the caterpillar out instead. Her slick longjohns made her look even smaller than she actually was.

Liege ran her scanner over the corporal, finally able to get a full reading. To her relief, the corporal was in good shape. She'd suffered some major bruising to her leg and hip, and she'd had a slight concussion. The PICS' AI had induced her state of unconsciousness as it sent anti-inflammatories coursing through her body. It was a precautionary measure, one that Liege could reverse. She adjusted her injector and gave Jones the injection. Ten seconds later, the corporal stirred and opened her eyes.

She seemed to have a hard time focusing on Liege's face, but after a few seconds, everything seemed to dawn on her, and she half-sat, her elbows propping her up.

She saw her PICS, then muttered, "Shit, Annabelle! You're all fucked up."

Liege broke out laughing, receiving a scowl from the corporal in return. It just seemed too funny. The huge, frightening PICS was not only controlled by a 35 kg Marine, she called her PICS "Annabelle." That didn't invoke fear.

"Sorry about that, Corporal," Liege said, trying to regain control. "You're a little banged up, but you'll be fine. Three days bedrest, I think, and you'll be as good as new."

"What about Anna. . .my PICS?"

"Your PICS? I don't know. I'm not an armorer."

"Doc Neves, what's the status of Corporal Jones?" Sergeant diTora asked over the P2P.

Liege looked up to see a PICS heading her way.

"She's fine. A little bruised up, and she'll need to be checked for a slight concussion, but she's good to go. We'll need to get her some transport back, but this is only a Class 3 CASEVAC. No emergency."

"Roger that. I'll get on it," the PICS squad leader passed.

"Some shit, huh?" Korf asked as Liege stood up and looked around. "One of the rockets was diverted into the ground, and another ricocheted off a PICS and hit that Wiedner. Took out half of the back."

"Is the driver OK?" Liege asked, suddenly remembering that she might have more work to do.

"Not even scratched. Pissed as all git out, though."

Liege could see the man, pacing up and down the length of his truck, which wasn't very long now with half of the cargo van blown off. Demolished bits of what looked to have been rolls and rolls of toilet paper were scattered around the ground, some still slowly burning, other bits still shades of subdued coral and white.

"There's going to be some shit to pay for that," Liege said, not able to help herself.

"Yeah, I know...oh, I see what you did with that," Korf said, suddenly laughing.

Liege was more of a sonic cleanser kind of girl, not toilet paper, but still, the opening had been too sweet to pass up.

Chapter 15

"You should join us," Liege told Rene as they finished up their field rats.

"Ah, the enthusiasm of the newly-converted," Vic said from where he sat, pulling up his peaches pouch and draining the last of the juice into his mouth.

Liege gave him a frown, even if she knew he was right. She'd been hitting the gym for only three weeks now, yet she was pushing it more than anyone else.

"Don't mind him. Just look at this," Liege told Rene, flexing her biceps.

Rene looked, then nodded before digging into her chili mac. She hadn't looked convinced.

Liege looked at her flexed bicep, then wondered if it really was more cut or if that was just her imagination.

No, it's more cut, she told herself.

With Rene, there were four women in the squad—well, five if she counted Sergeant Vinter, but Vinter was in another class. She was a *sergeant*, and that transcended gender or anything else. Liege and Fanny were very close, and Liege wanted to bring Rene and Lassi Rassiter into the fold. Lassi, though, didn't seem ready to reach out to anyone, so that left Rene if Liege was going to form a squad Three Musketeers. Besides, Rene was the first person Liege had ever known who came from Mother Earth, and it was almost as if by being her friend, some of that might rub off on her. That was ridiculous, she knew, but Earth was considered as almost some sort of heavenly paradise to those back in the favelas of Nova Esperança.

Rene's lack of enthusiasm didn't deter Liege. She'd just keep pushing, and she'd eventually wear the girl down. She looked down at the pouch of tuna japonnaise in her hand. Half of it was still there, steam slowly escaping. She wasn't hungry, though. Field Rations D just didn't cut it with her. As a little girl when it was just

Leticia, Avó, and her, sometimes they went without food. Back then, she would have killed for rations like these. But now, they just didn't cut it.

The platoon was in the playground of Tracy Heskett Junior School. With high, strong walls and positioned alongside Camino al Norte close to its intersection with Route Gazelle, it made a good secure area for patrols to stop or for Marine staff to meet local bigwigs. For two months now, the battalion had been sending a platoon to take up residence at the school, for a week at a time, as a forward CP.

"The lieutenant's coming," Corporal Sativaa told the rest of the Marines as he stood up. "Time to boogie."

Liege folded shut her rations, activating the seal, and putting them in her assault pack. She told herself she'd save the food for later, but "later," they'd be back at the camp where Gunny Coventry could run them some fresh fab-chow, not this petrified crap that had probably been processed back during the War of the Far Reaches.

The platoon had been on a patrol-in-force, leaving the battalion lines last night at 1930. Surveillance had indicated an increase of subversive activity, and the platoon had gone out as a reminder that the Marines were ready and willing to respond to any provocation.

Three other platoons from the other rifle companies were on their own patrols-in-force throughout the AO, and two of them had contact during the night. Surprisingly, one of the attacks had been on India's PICS platoon, which had been entirely ineffective and had cost the attackers at least four KIA and an unknown number of WIA.

There had been no challenges to Second Platoon during the long night, however, and the short break at Tracy Heskett had been a welcome interlude to get off their feet and get a bit of chow into their bellies. Now, they had a decent-enough hike down Camino al Norte, then a right turn to get back to port. Four hours tops, and they'd be back in their squadbays.

"Naptime's over, children!" Staff Sergeant Abdálle shouted, making the rounds of the three squads. "Let's start earning our salaries."

It took a good three minutes, with the platoon sergeant pushing hard, for the platoon to be ready to step out. Lieutenant Alamien twirled his forefinger in the air, and the platoon sergeant shouted, "Step it off, Sergeant S."

Sergeant Sasoon, the Third Squad leader, didn't have to say a thing. His lead fire team stepped out the school gate and onto the road. First Squad was second in line, and the lieutenant positioned himself with them. Behind Liege, Second Squad would pull up the rear.

The morning air was clear and crisp as Liege stepped through the school's gates. Once again, she was struck by the beauty of the city. It wasn't just the bay and the tree-covered hills; the city itself had been carefully planned. Camino al Norte in this sector was a wide, lovely boulevard with stately buildings on each side of the road. A center median had been landscaped with statues and vegetation. There were signs of the violence with more than a few destroyed buildings, but it was easy to see how nice it must have been before the fighting. Closer to the center of town, the east side of the boulevard would be taken up by the massive Barrio Blanca, but up here was a different story. Even the barrio wasn't that bad, at least to the favela-raised Liege (although most of the Marines said they found the place oppressive).

The platoon was in a dual column as it marched. There were far more secure formations, but the intent of the patrol was to be seen. Still, the Marines weren't stupid. Flank security was running parallel to them as they marched, drones and nano-drones flooded the air, the Marine's lone Wasp was on station, and up above in orbit, the *Josh* had her eyes along every centimeter of the route.

The street was fairly busy with pedestrians. People were going about their daily lives. Some of them glared at the Marines from windows and backed up alongside the buildings, but others either ignored them or even smiled. A handful of youngsters seemed to get a kick out of marching along the median and between the two columns.

Still, the Marines couldn't let their guard down. This was primarily a Svea area, and the Arm of the North was the newly formed Svea militia that had instigated a number of attacks, including the firefight with Hotel Company that had resulted in ten WIAs, four of them serious. Things might seem peaceful and routine, but the platoon could not be complacent.

Many of the landmarks in the city had designations to help their identification. The outward-leaning plastiglass bank that Liege walked past was the "Glass Cliff," and just up ahead, she could see the top floors of the "Pyramid." Liege had thought it somewhat silly, at first, that in the era of electronic identification and individual battle AIs, they needed nicknames for landmarks, but she quickly learned that in basic conversations, the nicknames worked well. Humans were humans, and they still used speech as their main means of communications.

The Pyramid was on the west side of the road, still in a Svea area, but it pretty well marked the beginning of Barrio Blanca on the east side of the boulevard. As the patrol wended its way past the building, Liege could feel her stress level lower. She knew that the Tinos were not really friends of the Marines, but the two attacks during the night on the other platoons had occurred in Svea neighborhoods.

Even without the Pyramid, it was pretty evident that the complexion of the area had changed. The buildings on the east side of the road became more uniform with less architectural variety. The median lost its trees and major pieces of art. Some art remained, but most of it looked rather worse for wear. The "Duck Walk" was a good example of that. The first piece of art after passing the Pyramid from the north, it consisted of a meter-tall mother duck with nine baby ducks following her. Liege didn't know how many ducklings had been originally sculpted as there were a number of gaps in the line, and in one of the gaps, two little legs still rose from the ground. Two ducklings were missing their heads, and another duckling had been torn out of place and was now mounting the duckling ahead of it. The Marines had named that duckling "Hank," and they saluted him each time they marched past. Most of the buildings were in pretty good shape, but Liege guessed that with the Tinos on one side and the Svea on the other, no one wanted to take ownership of the median.

There were fewer people on the street in this section of the boulevard. More of them ducked into doorways as the Marines patrolled past.

Liege brought up the patrol route on her display. Another 1200 meters of march, then the column right that would bring them back to camp. She was focusing on the route when a cloud of dust shot out of the bottom of a building just ahead of her. She immediately cleared the display a split second before the low rumble of an explosion, followed by a blast of pressure, reached her. Almost in slow motion, the entire side of an office building up ahead seemed to fall over onto the boulevard. Liege watched in shock as the road ahead disappeared into the rising dust and smoke.

It wasn't just the road that had been covered with debris. There were Marines there!

She toggled her bio-scans. Wheng was greyed out, Korf, Fanny, and Goodpastor were light blue.

Without thinking, she broke into a sprint, barely acknowledging the firing that erupted around her, both incoming fire and outgoing as Marines took cover and engaged. Her mind was on one thing: get her Marines.

The dust was still heavy as she reached the rubble. She saw Fanny first, sitting on the ground, looking dazed. A quick scan showed she was not seriously hurt, but rounds were pinging around them. Liege grabbed Fanny by the shoulder harness and pulled her to the cover of a big piece of wall.

"You're OK. Just stay down," she yelled at her.

She ran back to see another Marine helping Goodpastor out of the fire. A quick scan and she could see his injuries weren't life-threatening.

"Doc, take cover!" someone shouted as she tried to get a picture of the rubble covering the street.

She switched to her battle overlay. She could see where Wheng was—under the deepest pile of rubble. His bio-scan showed nothing, no signs of life. Korf, though, while he was in big trouble, was still hanging on to life. Liege oriented her display, then started scrambling over the broken chunks of building.

A heavy chatter of fire sounded overhead, and she ducked, but it was the Wasp, its 20mm chaingun chewing up one of the buildings on the barrio side.

Liege reached where Korf should have beeen, but she saw nothing. Two rounds hit the slab of plasticrete upon which she was standing, sending small splinters into her calf.

"Keep them off me!" she shouted into the squad circuit, hoping someone would cover her.

She took in a deep breath, then bent over to start heaving off whatever piece of rubble she could. Korf's vitals were on her display, and she could see him fading quickly. The display couldn't tell her everything, but the readouts were pretty indicative that he didn't have much time.

"Doc, I'm coming to help," Pablo passed to her.

"No! I've got it. Just cover me."

Liege knew she could use the help, but there wasn't much room where she was balanced precariously between two plasticrete slabs. But more than that, she didn't want anyone else exposed. She could feel enemy crosshairs centered between her shoulders, and she expected to be hit at any moment.

She renewed her digging, and when she pulled up a piece of sheeting, she saw 30 centimeters of Marines between her feet.

"Korf!' she yelled out, despite knowing he was unconscious.

She bent over to tug on him when she was hit with an agonizing shock. Her head flew back as her body arched in agony. She wanted to scream, but her lungs wouldn't cooperate.

And just as suddenly, it was gone.

She knew she'd been hit with an energy weapon of some sort—luckily by a side lobe of the beam. A direct hit, with only her skins and bones for protection, and she'd have been completely scrambled.

Liege tried to take some deep breaths to gather herself. She brought up her right hand to her face. She couldn't keep it still. The shaking told her that she'd suffered some serious damage.

Screw it!

She bent back down. Liege couldn't hold her hand steady, but by forcing it into movement, she could mitigate the effects. She tore into the rubble like a badger, throwing pieces of building around like they were made of polypuffs.

Maybe the gym's paying off, she thought, almost as an observer as her body simply went on autopilot.

She was only dimly aware of the fight going on, of the Wasp making run after run. She was hit four times by kinetics, her bones hardening and protecting her. The rounds felt like mule kicks, but except for the round that hit her shin and might have done some damage, she doubted that she'd been hurt by them. She was kissed by another energy weapon, but either the beam had ablated too much to have a significant punch, or she was even farther out from the main beam.

She'd cleared Korf's back first, so she focused on his head. A huge piece of plasticrete had his head trapped, and Liege couldn't budge it. She was about to call for Pablo to help when she remembered her M99. She'd slung it over her back when she started clambering over the pile. She pulled it back around and jammed the muzzled between the bottom edge of the piece of the wall and some rubble underneath it. She took a deep breath, and then bracing her feet, pulled down with everything she had. The slab lifted ever so slightly, and still straining to hold it up, she quickly grabbed Korf's harness and yanked him back. His head came free, and Liege pulled him upright.

I'm probably doing all sorts of damage here.

For injuries such as his, the protocol was to keep a patient as still as possible and secure the neck and head. But that protocol didn't consider people trying to kill both the patient and caregiver.

She put her arms around Korf from behind, locking her hands across his chest. Her nerves were on fire, but she pushed up with all the force she could muster. There was a nasty crackling sound from one of his legs, but he jerked free, sending Liege down on her ass with him on top of her. Liege pushed him aside, stood, and managed to get him into a fireman's carry. She stumbled off the rubble pile when a string of automatic fire laced both of them. The round that struck her side was a much bigger round than what had hit her a few minutes ago, and the force drove her to one knee. She knew that Korf had been hit as well, and she hoped his bones were still functioning.

Liege got back up just as Pablo and Vic rushed out from cover and pulled Korf from her shoulders. Vic took Korf, and Pablo helped Liege escape the line of fire.

They almost dove through the broken door of the adjoining building. Liege didn't know if the explosion next door had blasted the plastiglass door or if the Marines smashed it, but she didn't care. Korf and she were out of direct fire.

What she'd done suddenly hit her. She'd been working almost from muscle memory out there, somehow ignoring the fact that she'd been a very obvious target. She shouldn't have survived.

Liege leaned over and vomited the small amount of field rats she'd eaten.

"That's our Doc," Vic said, a smile on his face, as he leaned over to hold her head so she wouldn't get the vomit on herself.

She hadn't eaten much, so after a couple of heaves, she was able to sit up and wipe her mouth.

"You both OK?" she asked as she pulled out her scanner to check Korf.

Her hands were shaking, but whether from the energy blast she'd absorbed or from simple relief, she didn't know. She tried to focus on the readouts, which didn't look good, but she was having a hard time concentrating.

"What do we got?" Doc Gnish asked, rushing into the store.

"Korf looks fucked up, and I don't think Doc's in too good a shape," Vic said.

Liege wanted to protest Gnish taking over. Korf was her squadmate, her responsibility. But as shock was taking over, she realized that she was not totally all there. Gnish was a good corpsman with plenty of experience, and he'd be able to take care of Korf.

Liege leaned back, not caring that she'd just put her butt in her vomit. She watched Gnish work on Korf, trying to professionally evaluate her fellow corpsman's work, but not being able to make much sense of it.

She wasn't aware when the fighting outside stopped. The rest of the squad came in to check on Korf and her, but she waved off their concerns. She did try to stand up when Korf was CASEVAC'd, but Vic calmed her down. Korf was in good hands, he kept telling her.

Wythe and Vic helped Liege to her feet, and with legs that didn't want to obey her commands, they supported her while she left the store. Five Marines were standing on the rubble pile about where she'd thought Corporal Wheng was buried. She tried to change direction to reach them. Maybe Wheng was resurrectable.

"No, Doc, let them get Killer. You need to get back to the aid station," Wythe told her.

The battalion had one Armadillo tracked fighting vehicle, an ambulance variant, and it had arrived to pick up the wounded. Liege was helped inside where HM1 Knight met her and sat her down. Two other wounded Marines were loaded as well, but Liege couldn't make out their injuries.

"How're you feeling, Neves?" Knight asked, running a scanner over her.

"Not too bad," Liege told him. "I'll be—"

And that was the last thing Liege remembered.

FS JOSHUA HOPE OF LIFE

Chapter 16

Liege came to under harsh, bright lights. Her head felt fuzzy, and she was confused.

"You feeling OK?" someone asked.

Liege turned her head to the left to see a young man in scrubs standing over her, looking expectantly.

"I'm fine," she croaked out by force of habit.

But she wasn't fine. Her thoughts were not particularly clear.

"Good. You got quite a jolt down there, close to a level three. You've got a hairline fracture of the right tibia. But I think you're going to be fine, given time. No need for regen, at least."

Regen? Why?

Then slowly, things began to coalesce into something that made sense. They'd been on patrol, and they'd been hit. She'd gone to recover Korf.

Korf!

"How's Korf? Is he OK?"

The nurse, for that's who the guy had to be, repeated "Korf? Let me see. Ah, yes. Lance Corporal Reynaldo Korf." He paused a moment while she looked at his PA. "Oh, pretty serious."

Liege's heart dropped as she tried to sit up.

"He's suffered severe internal trauma and will probably lose a leg. He's in stasis now for transport back to Tarawa where he's going to face some serious regen time."

"But he'll make it?"

"I don't see why not. You never know, of course, but I would imagine he'll make a full recovery."

Liege sunk back down relieved. At least Korf had made it.

"And Corporal Wheng?" she asked.

The nurse didn't have to look at his PA for the answer.

His face fell as he said, "I'm sorry, Liege. Corporal Wheng didn't survive."

"What about resurrection?" Liege asked.

"His head was crushed when the building fell on him. No chance for that."

Liege felt as if someone had poleaxed her in the gut. She was serving with the Marines, and that was a hazardous job. She knew on an intellectual level that Marines died. But not her Marines. Corporal Wheng—Killer Wheng—was someone she knew, someone she trained with, went on missions with, sat around the Vineyard and shot the shit with. He wasn't some sort of abstract. He was a living, breathing compatriot, even a friend. She'd never hear his wry take on life again, never hear him offer an observation that sounded complacent, but as it sunk in, would cause Liege to laugh out loud.

". . . out as soon as he's free. So until then, if you need me, just ring your buzzer."

"Pardon?" Liege asked the nurse, missing half of what he'd just said.

"Doctor Mannerheim. He'll be in to check you out and let you know what's happening."

"Oh, OK," Liege said.

Doctor Mannerheim was the ship's surgeon. He was junior in rank to the battalion's Doctor X'anto, but on the ship, his medical decisions ruled. He could even overturn a decision by the ship's commanding officer if it pertained to health.

Things were still a little fuzzy, but the pieces were falling into place. She remembered the frantic digging to pull out Korf. She remembered getting hit by an energy weapon of some kind.

What did he say? Almost a Level 3?

Level 3 wasn't necessarily lethal, but it would effectively fry out a person's nervous system and cause significant tissue damage. Getting hit with a Level 3 for more than two seconds meant long term regen, and the process might not be 100% effective.

He'd also mentioned a fractured tibia. She looked down at her leg, which was enclosed in a regen chamber. The chamber was probably overkill. The B nanos would be weaving their lattice around the broken bone, injecting small regen pellets around the fracture, and she knew a couple of session in the Electrolavage System, the ELS, would be more beneficial. The regen chamber might optimize healing, but with this kind of injury, the nanos, aided by the ELS, could repair the bone within a couple of days.

She wondered where she'd broken it. Probably the shot she'd taken, but it could have been while she was climbing around the rubble.

"So how's our hero doing?" Doctor Mannerheim asked, pulling back the curtain.

Hero?

"Um, I'm fine."

The doctor looked at the readouts in the regen chamber clamped around her leg and then nodded approvingly. He ran his PA across her repeater and took a moment to read up on her chart.

"Well, HM Neves—can I call you Liege?" he asked, not waiting for a response. "You came close to some pretty serious damage, but close doesn't count. I watched the battle recordings, though, and I don't see how you escaped with so little. You were very, very lucky. Commander Barnes ran the CIC-W on you, and he counted no less than 29 rounds that either hit you or came within 15 centimeters. Four of those that missed were .50 cal rounds."

.50 cals? Liege thought, her eyes widening.

A Marine's skins and bones were pretty good defenses against most small arms, but they offered no protection against a .50 caliber slug.

"In fact, the .42 cal round that hit your side should have penetrated into your lungs, but somehow, it deflected off. It must have been just at the right angle. Another belt of fire, and I'm afraid you might not have made it. Lucky for you, that sniper took out the machine gunner before he could fire again."

Machine gunner? Sniper?

Liege's thoughts were getting muddled again. She remembered a blow to the ribs, but she had no idea what the doctor was talking about it.

"What sniper?" she asked.

"Oh, I saw the recording of her, too. At one point, she was dangling off a building with another Marine holding her up like a marionette."

The doctor looked excited as he recounted what he'd seen. The *Josh* would have been recording the entire battle, and evidently, the visuals were open to the staff.

"Which sniper?"

"Oh, the one with the odd name. Medicine Crow or something like that."

Liege raised her eyebrows. Corporal Medicine Crow had been the one to save Tamara Veal's ass, and now it looked like she'd saved her ass as well. Maybe there was something to this guardian angel stuff.

"So anyway, back to your medical situation. Your leg will be fine in another two or three days. You've suffered minor tissue damage; you know, the typical cuts and scrapes—nothing serious. Your main issue is the peripheral nerve damage. I don't want to put you into regen if I can help it, but I'm sending you back to Tarawa for a full work-up. I'll let one of the staff neurologists make that call."

"Tarawa? Back at the hospital there?"

"Yes, of course at the hospital there. We've one of the finest staffs there in the Navy. Hell, the entire Federation, I'd say."

"But you mean after the deployment, right?"

"No, Liege. You're going back on the next picket. You've grabbed the Golden Ticket back home."

"But, I can't go back now. I've got to be with my squad."

"That's an admirable emotion, Liege, but there's no need. There are more than enough corpsmen to cover for you. I know it's not very comfortable down there. I came down for a day, after all, so I've seen what they feed you," he said with a knowing laugh. "No, in a few days, you'll be back with the Navy—on Tarawa, of course, but at least in the hospital. No more gung-ho Marines for a while."

Liege felt a rise of anger that she had to push back down.

"Is there a medical reason I have to go back now?" she asked, her voice calm.

"No. Well, yes. You can't risk getting hit again for at least a year. As you know, energy disrupters like what hit you have a cumulative effect. If you get hit again within a year or so, it could end up much worse. Technically, you're non-deployable until cleared."

Liege had been taught that at A Schools, but she'd forgotten it.

"But other than that, is there a reason I can't stay until the battalion rotates out?"

"Well, no. You won't suffer any more damage. But I'd feel better if you were evaluated by the neurosurgeons."

"But in your professional opinion, you think I'm stable?"

"Well, yes."

"I trust your expertise, Doctor. If you think I'm stable, that's good enough for me. And I'd really like to get back to my battalion. I don't have to go out into the ville, if you require that. But I can at least run sick call and help in the aid station. Chief Soukianssian can use some help. You can ask him yourself."

The doctor seemed to waver, and Liege wondered if she'd laid on the compliments too heavily.

"Chief needs you?" he asked, sounding unsure.

"Yes, sir. You can call him up. If I'm out of action, he's going to have to pull someone else to go out with my squad. If he does that, he'll be even more shorthanded. "

"But don't you want to get back to Tarawa? It can't be that comfortable serving with the Marines. Wouldn't you like to get back to the blue side?"

"I appreciate that, sir. But as they taught us at FTCS, the Marines count on us. So I'd like to uphold Navy tradition of giving it everything I've got."

Shit, that sounds fake.

The doctor seemed to be swayed, though.

"Well, Liege, I have to say, I'm impressed. I thought I'd give you an easy out, but I forgot the big picture. Yes, we need to support our green brothers.

"OK, two more days here on the ELS to get your leg healed, and I'll run another eval on you. If everything's still green, I'll let you return to the battalion."

Liege was surprised at how relieved she felt when she heard that. Sure, it would be nice to be back on Tarawa, and not just from the comfort aspect. She'd be an HM3 soon, and she'd need to work out the details to bring Avó and Leticia there, so the extra time could be a godsend. But she couldn't leave the battalion while there was still a mission. She'd come with them, and she'd return with them. Nothing else was an option.

JERICHO

Chapter 17

"Grab a seat, Doc," Wythe said, kicking out a folding chair. "You looked pretty copacetic out there, standing proud."

"True that," Pablo said. "Copacetic to the max."

"Thanks," she said as each of the Marines lifted a fist for a bump, even Doc Opah, her replacement with the squad.

Opah wasn't a total replacement. Liege hadn't moved out of the Vineyard, and Opah hadn't moved in. But when the squad went on a mission, Opah took her place. Doctor Mannerheim, and supported now by Doctor X'anto, had insisted on no combat missions for her.

Liege had been surprised at how she'd just felt. When the chief asked her to be part of the color guard, it had just been one more task. But holding the Navy colors had been more emotional than she would have guessed. She felt honored. She might be serving with the Marines, but she was still a sailor, and pride ran deep.

"Did they read the commandant's birthday greeting yet?" she asked, having marched out of the warehouse after posting the colors and having only just returned.

"Yep," Wythe said. "All Marines, blah, blah, blah, tradition, blah, blah, blah, I'm proud, blah, blah, blah, Joab Ling, General, Commandant."

"Oh come on, Wythe," Fanny said. "It wasn't that bad."

"I'm not saying it was. I gots me a tingle, I did, by jove," he said, the last "gots me a tingle" in a comically weird old-timey accent of some sort. "But are any of the birthday messages any different?"

"Fucking Wythe," Vic muttered. "I liked the message."

"I liked it, too," Wythe said, suddenly sounding defensive. "But if any of you can recite the entire thing to Doc, be my guest."

Liege looked around the Warehouse D. Almost half of the battalion was gathered inside the warehouse, one of the port's two largest and the one not chock full of cargo. It didn't matter where they were or the mission, the Marines did not forget their birthday. The entire battalion was not gathered together, however. The "police action" (it was not to be referred to as a "war") had only gotten more intense, and the battalion XO had taken a heavily reinforced Hotel Company to create a secondary camp on the south side of the city. Other Marines were out on patrol or manning positions, so half of the battalion was most of the available Marines. During the second seating, Marines now on post would be relieved for a second ceremony.

Liege's duties were over for the moment, but there was more to the birthday ceremony. There was no official guest of honor, so the CO stood in, giving a short speech. Liege tried to listen, but the acoustics in the warehouse left a lot to be desired. She did catch the end, though, where the CO told the S-3 to get on to the birthday cake.

"Present the cake!" Major Cranston shouted out.

All hands stood as four Marines solemnly marched forward, carrying a good-sized birthday cake.

Gunny Coventry has outdone himself, Liege thought.

It looked like it could have been bought from a professional bakery.

Once the cake had been placed on the table, the major called forward the oldest and youngest Marine to get the first pieces of cake.

"Sergeant Major Jassus Douber-Link is the oldest Marine in the battalion. He was born on 13 July 338. He enlisted in the Corps on 14 July 346," the major called out.

The sergeant major graciously accepted his slice, taking a bite and nodding that it met with his approval.

"And, also per tradition, the next piece of cake goes to our youngest Marine. Private Klip Poussey was born on 9 May 367. . ."

There was a collective moan from the Marines in formation. Wythe and Pablo bumped fists while rolling their eyes.

". . . and enlisted in the Corps on 9 May 384. He joined the Fuzos on 12 August 384, 11 days before our current deployment."

Poussey, standing proud but looking slightly nervous, accepted his piece and took a tiny bite.

"I can't believe they are letting babies serve now," Corporal Sativaa said.

Liege had been the same age as Poussey when she enlisted, but she felt much older than Poussey looked.

Normally, the guest of honor would get the next piece, but as expected, the CO refused. The S-3 put the body of Marines at ease, and Gunny Coventry started cutting up the cake. Table by table, the Marines and sailors rose and joined the line to get their piece.

Liege was standing next to Fanny and Lassi when a familiar face made her way back to them.

"Corporal Crow, happy birthday!" Liege said.

"Happy birthday to you, too. You're looking good. I didn't see a trace of a limp."

"Oh, I just got kissed a little. Doc Gnish sent me up to the *Josh*, and a couple of sessions on the ELS, and I'm good as new."

"ELS?"

"You know, the Electrolavage System."

"I just wanted to say that what you did was pretty ballsy. I. . .I. . ." the corporal said. "Well, I just wanted to tell you that."

She started to turn away when Liege said, "I heard it was you on one of the buildings keeping the jericks off my ass."

"It wasn't just me. And your platoon was showing their fight, too."

"Maybe, but I appreciate it," Liege said, holding out her hand.

Corporal Medicine Crow took it, then asked, "The Marine you pulled out. I know he got CASEVAC'd, but how is he?"

"Korf's gonna make it," Wythe said, answering for Liege. "He's back on Tarawa in regen, but that son of a bitch will be back before we know it."

"Good to hear. Well, I, uh, I need to get back in line if I want to get my cake. All of you, happy birthday."

"You, too," Liege told her.

"That was decent of her," Fanny said.

"Maybe she was lording it over us," Wythe offered.

"Maybe, maybe not. But she zeroed a shitload of jericks, and she probably saved at least half of our asses."

"Yeah, but from up on the roof tops, out of danger. Not like Doc here. That's why Doc's getting a Navy Cross, and the Ice Bitch's getting nothing."

"I don't know. I saw the recording where she had her a-gunner hold her over the edge of the building. That had her more exposed than any of us, and that's when she zeroed the crew-served gunner who had me in his sights. I don't know about you guys, but I think she saved my pretty ass, at least," Liege said.

There was laughter when she said "pretty ass," as she had hoped. Yes, everyone knew she'd been recommended for a Navy Cross, but she still felt awkward about discussing it. And she felt more than a little unworthy. When she'd been out there digging Korf out, her mind had been on autopilot. She hadn't really contemplated that what she was doing was dangerous. It wasn't until later, when she'd watched the recordings, that she'd really processed the fact that she could easily have been killed.

The heavy beat of "I Want It" by Grayson Parade suddenly blared out into the warehouse to the cheers of most of the Marines. The song was probably not on any Marine Corps approved list of music, but it was popular.

"Come on," she said to Vic, grabbing his hand and pulling him out into an open area in the warehouse.

"But I want my cake," he protested.

"You'll get some, but not now. Now, you dance!"

Within moments, other couples were out on the make-shift dance floor, bopping to the music. Vic was a good-looking guy, but he danced like a possum with a corncob stuck up his ass. It didn't matter, though. It just felt good to let loose.

Wythe followed Vic, then Corporal Sativaa, then Pablo, who was a surprisingly good dancer. They were followed by a string of men, most of whom Liege didn't know. She didn't care. Liege was a party girl at heart, and this was her first party since landing on the planet.

There were far fewer women than men in the battalion, and while male Marines danced alone or with each other, most waited their turn to dance with a woman. Even the CO got out to shake her ass, first with the XO, S3 and chaplain, then with a very embarrassed PFC Poussey, much to the delight of the battalion.

The warehouse wasn't the most elegant place for a birthday ball, but it was the Marines and sailors who made a ball, not the venue. And Liege was having a great time. She was sad when two hours later, the music was cut off.

"Sorry to pull the plug, but all of you on the port watch, you need to get ready. We've got to let the starboard watch come in for their ball," the sergeant major passed on the mic.

The squad filtered back to their table, picking up their covers and the plastic cups with:

United Federation Marine Corps
398th Birthday Ball
Second Battalion, Third Marines, The Fuzos
Skagerrak Point, Jericho

stamped on the side.

"I never did get my cake," Vic said to Liege as they started to file out of the warehouse.

"Neither did I," she answered.

She didn't care. This was only her second Marine birthday ball, but she thought she would remember it well for the rest of her life.

TARAWA

Chapter 18

Liege had Vic put another five kilos on the bar. Flattening her shoulder blades, she took a breath, lifted it free of the cradles, then slowly brought the bar down to her chest before pushing it back up. It was more difficult this way, the slow lowering, but Liege was able to complete the eight reps, withVic hovering over her, hand poised and ready to assist if she needed it.

"Good job," he said as the bar settled back into the cradle.

Four months earlier on Jericho, Liege would never have imagined she'd become a gym rat, and she certainly couldn't imagine benching 60 kg. She felt better physically—no hint of her kiss by the energy weapon anymore—but more than that, she felt better mentally. She had a new level of confidence.

She got off the bench, raising her eyebrows to Fanny, who usually lifted heavier than her. Fanny just nodded and got on the bench as it was. Liege felt a small surge of pride. She'd finally reached Fanny's level.

"So, as I was asking you, you really didn't know what the Corpo de Fuzileiros meant?" Vic asked.

"No, I told you. I could figure out "corpo," but "fuzileiros?" What the heck is one of them?"

"But it's our nickname. You never wondered what a "Fuzo" is?" he persisted.

"Not really," Liege said as she moved to spot Fanny.

"And you're from Nova Esperança, right? Settled by Brazilians. And you can't speak Portuguese?"

"Hell, Vic. I'm from DeBrussey, and we don't speak French," Fanny said as she settled her grip.

The night before had been the battalion's patron day celebration. The battalion's patron was the Portuguese Marine Corps, the Corpo de Fuzileiros, formed in 1618 and one of the first Marine Corps in existence. When the Federation Marine Corps was formed, each of the infantry battalions adopted one of mankind's extant Marine Corps as its patron unit as a way to carry on hundreds of years of traditions.

Vic had asked Doc if the battalion's motto, *"Braço as àrmas feito,"* was well-known on Nova Esperança, and he'd been surprised that she'd never heard of it, nor did she know what it meant. He brought it up again that morning at the gym.

"Yeah, but Doc here, I've heard her swear in Portuguese, so I thought she must speak some," Vic said as Fanny started her set.

"But I'm not Portuguese. My ancestors were Brazilian, but we speak Standard at home," Liege said.

Actually, there was a flavor, so to speak, of old Brazil in the favelas. Liege's Avó could speak some Portuguese, and quite a few words had become absorbed into Standard, not the least being her gang's name, *Commando Meninas,* which simply meant "Commando Girls" in Portuguese, but using a few words in daily life was a far cry from knowing how to speak another language.

"Anyway, it's not like we're the same as Portuguese. Brazil had its own Marine Corps. I looked it up last night. 3/8 has them for their patron, so if I'm supposed to have some historical connection to Earth, maybe I should have been assigned to them."

Fanny finished her set, and Liege helped Vic add 40 more kilos to the bar.

"So do you have any of the old customs at home?" Vic asked as he lay down on the bench. "What about food?"

"Food? We eat what the fabricators put out," Liege said with a laugh. "Nothing too fancy in the favelas. Maybe the suits get more, but we make do with what we can afford. But, I guess we do like Carioca red beans and rice, and I think that's Brazilian."

"Oh, I know that. They serve it at a rodizio my family likes.

"Rodizio?" Liege and Fanny asked in unison.

"Sure. Rodizio. There's another word for it, too, churrascaria. You sit down, and waiters come out with big long swords with roasted meats on them. The servers cut the meat off right onto your plate."

"Ha, I don't think our fabricators have those kinds of recipes," Liege said.

"No, not fabricators. I think it has to be real meat. And lots of it," Vic said just before he started his rep.

"Oh, aren't we high society, only eating organics," Fanny said, reaching over to fist bump Liege.

In the favelas, Liege had eaten real vegetables at some of the festivals at the cathedral, but never to her knowledge meat. She had organic meat a few times with the Marines, but she'd mostly toyed with it on her plate. To be honest, the thought gave her the willy-wallies.

"You don't know what you're missing. Tell you what. There's a rodizio in Kentville. Let me see what they have, and if it looks good, we'll all take a weekend and hit the town."

Kentville was Tarawa's main resort. Tarawa didn't get a lot of off-planet tourists, so it mostly serviced residents. But it was supposed to be nice, and there was even a Marine Corps Lodge there. The room rates at the lodge were based on rank, so Liege, still an HM, would have to pay very little. Liege was saving up to bring her family to Tarawa, but she'd always wanted to check out Kentville, so if she could share expenses, that might be fun.

"OK, you check it out, and we'll think about it," Liege said, speaking for both Fanny and herself. "But right now, you're hogging my bench. I think I'm good for 65 kilos, and you're in my way."

Chapter 19

"When's she supposed to get here?" Wythe asked.

"She'll get here when she gets here," Fanny told him.

Most of the squad had parked themselves on the steps to the barracks, waiting for Tamara Veal to show up. Liege was pretty excited. She'd watched the fight on Halcon 4, of course, almost beside herself as Tamara stepped into the ring.

Tamara had always been a big girl, but the gladiator Tamara was almost unrecognizable compared to the lance corporal squadmate she'd been. She looked huge, even on the holo projector, but she moved with a sense of grace that was surprising for someone that large.

When she'd moved into what everyone now knew was a Maori haka, Liege couldn't remain sitting. She'd gotten up in the barracks common room where at least 60 Marines were packed in to watch, giving up her seat and starting to pace back and forth.

When the fight with the Klethos queen commenced, Liege couldn't tear her eyes away, but she feared what she'd see. The battle went back and forth for a few moments, and it looked as if the Klethos had kicked Tamara to the ground, but suddenly, the Klethos' neck was spouting blue blood, and the fight was over. The cheers that filled the common room threatened to shake the building's very foundation.

And now, for the first time since she'd left, Tamara was coming for a visit.

They'd already had a formal parade that morning, with the commandant himself presenting Tamara with a Single Combat Service Medal. Liege tried to catch Tamara's eyes as they passed in review, but she wasn't sure the gladiator had seen her among all the Marines marching by.

Liege was a little nervous to be meeting Tamara. They were friends, but not bosom buddies. Tamara had left before the bonds had grown too strong. And now Tamara wasn't even a lance coolie anymore; she was a warrant officer. Maybe she was above them now. Fanny and Liege had been tasked with escorting Tamara to a room to get her into some over-sized Fuzos PT gear the battalion had specially made for her, but maybe with her new rank, she'd want another officer to help her instead of two non-rates.

Fanny and she had discussed that possibility, and they'd decided that if Tamara objected to them, they'd ask Lieutenant Southerland, one of Hotel's platoon commanders, to take over.

Liege leaned back, elbows on the step behind her. The sergeant major had passed that Tamara was visiting the Wounded Warrior Battalion, so it was just a matter of waiting. Pablo and Lassi were sitting on the next step below her, playing Next. Liege could never quite grasp neither the rules nor the attraction of the inane word game, and she only listened in with half an ear.

Her mind was drifting when the low murmur rising from the battalion let her know Tamara was coming. A large, custom van pulled in front of the battalion CP.

"Come on, Liege. We've got to get up there," Fanny said, pulling on her arm.

The two wove their way through the Marines as Tamara, looking sharp in her alphas, stepped out of the van to the cheers of the battalion. She stood there for a moment, looking a little embarrassed, when they reached her.

"We're guessing you might want to get more comfortable, ma'am?" Fanny said, holding out the PT gear.

"I'll 'ma'am' you, Fanny, but yeah, let me get changed," Tamara said, looking happy to see them.

Tamara scanned the crowd, then pointed to the rest of the squad, now standing on the steps.

"About time you showed up, ma'am! We're starving here!" Wythe yelled out to the laughter of the crowd.

Tamara followed Liege and Fanny, high-fiving Marines as they went. Tamara had to duck to get into the CP, and they led her back to the sergeant major's office. In the constrained space for her bulk, it was a little difficult for the gladiator to shuck off her alphas, which Liege took and hung up on a large, but still too-small hanger.

She slipped on the PT gear with the 2/3 emblem emblazoned on the front of the shirt. They didn't have any shoes big enough for her, so she kicked off her florsheims and simply went barefoot.

"I heard Jericho was pretty rough," Tamara said.

"Yeah, it kind of sucked," Fanny admitted. "The ROE[12] was messed up, you know."

"You heard about Wheng, right?" Liege asked.

"No, what about him?"

"They brought a wall down on him, him and Korf. Korf was messed up, but he pulled through and was CASEVAC'd, but Wheng didn't make it," Liege said.

Tamara looked gut-shot when she heard.

"Don't let Doc downplay it. When the wall went down, we got hit bad, and she went all badger there, digging like crazy while rounds were bouncing everywhere. She pulled Korf out and saved his ass. She's getting a Navy Cross for it."

"Really?" Tamara asked.

"It was no big thing," Liege said, trying to be humble, but feeling more than a bit of pride.

What she'd done was nothing like what Tamara had accomplished, but still, she was proud to see that Tamara seemed impressed.

"Well, your fans are out there waiting. Shall we?" she asked Tamara.

The three left the CP and rejoined the massed Marines and sailors. The sergeant major called Tamara forward.

"I'll talk to you later," she said to the two of them as she strode up to join him.

The sergeant major welcomed her "home," and gave a brief synopsis of her time with the battalion, with focus on Wyxy—as if no one there had already known it all. He only talked for a few minutes before giving the mic to her.

"Thank you for your welcome," she said, stumbling a bit on the words. "I. . .I'm glad to see some friendly faces. And some not

---

[12] ROE: Rules of Engagement

so friendly, Staff Sergeant Abdálle. Yeah, I see you there," she said, pointing down at him.

"Oh, she didn't!" Lassi said, as the squad fist-bumped each other and the battalion broke out into laughter.

The platoon respected their platoon sergeant, but it was fun to hear him take a little shit.

"I've followed your deployment on Jericho, and I have to say, I'm proud of you, all of you. I just found out that my friend, Doc Neves, is up for a Navy Cross, and I'm, well, I'm bursting with pride at that. I just wish I'd been with you in person instead of just in spirit."

Liege turned red at the mention. This was Tamara's day, not hers.

"I'm detached from the Corps right now. But there are eight of us serving as gladiators, and we remember our roots. And my roots, where I feel at home, are with Second Battalion, Third Marines! Fuzos!"

Her saying "Fuzos" opened up the faucet as over a thousand voices opened up with "Fuzos, Fuzos!" Finally, it looked like Tamara gave up and handed the mic back to the sergeant major. He gave up as well, and signaled to the food line to start serving.

Liege and the rest of the squad started heading over to where the chow hall had prepared a pretty good layout. With recent promotions, Lassi Rassiter was the only PFC left in the squad, and she could have gone up ahead, but she stuck with the rest.

When Liege and the other E3s reached the head of the line, she was surprised to see that Tamara was there slinging macaroni salad. Liege held up her plate and received a scoop while Tamara told her to save a place for her. She gave Wythe two scoops, telling him that was for making him wait.

By that time, Liege was accepting a roll from the battalion CO herself, who had taken a position serving on the line as well.

"Here you go, Doc. Get yourself a dog from the XO. They look pretty good."

Liege was in her PT gear, not in uniform, and it still surprised her when senior officers singled her out. She knew with the Navy Cross recommendation she was somewhat of a rising star, but that boggled her mind.

"Thank you, ma'am," she said, hurrying to where the XO was dishing up hotdogs.

Once through the line, Liege followed the other E3s back to their position on the steps. Tyrell started to take a bite of the choconudge cookie when Wythe smacked his hand.

"Wait for the warrant officer. She said she's joining us."

A few minutes later, the corporals showed up, and after that, Sergeant Vinter made her way back to join them. They sat around making small talk, their attention on the big gladiator still dishing up food.

Tamara was a chief warrant officer, higher ranked than any enlisted Marine, but lower than even a boot lieutenant. So if she was going to go by rank to get fed, she'd be right after the sergeant major. As the guest of honor, she could have been first, but she'd thrown that out when she decided to serve.

"She's going last," Wythe said, looking back to the serving line. "She just made Gunner Morrey go before her."

Gunner Morrey was a Chief Warrant Officer 4, so he was senior to her. There weren't that many officers though, even if there were some visiting O5's and even an O6. It didn't take long before the four servers made a big show of serving each other, and Tamara made her way back to join the squad.

Wow! For such a big girl, she sure doesn't have much on her plate, Liege noticed.

Tamara looked around, then folded her legs, and as graceful as a cat, sat down on the grass so her face was almost level with those sitting on the steps.

There were a few hesitant words spoken, and more than a few "ma'ams," before Tamara broke out with "Let's cut the formal stuff for the duration, OK? I got promoted, but it's more of an honorary position. And I really just want to relax and get all the scuttlebutt."

The squadmates looked at each other awkwardly. Honorary position or not, she was still a chief warrant officer.

"Like what?" Corporal Sativaa asked hesitantly.

"Well, for starters, who's hooked up with who? When I left, Tyrell, you were madly in love with some cashier at MakerMart. Is that still on?"

"Oh, tell her, Lover Boy," Fanny said excitedly, but not giving him the chance to respond. "His little cashier was 16 years old, and get this, her dad was the logistics group chief of staff."

"No!" Tamara said, her eyes alight as she leaned in.

"Hey, I didn't know that when I met her. She said she was 19 and that her family were tech monitors at Cool Air. As soon as I found out, I cut her off," Tyrell protested.

"Lucky you did, or you'd still be in the brig," Wythe said. And then to Tamara, "But never fear, ma. . .uh, Tamara, our Casanova wasn't alone long. Next thing we know, he's hooking up . . ."

With that, the barriers were broken, and it was like old times. Several other Marines came over for short stints, and the CO came to give her regards before she left, but most of the rest of the battalion gave the squad their space. As much as they might take pride that one of their own had been elevated, they knew this was a chance, maybe the last chance, for the gladiator to just be one of the gang.

It was 0200, and the quad was long deserted, before they finally broke up. Tamara stood and gave everyone a hug. Liege felt her eyes water just the tiniest bit as Tamara enveloped her.

They walked her over to the van, where Tamara apologized to the lance corporal driver who'd been patiently waiting. Tamara got in, and the vehicle slowly rose, pivoted, and took off. Liege and the Marines watched until the van turned the corner out of sight.

Without a word, each of them turned and silently walked back to the barracks.

Chapter 20

I, Liege Anna Neves, do solemnly swear that I will support and defend the Articles of Council of the United Federation of Nations against all enemies, foreign and domestic, and that I will bear true faith and allegiance to the same; that I take this obligation freely, without mental reservation or purposes of evasion, and that I will well and faithfully discharge the duties of the rank of which I am about to enter, obeying the lawful orders of those appointed over me and leading those of lesser rank to the best of my abilities. So help me God.

Liege lowered her right hand as Rear Admiral Giscard said, "Congratulations, HM3 Neves. Your promotion is well deserved."

The admiral stepped forward to take off the HM stripes that Liege had simply tacked to the right sleeve of her alphas. He pressed the new crow[13] in its place, then stepped back. Liege saluted him.

"Chief, I think you're up?" he asked.

"Yes, sir. And it's my pleasure."

Chief Sou stepped forward, took off the stripes of her left sleeve, and pressed the crow home.

"Looks good, Hospitalman Third Class Neves."

"Thanks, Chief."

The admiral stepped to his right where another corpsman from 1/2 was getting promoted. Liege let out a deep breath. She was now an E4, and more than the prestige, that now meant she could bring Avó and Leticia to Tarawa. This was for what she'd been working.

---

[13] Crow: slang for the insignia of a Navy E-4 to E-9 due to the prominent eagle in it.

Still, she was proud of the promotion, and she was proud that she'd been selected to get promoted by the admiral himself. Rear Admiral Giscard was the Medical Officer of the Marine Corps, and it was tradition that on June 17, the birthday of the medical corps, he promote a handful of corpsmen. Liege, whose official promotion date was not for another 14 days, had been one of two non-rates to be so honored.

Her alpha blouse was tight across her neck, but she resisted the urge to lift her chin. With her time in the gym, she was getting a bit bigger, and her alphas no longer fit as well as they should have. She could have worn her looser fitting Navy service dress, as one of the corpsman getting promoted to chief had, but she was serving with the Marines, so she had gone green with her Marine uniform.

When HM Paulsen, the corpsman from 1/2, received his crows, the six corpsmen (two former non-rates, two petty officers, and two chiefs) conducted a left face and marched off from in front of the admiral. Their exit petered into nothing as they simply broke apart and joined the rest of the gathered corpsmen.

The medical corps' birthday was not a major observance as those celebrated by the Marines for their birthdays or patron day celebrations. It consisted of the promotion ceremony, a quick speech by a senior officer, and then a short reading pertaining to the medical corps. That was followed by the inevitable cake and a short period of socializing. The Marines tended to rehearse their celebrations until they had each movement and event down cold; the Navy tended to fly by the seat of their pants.

Since they were on Tarawa, the assistant commandant of the Marine Corps was the guest speaker. Liege had never seen the great man in person. She didn't think she'd seen any flag officer. Now, with a four-star Marine and a two-star sailor, she'd broken that drought.

Hell, he looks like my Avó, she thought as the general stepped forward.

The general undoubtedly was in full control of his senses, unlike her grandfather, but from a physical standpoint, they were not too different. That hit Liege a little hard. With her Avó's condition, she tended to think of him as old, but in reality, his chronological age wasn't that high. Looking at the general, who was delving into how much the Marine Corps valued their corpsmen, she realized that her Avó should be the same vibrant, competent man. He was too young to be an invalid. The thought made her sad.

As her mind went to her Avó, she missed most of what the general said, only coming back to the present as the crowd broke into polite applause.

The general stepped back, and Command Master Chief Hospital Corpsman Lin Follette stepped up onto the podium.

He looked over the gathered sailors and Marines, then asked, "How many of you have heard of The Sovereign Hospitaller Order of St John of Jerusalem, of Rhodes, and of Malta?"

A few people raised their hands.

"They're more commonly referred to as the Knights of Malta."

Quite a few more people raise their hands as well.

"Why am I asking you this? It's simple. We owe our very existence to them. The Order of St John, the Knights of Malta were most known for their wars in the Holy Land. Probably most of you don't know that they still exist as a sovereign nation, inside a single building in Rome on Earth, but that's beside the point. As far as the medical corps, I want to point out something. Look at their name: The Sovereign Hospitaller Order of St John of Jerusalem, of Rhodes, and of Malta. What was that third word? *Hospitaller.*"

Liege had heard of the Knights of Malta, but if she'd heard of their official title, she'd certainly never noticed "hospitaller." She focused her attention on the command master chief, wondering where he was going with this.

"That word is the key. The knights weren't doctors. They were medieval versions of medical assistants. They were founded about fifteen hundred years ago to serve sick and wounded crusaders and pilgrims, helping the doctors and doing all the care such as changing bandages, feeding patients, cleaning them up, lancing boils and whatnot. In other words, they were the world's first corpsmen.

"But, and this is a big but, they were different from all the other medical assistants of the era. The knights were the first chivalrous order, and from them, we get all our ideas of how knights are supposed to act. They also took vows of poverty and chastity, though, and to serve the Pope. What they didn't do was take vows of non-violence. Quite the contrary, they were perhaps the fiercest warriors of the Crusades.

"When Suleiman the Magnificent attacked the fortress on Rhodes, the home of the knights, he attacked with over 200,000 men. The knights were only about 500 men. But they held out for six months, beating back every Ottoman attack. What finally got them was when they ran out of food. Starving, they surrendered, and Suleiman let them keep their arms and sail away in recognition of their courage and tenacity.

"The reason I'm relating all of this is because I want to stress one thing: the Knights of Malta set the stage for us. They might have been hospitallers first, but they were still warriors, noted warriors. And that is the same with you. You are corpsmen, and your mission is to treat your Marines. They depend on you for that, and that, as General Cusak said, is why they hold all of you in such high esteem. But they also count on you to fight alongside them. You are healers, keeping death at bay, but you are also dealers of death when the time comes."

Liege had never really considered that, and she had to take stock of her thoughts. She'd been in combat, but except for an un-aimed burst of fire back on the *Imperial Stabiae,* she didn't think she'd fired her weapon in anger.

"Over the years," the command master chief continued, "Navy corpsmen have answered the call. Corpsmen have been awarded all the old top medals, from American Medals of Honor to British Victoria Crosses to Heroes of the Russian Federation—and just about every other medal from every other country. Since the founding of the Federation, 18 corpsmen have been awarded the Federation Nova. Thirteen of those Novas were awarded posthumously.

"Corpsmen have been answering the call for centuries. You are the latest in that long line of service and tradition. All of you volunteered for this duty, and you are the best the Navy has to offer. And all of you here are lucky enough to serve with our sister service.

Some of you may never hear a shot fired in anger, but most of you will, and how you react will prove the temper of your steel."

The command master chief paused to look out over the crowd.

"You really are the best we have to offer, and I'm proud to serve with you. *Semper fortis*, sailors, *semper fortis!*"

The Navy didn't have a set war cry like the Marine's "ooh-rah" or the Confederation Army's "hoo-yah," but the shout that burst forth from a hundred throats was no less formed out of raw emotion.

Chapter 21

Liege waited impatiently outside of arrivals.

What's taking them so long? she wondered, checking the time yet again.

"Take it easy, Liege," Fanny told her.

Liege nodded and reached out to take Fanny's hand and give it a squeeze.

She almost didn't recognize her as she came out of customs.

Oh my God, she's a woman now! she thought as she took in the sight of her.

"Leti!" she shouted, jumping up and down and waving her hand.

Liege had seen her sister on camchat, but the little screen on her PA hadn't been able to fully display the change in Leticia. The word "blossom" was used too often, but Liege didn't know of anything better. Leticia had blossomed, pure and simple.

Leticia looked up, caught her eye, and waved back, then turned to the elderly man beside her to say something.

And Liege's heart fell.

That elderly man was her Avó, and he looked far, far too old for his years. The joy in seeing Leticia evaporated like desert dew.

Liege pushed through the waiting people to reach the bars that kept friends and family from customs. She reached over the bar to hug her sister, squeezing her tight. She didn't want to let go.

"Avó, it's Liege," Leticia said, pulling her grandfather around.

The old man looked confused for a moment until recognition seemed to dawn in his eyes.

"Criceto," her grandfather said, "Where have you been? Your mama's looking for you."

Liege's mouth dropped open, and tears began to form in her eyes. "Criceto" was an old nickname he used to call her when she was a child. She'd managed to get a hamster from somewhere, and she'd loved the little rodent. Her grandfather said she spent so much time with it that they must be sisters, so she must be a criceto, too.

"Now Avó, I told you. Liege is all grown up. She's in the Navy now, and we're coming to live with her," Leticia said with a well-seasoned patience.

"But her mama is looking for her," the old man said.

"How did he. . ." Liege started.

"It hasn't been good. He's slipping."

"Why didn't you tell me?"

"For what good?" Leticia asked. "So you could run home and do what, exactly? No, you were here doing what you had to do."

She turned to her grandfather and buttoned the old man's top shirt button, then brushed off his shoulders.

Just like mama, Liege thought. *My little sister's become the mother of the family.*

"Hi," Fanny said, reaching across the bar to offer a hand.

"Oh, yeah. Leti, this is Fanny. I've told you about her."

"Oh yes, good to meet you."

"Move it along," one of the security guards said, sweeping his arm as if to shoo them along.

"Come on, you're blocking the others," Liege said.

She paced them as they reached the end of the barricade and stepped out into the open area. She took the hovercart with their luggage: four battered suitcases, representing all their worldly possessions.

"I'm taking three days leave. Right now, we're going to get you moved in, and tomorrow, I've got Avó his first appointment. After that, we'll see what our options are," she told Leticia as Fanny led the way to the rental hover.

"You're getting us moved in?" Leticia asked with emphasis on the "us."

"Uh, yeah, about that. I wanted to get you closer to the hospital, and I can't really afford a three-bedroom anywhere near there. I've leased a nice two-bedroom, so both you and Avó have some privacy."

"I thought we'd all be together here, like you said. What's wrong with you and me sharing a room?"

"I know you thought I'd live there with you. And I'll be there as much as I can. The couch is a sleeper, and I can use that. But there isn't much room, and I've got all my gear, so the first sergeant said I can keep my room in the barracks. I'll leave my military gear there, and depending on what's going on, I might sleep there sometimes. But I'll be with you whenever I can. Just not all the time."

Leticia seemed about to say something, then made an obvious effort to stop herself.

"What were you about to say?" Liege asked.

"Nothing."

"No, really. You need to tell me."

Fanny turned back to say something, realized there was an issue, and quickly introduced herself to their Avó, taking him by the arm and leading him forward.

"OK, now, what were you going to say?" Liege asked as Fanny moved on ahead.

"I just thought, I mean, since you've been gone, it's been all on me. I. . .I haven't had a moment to myself in two years. And I thought you could finally help me."

Tears welled in Leticia's eyes as emotions broke down.

"Oh, Leti," Liege said, pulling her sister into her arms. "I am here, and I will be here. I'm not trying to stay away. But I've got my duties, you know? I can't ignore them. We're getting Avó his care because of my job, but that means I have my responsibilities."

"I know," Leticia mumbled into Liege's shoulder, hot tears soaking through the jumper Liege had on. "It's just, well, you don't know how bad it's gotten. And he knows it sometimes. He sees his mind slipping away, and he acts out."

"Has he hurt you?" Liege asked, pushing her sister back so she could see her face.

"He doesn't mean to," Leticia said before hurriedly changing the subject. "And now with moving here, and I don't know anyone, I. . .I'm afraid."

The favelas were not the best place to live, but within each small neighborhood, there was a support network. And Liege had yanked Leticia out of hers. No wonder she was on edge.

Liege pulled her sister's head back to her shoulder and said, "Don't worry, little Leti. I'm here for you and Avó. Don't worry."

She wasn't sure how she would juggle her duties as a corpsman and as a caregiver, but she'd somehow figure it out.

Chapter 22

Liege looked down at the Navy Cross hanging from her chest. For the last four hours, she'd barely given it a glance, not wanting to look vain. Now, however, sitting at the table at Porcao de Rio, she thought she could risk a quick look.

It was an old design, a bronze cross pattée hanging from a dark blue ribbon with a white stripe running down the middle. It was not very flamboyant, but there was a long history to it, being one of the two medals that conveyed almost unchanged from the old US Navy and Marines into the Federation armed forces.

The ceremony had been impressive. The commandant himself, General Joab Ling, had presented it to her in front of a battalion formation. Liege had felt a little guilty making her battalion go through the hassle of a parade—but only a little.

She'd been honored by the effort, honored by the award, but perhaps the best part of the day had been when her Avó came up to her immediately following the ceremony.

At first, Liege had been afraid that he'd say something weird to the commandant, but to her intense joy, he touched the medal hanging from her chest, then said, "Liege, I'm so proud of you."

It wasn't much, and perhaps no one other than Leticia noticed it, but it had been a huge step for her grandfather. He'd only just begun to receive treatment, but it looked like it might have been having an effect. He still had a long journey in front of him, but for a brief moment, at least, he was back.

And now he was back at the apartment, she thought guiltily. *Alone and not with Leti and me.*

As part of a celebration for her Navy Cross ceremony, Vic had offered to finally take her to Kentville to try that rodizio he'd mentioned after the patron day celebration. She'd demurred, telling him she had her sister and grandfather to take care of. In reality, however, she had longed to go. She wasn't spending as much time in the apartment as Leticia, but it was already grinding on her. Between her work and her grandfather, her social life had ground to a halt.

Vic hadn't accepted her refusal. Before she quite knew what was happening, he had arranged for a caretaker, and Leticia, Fanny, Pablo, Tyrell, and she were on the maglev heading to the beach. Liege had protested that she couldn't afford it, but he insisted it was all on him.

Liege realized that despite their time in the squad together, she didn't know that much about his personal life. An oblique question to Fanny let her know that, despite only being a newly promoted corporal, he could afford pretty much whatever he wanted. She knew she shouldn't accept. It was too much no matter how rich he might have been. But she really needed a break, so she accepted.

They'd checked into the Marine Corps Lodge. Vic had offered the Hilton, but Liege had put her foot down. The Lodge was good enough, and far cheaper. She, Leticia, and Fanny were sharing a room, and she assumed the boys were as well.

She'd wanted to change clothes, but they'd all insisted that they all stay in uniform. This was a military planet, after all, and it wasn't every day that someone was awarded a Navy Cross. Vic had laughed that someone might comp them the meal. Liege didn't know about that, but as they waited in the bar for their table, some retired colonel paid for their drinks, and no one thought to card Leticia, who was still two months too young to drink.

Now, after the ceremony and after catching the maglev, she finally had a chance to sit and catch her breath. She still wasn't too sure that she wanted to eat, but she had to admit, the smell was pretty enticing.

Porcao de Rio proudly advertised that they served Higgensworth and Griselda. Higgensworth was Higgensworth of Parker Manor, one of the more famous beef cultures. Griselda was Sweet Griselda Blue, one of the more famous pork cultures. Liege had never imagined eating at a restaurant with a patented culture, much less one with two.

Now, the smell of cooking meat warred with her image of thousands of slabs of living flesh growing in farms around the galaxy. Higgensworth wasn't even alive anymore. The Blue Angus steer had died 50 or more years ago while slabs of his flesh, like eternal zombies, kept marching on.

No one else seemed to have her squeamishness, so she thought her reaction was odd as she was a corpsman, supposedly inured to mangled flesh. Leticia was sure excited, at least, although that could be due to this being her first social outing in a long, long time. Liege looked up across to the table to where Leticia was laughing at something Vic had said. She placed her hand on Vic's forearm, leaning in to whisper something into his ear.

What? Is she flirting with him?

Vic whispered something back to her, and she laughed as she leaned back and playfully slapped his shoulder. Liege watched for a moment longer, but Fanny said something about getting another drink, and Leticia turned from Vic to listen to her.

No, she's just happy to be out, Liege decided.

Liege had been a little wary of Tyrell and Leticia coming on the same trip. She dearly loved the guy, who'd do anything for any one of them, but it was also well understood that he'd fuck a dead dog at the side of the road, if it came to that. Leticia was still young and still getting used to living on Tarawa, and she could be a little vulnerable.

A waiter dressed in some sort of gaucho outfit came to the table and explained the process. Each person had a small wooden cylinder, one side painted green, the other side red. When they wanted meat, they flipped the cylinder so the green side was up. When they were done, it was red side up. He then took their drink orders. For that, Liege didn't need any explanation. They might not have rodizios in the favelas, but they have caipirinhas, the lime and rum drink that might have originated in Old Brazil but had spread across the galaxy.

After the explanation, they stood up and went to a very large salad bar. Liege, not sure how much meat she was going to eat, loaded up on the salad. Little signs indicated which ingredients were organic and which were fab, but she didn't have a mental problem with organic veggies and fruits.

As they returned to the table and sat down, Vic kept standing.

He lifted his glass and said, "This is in honor of our good friend and brother-in-arms Doc Neves, and we'll get to that, but first, I think we should offer a toast to another brother-in-arms, Chief Warrant Officer Tamara Veal!"

They all stood up and lifted their glasses. People at several tables surrounding them heard Vic as well, and to a person, they all stood up, lifting their glasses high.

"Here, here!" emerged from a couple of dozen throats.

Liege felt a lump in her throat as she thought about Tamara, but she had already come to terms with what had happened. She was glad that Vic had thought to remember her.

"And now, to the reason for the season: to HM3 Liege Neves, our squadmate, our friend, in honor of being awarded the Navy Cross today, we salute you!"

"Ooh-rah!" shouted her squadmates, joined by at least half of the tables in the restaurant.

Liege reddened, embarrassed by the attention.

"He's going to get someone to pick up the tab for sure now," Fanny said to Liege. "Smart guy."

"OK, OK, sit down," Liege insisted.

She tried to focus on her salad, but she was extremely conscious of the eyes on her. No one approached her, thank goodness, but every time she looked up, someone caught her eye and lifted a glass in congratulations.

A gaucho-slash-waiter approached Liege, a flat wooden platter with a huge piece of beef ribs balanced on one arm. Liege glanced at her little wooden cylinder, but it was still red side up.

"Ma'am, this is our specialty, costela. Normally, this is by request only, but we'd like to offer it to you now."

Liege was hoping for her first piece of meat not to look so, well, like meat. The attentive waiter was looking expectantly at her, and she didn't want to seem ungrateful, so she just nodded and moved her salad plate to the side.

He quickly sliced off a fatty-looking piece of meat and laid it on her plate. Then he went around the table giving everyone else a piece.

"Say hello to Higgensworth!" Pablo said, looking down at the meat with covetous eyes.

Liege considered just sort of pushing the meat to the side, but she realized everyone was watching her, waiting for her to take a bite so they could begin. She cut a tiny piece of the beef, looked at it closely, took a deep breath, and took the plunge. She put the meat in her mouth. . .

. . .and it freaking melted! The taste assaulted her tongue, and she looked up at Vic in surprise.

"Not too grubbing bad, huh?"

"No, this is good!" she said, taking another bite.

Two hours later, stuffed to the gills with picanha, fraldinha, ancho, costeleta de cordeiro, and more cuts that she couldn't remember, and after more than a few caipirinhas, she was in love. She was in love with her ancestral culture, even if she had to travel to Tarawa to discover it, and she was in love with a 50-year-gone Blue Angus steer—her new boyfriend, Higgensworth of Parker Manor. All hints of squeamishness were gone. It wasn't as if the steer had been actually slaughtered for her pleasure. What she had eaten was simple cloned tissue, nothing more. At least that was how she reasoned it. The truth of the matter was that it was just so freaking delicious. She didn't know if she'd ever have enough money to make Higgensworth's acquaintance very often, but for tonight, she was happy.

And Fanny had been right. Whether Vic had planned it that way or not, the restaurant refused payment.

She gave out a loud burp, pleased with the volume of it. Fanny tried to follow suit, but what she got out would have embarrassed a mouse, much less a hard-charging Marine.

"Amateur," she told Fanny, patting her full stomach.

Across the table, Leticia was deep into conversation with Vic, who had that sparkle in his eyes that Liege well knew. He wanted to get into Leticia's panties, that was pretty obvious. But she also knew that Vic was an honorable guy. She could trust him.

But can I trust Leti?

"Hey, are we still going to the Deacon's Hat?" Pablo asked.

Liege groaned. The Deacon's Hat was a well-known dance club, and they had planned on checking it out after dinner. But that was before they'd put away a couple of tons each of beef, pork, and lamb.

"Of course we are, right?" Leticia asked, looking around at the others.

"If you want to go, then m'lady shall be granted her wish," Vic said with a horrible medieval accent.

Really? That's all you got? Liege wondered.

She was really too full to dance at the moment, but they only had one night in Kentville, and then they'd be back to the grind. She'd regret it if she simply went back to the room and collapsed on the bed.

"If they've got caipirinhas there, I'm up for it. Heck, if they've got beer there, I'm up for it," she said. "But first, back to the lodge. If I'm going to shake my ass, I've got to get out of this uniform and into something a wee bit more comfortable."

She got up to the cheers of the rest. Vic put down a pretty hefty tip, and they all started to file out of the restaurant.

"Thanks, Vic, for all of this. I appreciate it," she said, pulling him aside.

"Don't worry about it. It's been my pleasure, really, my pleasure."

If he glanced quickly at Leticia while he said "pleasure," Liege let it slide. Tonight was too good a night to worry about possibilities. Tonight was to celebrate the present.

Chapter 23

"If that's your decision, then of course I'll support you," Leticia said as they sat around their tiny kitchen table.

"Kitchen" might be stretching the meaning of the word. There was barely enough room to turn around, and except for a second-hand hotplate, there was nothing with which to cook. All their food came out of a Kiogi fabricator, and their cold items were run through a one-liter chiller. For the hundredth time, Liege reminded herself to look up Kiogi. It certainly wasn't a universal brand, and judging from the quality of the fabricator, she could understand why. Still, recipes were just programming, and the food it created was OK.

Liege reached across the table and pushed aside Leticia's school books to grasp her hands. She just squeezed them for a moment, thankful for her sister's support. Liege wasn't even sure what she wanted herself, and it was good to know that Leticia had her back.

Still holding her sister's hands, she swung around to where Avó was sitting in his chair, watching a holoserial. At least the living room in the apartment was good-sized, and Liege had sprung for a nice Samsung at the base exchange. Her grandfather seemed happy, more so now that he was getting his treatment.

"Well, I've got to get back. I need to tell the chief today," she said.

She'd skipped chow to return to the apartment and tell Leticia. This wasn't a decision to be made lightly—what she chose would affect all three of them.

Liege stood and leaned over the table, and still holding her hands, put her chin on top of her sister's head. She stayed there a moment, then giving one last squeeze, she broke free and turned away. Walking up to her Avó, she put her hand on his shoulder.

He reached up with his hand to place it on hers, saying, "Ah, Criceto, where are you going?"

Liege stood bolt-upright and looked back at Leticia.

Has he regressed?

"Oh, don't get excited. I know you don't think you're my little Criceto anymore, Liege. But no matter how old you get, no matter how many medals you win, you'll always be my Criceto."

Liege looked back at her grandfather for a moment, relief flooding over her as she saw the slight smile crook one side of his mouth.

She squatted beside him and put her arms in his lap, saying, "It's OK, Avó, I will always be your Criceto."

"I know you will. Now you're blocking my view. Come give me a kiss, then go back to work and leave an old man alone."

Liege stood up and kissed her grandfather on the cheek. He'd been in treatment for five months, and while Liege didn't want to fool herself into false hopes, it was obvious that the treatment was having an effect. Navy medicine really was first rate, and as a corpsman, that made her proud.

Liege waved to Leticia and left the apartment. She checked the time. Noon chow was over, but she'd told Sergeant Vinter she needed some personal time, so there was no hurry. Still there was no reason to dawdle. She'd made up her mind, and stewing over it wouldn't do her any good.

She jumped on the tram and rode it to City Center, changing to the Blue Line to get to the front gate. It only took 20 minutes combined, but it would have been nice to be able to afford even a Jetscoot. The economy scooters didn't have much power, but she could have cut right over to the gate and been there in five minutes.

Once on base, despite being adamant not to dawdle, it still took her 35 minutes to make it to the H & S Company CP. The battalion aid station took up one of the bottom deck wings, and she climbed the four steps and entered.

"Hey Liege, what's up?" Cal Zylanti asked from behind the receiving desk. "I thought First Squad was on the range."

Cal was a short-timer, already in his check-out, so he was killing time on sick-call duty. Not that the early afternoon time slot usually had much action.

"I have to see Chief. Is he in?"

"Yep, back in his office."

Liege started to walk past him, then she turned back and asked, "Cal, are you happy going to SRCC?"

"Hell, yeah, I am. This is what I've always wanted, to be a recon corpsman." He tapped the Fleet Marine Force Enlisted Warfare Specialist badge on his chest. "This is pretty good—and congrats on you earning yours, by the way. . ."

Getting "qualed" had taken more time and effort than Liege had imagined, especially while taking care of Avó, but she'd done it, and she wore the badge with a degree of pride. Only 30% of the corpsmen who serve with the Marines ever earn it.

". . .but becoming a Special Reconnaissance Corpsman, that's the ultimate. If I make it through—when I make it through, I mean, everyone will know I've got what it takes."

"But what if you don't? I mean, make it through."

"Oh, I will."

"But what if you don't? What if you get hurt in training?" she persisted.

"If I don't? Well, at least I know I tried. I couldn't go through the rest of my life wondering 'what if.' Not like your regen school, huh? Not much of a chance of getting injured in that course."

"No, not much of a chance," she agreed. "Well, like I said, I need to see the chief."

She stepped past the empty triage desks and knocked on the jamb to the chief's open hatch.

"Chief, you got a minute?"

"Neves, sure, come on in," he said from behind his desk. "I've got your class date here. November 3. We'll process your leave, and you should plan on arriving at Station One no later than October 28.

"And oh, yeah. I talked to my buddy at Navy Schools Command, and he's already got you on a priority list for housing for your grandfather and sister."

"Thanks, Chief, and I appreciate that. But about the school, I think I've changed my mind."

She stood back waiting for his reaction. He leaned his head back, closed his eyes, and took a few deep breaths.

"I don't suppose it would make any difference if I told you how many people went to bat for you," he said, eyes still closed.

"I. . .I really appreciate it, Chief. You and Doctor Wright and the CO, even."

"And Doctor X'anto, too. He may have rotated, but he still pushed pretty hard for you."

"Yes, Doctor X'anto, too. But my grandfather, he's doing pretty well in his treatment. He likes his therapist. My sister and I, well, we don't want to change him up again. It could push his recovery back."

The chief opened his eyes and stared at her. Liege started feeling nervous, waiting for an explosion.

"Well, I can't fault you for that. Family comes first, right? I think it's a shame, but it's your choice. I just hope you decide to keep in the reserves. The commitment isn't too onerous, and if things change in the future, well, you can come back in."

"Chief? The reserves?"

"Yes, the reserves. And I'll tell you what. The hospital hires some civilians, too. You won't be qualified for regeneration therapy, of course, but I can call around and see if we can't get you OJT for radiology or something similar. You can still get your skills while your grandfather goes through his regimen."

"Uh, Chief, I don't think you understand. I don't want the reserves."

"Why not? You've invested four years in the Navy. Why throw that away?"

"It's not like that at all, Chief. I've changed my mind about regen school, not about my re-enlistment. I still want to re-enlist."

The chief looked surprised and then leaned forward over his desk.

"Oh, OK, that's great! Sorry I misunderstood you. That's great. Really great. Great. I, uh, well, we don't have too many C-Schools here on Tarawa. Just rehabilitation therapy. Do you want that? Or maybe you want another C-School, a short one, and then come back here? I'm guessing you'll be re-enlisting to remain on station," he said, his words coming quick and his sentences jumbled together.

"Yes, I mean no," she said, unsure of what question she was supposed to answer first. "What I mean is, yes, I want to remain on station. I have to, if my grandfather is going to keep up with his treatment. But I don't want rehab, ortho, regen or whatever. I want to remain with the Marines."

"Oh," he said quietly, followed by a louder "Oh!

"With the Marines. So you don't want C-School?' he asked.

"No, I want C-School," she said.

"But you just told me you don't want rehab. That's the only C-School we have here on the planet."

"No, there's one more. I want SRCC. I want to be a Special Reconnaissance Corpsman!"

Book 2

Jonathan P. Brazee

TARAWA

Chapter 24

"Hey, boot! Get your butt over here!" Liege shouted at the newly graduated recruit.

The private double-timed over, centered herself, then said, "Yes, Petty Officer!"

Liege looked her over with a critical eye, then said, "Well, I guess they're letting anyone graduate now, Marine. So come give your sister a hug."

"Thanks for coming, Liege. I wasn't sure you could make it," Leticia said, giving Liege an awkward, but still heartfelt hug.

"Wouldn't have missed it for the world, Leti. I'm so proud of you."

And she was. Leticia had grown so much, had matured so much since Liege had left them on Nova Esperança. She'd become the mother of their little family, always giving, never receiving. Liege had always felt guilty that she had left her sister, even knowing why she'd done so, but while she was travelling the galaxy, enjoying the companionship of her friends, Leticia had been home caring for Avó. Not only that, but somehow, she'd found time to come close to earning her degree. A few more credits, and Leticia would be the first university graduate in the Neves family for generations.

And now, she was a Federation Marine. Avó's treatment had gone exceptionally well. He wasn't 100% and probably would never be, but he was more than functional. With home visits by assisted services, he could live as he wished. Leticia had at first resisted enlisting, but with Avó insisting, and with Liege's enthusiastic backing, she'd taken the plunge. Liege knew that this was the first time since their mother had died that Leticia was finally on her own, doing something for herself.

"So, you didn't tell me where you're headed," Liege said as they broke the hug.

"Well, after ITC, I'm out to 3/13."

"Oh, an Outer Forces Marine. Out in the booneys!"

"That's right, no soft living for me. I'm out to the frontier, where Marines are hard!"

"Dream on, little girl. The Inner Forces are where it's at," Liege said with a laugh.

"Who knows, maybe I'll ask for RTC[14] after that. See how you snake-eaters live."

Liege punched her sister in the arm, saying, "You got enough in the tank for that?"

Her thoughts briefly skirted the mass of memories of SRCC first, then RTC. Without a doubt, the two courses were the hardest, worst, and best things she had ever accomplished. Hardest was self-explanatory. Only 22% of those who started RTC graduated. For the few women who volunteered, the numbers were even worse. And while fit, Liege was hardly a super-stud.

Worst was because they came close to breaking her. She'd been pushed to the edge, and she'd seen that she was lacking. On more occasions than she wanted to remember, she'd come ever-so-close to quitting.

Best because actually succeeding had been the single most emotional moment of her life, to know that she had made it, that she'd been able to dredge up the raw material within her to be tempered into the steel that she was today—and that raw material was simple force of will. Physically, she didn't have all the same tools, but mentally, she was hard as a diamond, making it through when some monster physical specimens had quit.

It had been a very close thing with her, but as Liege looked at her little sister, she knew that if anyone could make it, she could.

"And what's going on with Vic?" Liege asked. "I saw him sitting with Avó in the stands."

---

[14] RTC: Reconnaissance Training Course

Leticia colored, looked down, then raised her face to look her sister in the eyes.

"He came to see me graduate, of course. And we're spending three days in Kentville—oh, when are you going back?"

"Tomorrow morning. I trust we can all eat together as a family tonight?"

"Oh, of course. But—"

"Yeah, invite him too. Then you can go play house with him."

"It's not like that, Liege."

Liege knew it wasn't, really. Maybe she was a little jealous of her sister—and a little jealous of Vic. Leticia was smart, beautiful, and level-headed. She and Vic had become close after Liege had been awarded her Navy Cross, and things had evidently heated up after Liege left for SRCC. Liege had been first assigned to First Recon on Tarawa, but when the billet with regiment on Gobi came open, along with a place in the Independent Duty Corpsman Course, that had taken Liege away from her family, and Vic had stepped in as Leticia's support. After Avó's improvement, when the option of Leticia enlisting was first broached, Vic had decided not to re-enlist. He'd said he did not want the complication of a corporal in a relationship with a private.

Of course, that hadn't too hard of a decision for him. Vic came from a very, very wealthy and high-placed family on Broadbent. Most of the high-society families sent their sons and daughters to the Navy, if public service was deemed appropriate, but Vic went Corps. No one had had expected Vic to make the Marines a career, though. He had many more options available to him.

When Leticia entered boot camp, Vic had gone home to "take care of some family matters." To be honest, Liege had thought he's been gone for good and had only used Leticia as a local hook-up. So she was surprised, and more than a little gratified, to see him show up for the graduation.

"So, Private, let's go pick up Avó and your boyfriend. I'm thinking Carlito's for dinner? Nobody on Gobi can make a decent pizza, and I'm dying for a couple of slices."

Taking her sister's arm in hers, she led her back to the bleachers. Walking like that might not be regulation, but family came first.

GOBI

Chapter 25

There was a soft plop from a few meters off Liege's right.

"Shit, Moose! Stay still!" she subvocalized into the throat mic.

She listened a moment longer, hearing nothing else.

Moose, Staff Sergeant Phil Warner, did curls with a ton on each arm and ran 50 klicks before breakfast—if you believed what he said. And he really wasn't that far off. He was an absolute beast. But he had a hard time with discomfort, and lying in the muck of the swamp was very, very uncomfortable.

Liege hated it, too, but that hate was shoved back in the recesses of her mind, and she simply ignored the smell, the knowledge that her skin was being attacked by millions of parasites, molds, and bugs, and the constant itch. She was on a mission, and that was what mattered. The party-girl Liege worried about appearances and could spend an hour getting ready for a night on the town, but the corpsman Liege was a different person, professional and confident.

That didn't mean she didn't hope the mission ended soon. They'd been parked in the heavy cover of the swamp for a day now, and the thought of a hot shower filled her with anticipation.

Another soft plop reached Liege's ears, and she was about to call out Moose again when she realized that the sound was from the wrong direction.

"I've got something from our six," she passed as she ran through her inputs.

"What, Doc?" Dannyboy, the team leader asked. "I don't have anything."

"I don't know, but I know I heard something."

If there was something out there, it wouldn't surprise anyone that Liege had heard it first. Her hearing, or rather her ability to discern the differences between sounds, was better than anyone else's. But the various scanners they had emplaced were quiet, showing nothing unnatural.

The team had eyes on the slightly raised dry hummock of grass and bushes that marked one of the few large dry spots in the huge expanse of morass. They'd wired the ground with explosives, ready to detonate if the enemy landed. No one expected an approach from the rear, but the unexpected often has a habit of sneaking up on a person, so they'd laid out interlocking sensors to warn of any approach from that direction.

Liege strained to listen, and just as she had convinced herself that there really wasn't anything back there, she heard the distinct sucking sound of a foot being lifted from the muck.

"I—"

"I heard it," Dannyboy interrupted her. "Fidor, why aren't we picking anything up?"

Fidor responded, but Liege couldn't make out what he said. Couple the subvocalization, which was hard to master, with Fidor's horrendous Almatty accent, and he was often undecipherable.

"Fuck it all, Fidor. Concentrate."

Dannyboy had somewhat of a mouth on him, and it still sounded odd to hear cursing in the calm monotone required for sub-v comms.

"I'm re-routing the Charlie band," Fidor said, much clearer than before.

Liege switched her display to the Charlie band, not wanting to wait even an instant for her AI to make the switch if something came through. There was a flicker in the display, then three figures appeared. Whoever was heading their way was at 150 meters and closing.

"Cross-polarization," Fidor said, "with freq-hopping. Clever."

I knew we should have hard-wired, Liege thought.

They'd had time to run shielded wires, and those were extremely difficult to jam or spoof, but they could be picked up by sensitive orbital scanners, and if they were, the wires might as well be big flashing neon arrows right back to the four of them.

Come on, Dannyboy, what do we do?

Dannyboy, Staff Sergeant Lu Tien-chieu, had never acted as team leader before, and Liege thought he was too cautious, too risk-averse. Unnecessary risk was foolish, but being too cautious could be just as bad, if not worse.

"I think they're going to give terminal guidance to whatever is incoming. We can live with that. Keep low and let the fuckers just walk on by," he finally passed.

Liege rolled her eyes. They had the islet loaded for bear with explosives, and while they were shielded from overhead scans, they would not stand up to visual scrutiny. But Dannyboy was the man with the plan, so Liege sunk deeper into the muck until only her nose eyes, and forehead were above the surface of the nasty glop.

Fidor and his AI kept playing with his inputs, trying to keep one step ahead of the enemy AIs. The enemy avatars flickered in and out as they got closer. It looked like they were going to walk right over the four team members, which wasn't too much of a shock considering that there was much deeper water on either side of them.

She didn't need the avatars as the enemy got closer; she could hear them. They were good, and they were mixing up their stride patterns, but they were still plunging through black muck that sucked at their feet.

Liege was feeling naked. She wished she'd had a tarnkappe[15] at least, to drape over her. Many of the active camo and light bending projectors were not as effective, or wouldn't even work in water, but she thought anything would have been better than nothing. As the footsteps got closer, she flipped her monocle back and out of the way. She was now cut off from her visual displays, but she could see movement—she didn't need her AI telling her that an enemy was just a few meters away.

Just keep on walking, she tried to force the thoughts into whomever just stepped past a bedraggled bush.

---

[15] Tarnkappe: a sheet of fabric that channels light rays through the hollow threads, rendering whoever was wearing it almost invisible from a front aspect.

Without consciously deciding to do it, she sunk below the oily surface, out of sight (she hoped).

Liege felt a swirl of water near her legs. She gripped her combat knife with her right hand.

A boot landed on her thigh, and Liege twisted, knocking the enemy off balance while she surged to her feet, black water pouring off of her as the lunged for the man who was only now gaining his balance. Knife hand forward in a Sukido, she reached for his neck—only to be blocked aside. She splashed into the water face-first, hand forward to stop her fall, only to have it sink 20 centimeters into the muck. A body landed on her, and she felt the whisper of the electronic blade kiss her neck.

"You're dead, Doc," someone said into her ear.

Her AI told her the same thing through her cochlear implant. Liege stopped struggling and turned around to see the grinning face of Gunnery Sergeant Warden Johansson, "Stein," before he winked and dove thorough some half-rotted skunk cabbage and out of sight.

Of all the people to kill her, it had to be Warden. The gunny was new to the team, but he had quite a rep. Sharp as a tack, he had an infectious sense of humor and was a physical beast. This was their first force-on-force since he'd arrived, and more so than usual, Liege had wanted to make an impression. A good one, that was, not getting killed when she'd had the jump on him.

She looked down at her combat knife. The electronic blade glimmered in a dull blue. With a groan, she slammed it into her belly, committing electronic seppuku. She almost wished it was a real blade.

There was a flurry of motion over where Moose had been. Liege flipped down her monocle, but it was now covered with muck. Being dead, she wouldn't be able to communicate, but at least she could see what was going on.

Liege kicked at the nearest skunk cabbage, which had made up most of her view for the last day.

Of all the plants to terraform a world with, why skunk cabbage? What possible environmental benefit do they have that outweighed their nasty smell?

She kicked another, knocking it off its stalk, then strode to the muck to sit on a small tuft of grass, a small throne in the midst of the morass.

Shots rang out, but Liege didn't bother trying to clean her monocle. She'd find out soon enough what had happened.

"OK, bring it in," Warden passed a few minutes later.

Liege didn't know where "in" was, given the state of her monocle, but she heard Moose splashing through the swamp, so she hurried to catch up to him. Another 30 meters, and Warden, Dannyboy, Gidge, and Teri were standing knee-deep in the water. Liege could hear the last two coming in as well.

"That was fun, huh?" Warden asked as the last of them gathered.

Liege wouldn't really call the last day "fun."

Warden was the Team Two leader. The captain had Team One. Warden had broken up the team into two smaller teams for this force-on-force. He'd told them he wanted to see how they worked together in the field before they left for the quarterly Dark Eye exercise. Liege had thought he could learn enough about them during the two-week exercise, but it was his team and his call.

"So, I have to nod to Dannyboy here. Looks like he's the only survivor."

Liege looked up in surprise. Somehow she'd assumed that Warden had to have made it through the exercise in one piece.

"So, I want to see how you laid out the explosives. . ."

Liege was suddenly glad that Dannyboy had insisted that they lay out the training aids in a sound tactical manner, not just throw them on the ground.

". . . so let's head on over and take a look. And I've got a Stork arriving in 40 to take us back."

"Oh, the crew chief's gonna be happy to see us climb aboard, dripping black snot like this," Moose said, to general laughter.

Liege's mood was getting better. First, Warden had been killed, so he couldn't lord that over her. Second, they were flying back instead of humping it. And it had been kind of fun, she had to admit. It would have been better if she had taken down the team leader, but the look on his face as she rose out of the water like some sort of zombie *Birth of Venus* had been priceless.

Chapter 26

"Some training, huh?" the gunny asked as he approached Liege, a pitcher in hand with which he topped off her stein.

Dark Eyes had just concluded, and it looked like the company had done well. They wouldn't know for sure until the debrief in the morning before they flew back to Portillo. Liege wasn't worried; Dark Eyes was a requirement to remain deployable, but in her two tours with regiment, she'd never been in a company that had failed.

"It was OK. We got it done."

"Sure, I know that. But it was fun, right?"

Is this guy ever in a bad mood? Liege wondered as she looked over at him.

She didn't really know what to make of her team leader. On one hand, he had a continual smile and an almost annoying habit of being eternally sunny. On the other hand, when he moved, there was no doubt that he was an extremely dangerous man, one you didn't want to cross.

Liege wasn't sure why the gunny put out that kind of vibe. He wasn't particularly large, nothing like Moose. Given the right kind of clothing, he could look somewhat inconsequential, in fact. With his shirt off, it was different. The first time Liege had seen him shirtless, she had been surprised to see how chiseled his body was. He looked really, good, something both she and Teri had remarked to each other at the time, Teri with her typical crudeness that made Liege laugh.

Even sitting beside her, leaning back in the bench seat, a stein in his hand, he exuded a deadly competence. His record backed that up. Liege hadn't bothered to delve into the details of his background, but he had three silver stars and five BC1s, and what he'd done on Indigo Seas was well-known throughout the Corps.

"Gunny Johansson, good to see you again," someone said from behind him. "Doc Neves, you too."

"Sergeant Major, glad to be back in a real billet. Headquarters was driving me batty."

Retired Sergeant Major "Crutch" Carruthers was a fixture outside of Camp Wister—really the only fixture. Wister was a temporary camp used for extended field ops, a thousand klicks from the regimental headquarters at Camp Portillo, and his appropriately named The Bar was the lone civilian dining and drinking establishment outside the gate. Just about every recon Marine over the last 20-odd years had spent more hours inside than he or she would want to admit. The walls were covered in memorabilia—anyone could tack up whatever he or she wanted. Behind the beat-up metal bar, pictures of Sergeant Major Crutch's highlighted his career. Centered was a prominent picture of him with none other than General Lysander, back when Crutch was a corporal and the general was a lieutenant. The sergeant major was Old Corps.

"I'm surprised you survived a full tour there, Gunny. Thank the gods I never had to suffer through that.

"Well, take care when you ship out. You've got a tough gig coming, but I know you'll do fine," he said, clapping both of them on the shoulder before leaving them.

"Ship out?" Liege asked the gunny.

"I don't know what he's talking about," Warden answered, looking confused. "He somehow knows some things before anyone else, but I haven't heard of any hot spots popping up right now. Maybe the years are finally creeping up on him.

"Well, if there's anything to it, I guess we'll find out. But anyway, I'm glad I caught you here before the rest showed up. I just wanted to tell you that you did well out there."

"Oh. Just doing my job," Liege said, but suddenly feeling good.

"Yeah, we're all doing our jobs, but I watched how you shepherded Moose. You're a good leader."

"Moose does fine," she protested.

"Yes, he does. But that's in large part due to you, from what I saw. You kept him focused."

There was more than a little truth in his words. Moose was not dumb—no one in recon could be called that. But he could be a little scatterbrained, and Liege had taken it upon herself to keep him on track. She and Moose went back quite a ways. They'd gone through RTC together, and Moose had been there for her, helping her through some of the rough spots. He was big, powerful, and had a huge heart—and he was her friend.

Friend or not, if he was a weak link, she couldn't carry him. The teams were too small and relied on each other for that. But he was a huge benefit to the team, and if Liege had to ride him a little, so be it. She wasn't going to admit that to the gunny, though.

"So, your sister is a Marine now, huh?" he asked, changing the subject.

"Yeah. I was back there for her graduation."

"You must be proud."

"Yes, of course."

Liege wondered why the 20 questions. They hadn't had a chance to talk much since he joined the team, so was this one of those show-the-troops-that-I-care evolutions?

"And I saw you have a dependent? Leandro Estacio?"

"My grandfather. On my mother's side."

Liege was feeling a bit uncomfortable. He could just be being sociable, but while Avó was much, much better, she didn't like to talk about his condition.

"Ah, OK. That explains it. It didn't make much sense from your records. I also saw that you were married?"

Liege put her stein down and turned to stare at the gunny.

"It was a mistake. Annulled," she said, offering nothing else.

Technically, Rex Klein Omarr had never been her husband. Oh, they'd been married in a moment of lust and complete brain shut-down, and they'd had a two-day honeymoon at the Golden Mountain Casino and Resort, where they'd met at the casino's Hundred Meter Bar, but when she awoke two mornings later, the alcohol that had fueled the marriage finally metabolized, she realized what a mistake it had been. Her husband was on his back, naked except for one shoe, snoring loudly. She couldn't even remember where he was from.

She'd shaken him awake, and to her great relief, he'd expressed similar regrets. An hour later, the marriage was annulled, and it had never officially happened. The marriage had already been registered, however, and the Navy had duly noted it. She was now listed as divorced despite two years of trying to get the marriage stricken from the records.

Gunny must have seen something in her eyes, and he quickly retreated from the personal lines of questioning. He almost seemed happy when Gunny Van Meter from First Platoon sat down to join them. Before long, the entire company was in the bar, ready to kick back and relax after the exercise.

Liege made her excuses from the gunny and went to join Teri and Fidor as they came in. She knew that a good leader is supposed to know his or her subordinates, but she'd felt uncomfortable with him asking personal questions.

Chapter 27

Sergeant Major Carruthers back at The Bar had been right. Less than an hour after landing back at Portillo, Major Stann informed the company that they were deploying to New Manitoba in support of Third MEB.[16]

New Manitoba was an industrial hub in the Second Sector, with only eight years as a member of the Federation. The results of the referendum to join the Federation had been close, with the "Feddies" gathering 53.7% of the vote. There had been protests and demands for a new vote, but nothing had come of that.

Until three days ago.

A large military force had attacked two of the industrial centers on the main continent and was now moving towards the capital. Initial intel was that the force had been drawn from much of the Army, supplemented by the security forces of several of the old business conglomerates. These conglomerates had supported joining the Federation, but now seemed to be having second thoughts as they proved unable to compete with the larger corporations that came in as the planet merged with the Federation.

Facing these forces were scattered elements of the Army that had stayed loyal to the government, two regiments that were consolidating their position around the capital, and several corporate security forces. They wouldn't be enough.

Enter the Marines. Two of the battalions that would make up the MEB were already deployed on routine cruises and had been diverted to the planet. The Immediate Reaction Battalion was in the process of embarking. Bravo Company, First Recon, and several other support units were to conduct a crisis action deployment; in 14 hours, they would be embarking for the transit over.

It was go time.

---

[16] MEB: Marine Expeditionary Brigade

FS VICTOR BILLINGHAM

Chapter 28

"As you can see, sir, the PIP has significant armor assets," the Navy lieutenant said, using his pointer to highlight the order of battle. "They could easily punch through the defending forces, and they might have done that already had the *Sunlight City* not reached orbit."

That made sense to Liege. The *Sunlight City* might be an older cruiser, but with her on-ship weapons systems, she could easily wipe out a fleet of armor.

"As far as friendly armor, the loyalist forces have 25 PTY-3 Armored Combat Vehicles, of which 16 are combat effective, and 14 TYNs, 9 being effective. The MEB has 15 M1 Davises and 12 Pangolins. Of course, as I've already noted, there are 28 PICS platoons and the five Wasps that will help even up the playing field."

The People's Independence Party's 127 TYN, "Tonya" tanks, were not nearly as advanced as the Marines' M1s, but at 127 to 15, and with a full 240 PTY-3 "Patties," they could overrun the Marines by sheer numbers. With the Wasps, PICS Marines, and most of all, the *Sunlight City* in orbit, the PIP armor should be taken out of the equation before it came to that, though, so if it came to full-on combat, it should boil down to the infantry.

Not that recon would be taking on armor. Their mission, which was still being tweaked, was to get out in front of the defensive lines and make sure the general had the full picture.

Liege looked down to where Brigadier General Lamonica sat in the front row. She wondered if he minded riding out to the battle with mere support units. With two battalions in the process of planet-fall and the Immediate Reaction Battalion preceding them, he wasn't going to be able to affect full command of the combat units until he got on scene. She didn't even know his reputation. He'd been plucked from some staff billet to command the ad hoc brigade, and none of the units had trained together. It would take some amazing managerial skills, she knew, to mesh all the units into a smoothly running force.

Her stomach rumbled, breaking her train of thought. The "*Vic*" was an old troop transport, built on the plans of a cruise liner. It wasn't a feasible option for an opposed landing, but in this case, it could transport lots of Marines, and more importantly to Liege at the moment, in comfort. Her kitchens were top-notch, and in fewer than nine hours, Liege and her team would be out in the badlands, eating field rats. She was bound and determined to get in two more good meals under her belt before that.

But the general wanted briefs, and with the *Vic's* large auditorium (a theater for the civilian liners built on the same hull) and the relatively low number of PAX, he wanted everyone to sit in on them with him.

Most of what the Intel officer was presenting had already been downloaded onto each Marine's PA, and Liege wasn't learning much of anything new. She almost wished that something would happen of which the general had to be informed, something above the security clearance of a mere recon corpsman.

But, no such luck. The lieutenant pulled up yet another image, this one detailing the personal weapons and equipment of each PIP soldier.

Liege sighed, put her hands on her belly, and settled into her seat.

NEW MANITOBA

Chapter 29

Liege was suspended in a sea of darkness. The wind brushed her face as she descended to the planet's surface. Out there somewhere, her seven teammates floated as well. She couldn't see them, and she wouldn't go active to try and spot them, because even if she had known exactly where they were, it really made no difference.

She'd been in free fall for only a few moments—the insert was using   HAHO,   or "High Altitude, High Opening." After the shock of her foil deploying, it was almost unnaturally calm as she floated down. Above her, the stars painted a panoply of bright points, but below her, the darkness was only broken by a few lonely lights in the far distance.

Liege was at the mercy of her AI. She could take over control of the foil, of course, but that would result in the slightest bit of power leak, enough so that anyone actively searching could spot them. Her AI had been programmed, and using passive measures to determine her position, should get her down to the DZ,[17] along with the rest of her team.

She glanced up at her stealthy canopy. The foil was designed to absorb waves, be they light, radar, or sound. With a 1.0 wing loading, the glide ration was excellent, reaching 18 to 20. Exiting the glider at 9,000 meters, their insertion range was outstanding, up to 30 klicks or so.

With a duck egg, of course, the teams would have had far more control as to their DZs. But the *Vic* didn't have launching

---

[17] DZ: Drop Zone

capabilities, so as soon as they landed at Williamson City, the three teams being inserted loaded the gliders for the lift by the *Vic's* shuttles returning to the ship. The shuttles could be tracked by even primitive gear, but the cohesion-board gliders would be practically invisible as they piggybacked up to altitude. And now, somewhere above her, the glider, having discharged the team, would already have disintegrated into tiny dust particles.

After descending to about the 4,000-meter altitude, Liege popped the supplemental O2 tubes out of her nose. New Manitoba's atmosphere was only 16% O2, slightly less than Earth-normal, but she'd be fine, and she didn't like the cannulas. All the cannula prongs were shaped exactly the same, and they were not flexible. For her, they were pretty uncomfortable hooked inside her nose.

The DZ almost surprised her as she reached it. She had to lift her feet as she cleared a line of trees, but her AI brought her in for a stand-up landing. Her chute immediately detached and fell to the ground. It started to collapse around itself, and within 30 seconds, what had been a 15-meter wide foil was a small hunk of solid polyestroline.

She jammed it into her cargo pocket, then looked around for the rest of the team. A ghost passed over her head, resolving into another Marine landing ten meters away. Liege waited for his foil to fall away, then pushed through the knee-high grass to him. Within two steps, she knew it was Moose. Even in the dead of night, his outline was immediately recognizable.

She flipped down her monocle, and Moose's features sprang into visibility. New Manitoba might not have had a moon, but the stars gave more than enough light for the monocle's night vision capability to work in passive mode. He pocketed the remains of his foil, turned and saw Liege, and raised a hand in greeting. Together, they moved to the south side of the DZ, and within a couple of minutes, the team was gathered. Warden gave the move-out signal, and Gidge took point, starting the 30-klick-long march ahead of them to their objective.

Every member of the team had multiple skills, both through formal training as well as simple genetics. Gidge, Staff Sergeant Dek Wisteria, was the team's school-trained EOD Marine. But, he had also been a well-regarded gymnast in his school days, and the small man could move like a wraith. Because of this, he was the point man whenever they moved. In line units, the point man was rotated to spread around the risk, but in the teams, operators simply took the jobs for which they were best suited. Gidge had gone through regen twice during his career, the result of being hit while walking point, but Liege knew he'd never considered someone else taking point. It was his job, and that's the way it was.

It was dark under the cover of the trees, the leaves blocking out the starlight. But, like most terraformed worlds, there wasn't much undergrowth. Both the genmodded oaks and maples which formed the top canopy and the tree-aloes at the second canopy level were planted to produce O2. As this area was mostly unpopulated, there was no reason yet to sow the ground-hugging plants that had commercial uses.

Liege followed Moose, his broad back easy to see through her monocle. She tried to keep alert, watching for any sign of danger, but unless she went into active night vision, her view was limited to eight or nine meters. The *Sunlight City*, though, had blasted the area with active scanning the day before, along with half of the landmass so as not to alert the PIP forces as to where actual areas of interest were, and this route of advance was deserted.

By the time daylight started to filter through the trees, they'd only covered ten klicks. Warden decided to push on. They had to get eyes on the objective, and he felt the chance of being spotted was small. They covered another five klicks before the team leader called them to a halt near a small stream. Without underbrush, it was hard to keep concealed, but the stream had undercut the soil just enough to offer a tiny bit of cover. Liege and the Marines settled in for the rest of the daylight to eat and sleep the best they could. Liege was assigned one of the middle watches, so her restless sleep was broken into two sections.

They could have taken their stimtabs and kept straight on to the objective, but without knowing what they faced, or how long they would face it, the gunny didn't want to waste that silver bullet just yet.

At nightfall, the team was roused, and after another 20 minutes to eat and shit, they moved off again. Their movement was routine, and, well before dawn, the growth started to thin out as the terrain rose. Their objective was a 40-klick long finger of low hills that rose out of the surrounding plains. The main PIP force was spread out starting another 50 klicks beyond the hills to the north, but they would have to cross or go around them if they wanted to advance on Williamson City. This high ground was the strategic center of the AO, and if the Marines couldn't control it yet, they at least had to have eyes on it.

The problem with that was that the PIP Army knew that, too. There were PIP forces scattered throughout the line of hills, and they controlled a small waystation located at the northern end where the main highway passed through them. Warden brought the team to a hasty halt while he tried to confirm where they were.

A recon Marine's main advantage on the battlefield was to remain unseen. A good part of that was not to emit nor receive emissions. Their monocles functioned as mini combat displays, but all the information in them was uploaded before a mission. They could be switched to full net capability, but that was done only if the situation required it, and the monocle screen was small and couldn't display very much. This, of course, meant that navigation was not as simple as having an active AI guiding them, so all recon Marines underwent modification, both to have their hippocampus stimulated to over-develop and to have two Neulife bridges inserted, one connecting each hemisphere of the brain and one connecting the hippocampus to the cortex, which enabled the Marine to make use of that input in a more cognitive fashion.

The Neulife bridge was essentially a bundle of KD crystal connectors, bundled together much like dried spaghetti in a hand before putting it into the boiling water. But KD crystals cannot connect into brain cells themselves. There has to be some sort of interface. So, on each end of the KD bundle, Neulife "caps" were attached which could take the input from the hippocampus, transmit it to the crystals, then interface back into the entorhinal cortex, bypassing the fornix, in a usable format.

The result was that recon Marines pretty much knew where they were at any time, and like waterfowl migrating to a specific pond to lay their eggs, they knew where they were going. Still, it was dark and without visual cues, and the gunny wanted to make sure they were on the right path, so he conferred with Dannyboy and Teri.

Liege was in recon, so she'd had the modification as well. Once, she'd tried to describe to Leticia how it worked, but she couldn't put it into words. She knew the science of it, but it was like describing hearing to someone who'd always been deaf. She could describe how sound waves vibrated the hairs in the inner ear, but to someone who'd never heard before, the context would not resonate. It was the same with navigation. She simply knew where she was and where she was going. Of course, just as someone might mishear something, so could the inner navigation be off.

But evidently, all three of them agreed, and the team moved off again. They were going to the steep side of a hill that didn't offer a direct view over the entire highway as it crossed the hills, but it did provide observation of both the north and south side of the highway at either end. Being on the side of the hill, it was unlikely that a casual patrol would just happen to come across them, and without a direct view of the entire waystation, the hope was that the PIP forces would not flag the position as a possible observation point.

It was still dark, but the orange fingers of dawn were visible over the horizon as the team eased into position. The team was broken into two-man groups, positioned 20 or 30 meters apart, and as the night turned into day, they settled in for what could be a long mission.

Chapter 30

"There's another one," Warden said, pointing to his right. "Just downhill from the Seagull."

Liege turned to look. The "Seagull" was the name they'd given a white outcropping of rock 800 meters to the northwest. It looked nothing like a seagull, but just having a quick reference point was what was important, not that the descriptions were accurate.

Her Zeis binos were top-of-the-line for mechanical binoculars, almost as good as electronic binos, and they brought the four PIP soldiers into stark relief. The soldiers were making their way along a narrow trail, and they looked much more interested in their footing than in the possible presence of Federation Marines.

No one they had spotted so far seemed to be on a combat footing. The PIP command had to know the Marines had landed, but the idea that the Marines would send forces forward didn't seem to have occurred to them.

Liege noted the numbers, weapons, position, and direction of movement in her journal. At least two of the other two-man teams probably had the four soldiers in sight as well and would be recording their sightings. Writing down observations in a physical journal might have been pretty primitive, but until they needed to, they would use no electronic equipment.

When the time came to report to the MEB, they wouldn't even have to break radio silence, at least from their current position. They could take micro images of their journal entries, stuff them into a small carrier pod, then shoot the pod from a small handheld crossbow. The little crossbow could shoot a pod over 10 klicks, and once it hit the ground, it would emit a tiny microburst, sending the intel back to the MEB. The message would be highly scrambled, and the transmission shielded, but still, most advanced surveillance measures could tell that something had been transmitted and approximately from where, but the contents should be secure.

The little crossbow could also send a PCC-4 out to about half that distance. They could then "shoot" the transponder with a small encoded low-watt laser, and the transponder would redirect the message back to the MEB. The only issue with that was that the PCC-4 had to be in direct line-of-site, so when employed, it was rarely at the full five klicks. Both of these methods were used when they wanted to keep their presence, or at least location, from being discovered. Once compromised, or when back-and-forth comms were needed, they would break radio silence. At that point, though, as Fidor kept reminding them, they might as well erect flashing neon signs shaped like fingers to point out their positions.

The team had been in position for a little over ten hours so far. Liege and Warden had spotted 18 foot soldiers during that time, but only eight had been mobile. The rest were as a makeshift barricade at the north end of Route Grape—Highway 21—as it entered the range of hills right at what used to be the small waystation, rest-stop, and resort, now abandoned and destroyed by previous fighting. One of the Gentry-made Patties stood guard at the barricade, its short-barreled 50mm chaingun aimed down Grape to the south. Without active AIs, Liege thought the Patty was an R-variant—Warden was pretty sure it was an S. It didn't make much difference, especially as it was acting as a pillbox, but Liege was sure the slight indentation of the skirt over the road-wheels proved it was an R.

An ancient, but still impressive, Koft 79mm field gun guarded the approach from the north. The old canon had very primitive target acquisition, but no one could deny the efficacy of its chain-delayed shape rounds. A direct hit could take out a Davis.

Neither Liege nor Warden could figure out why the barricade was on the north side of the range. It would seem to have made more sense for it to be on the south side, where the Patty could take any approaching Federation armor under fire. Even at its present position, they both thought it made more sense to turn the big Koft around as well, oriented to the south.

"How do you think the captain's doing?" Liege asked as the two scanned for more activity.

First Team had been inserted far to the west, and they had a longer march to get into position, mirroring Second Team on the other side of Grape. The rest of the company was scattered over the continent at the most likely avenues of approach toward the capital.

"I doubt they're in position yet."

"You don't think so? I'm guessing he had them move through the day," Liege said. "If I had to bet, I'd say they are in position now."

"Well, then bet on it?"

"What?"

"I think they'll make it in tonight. You think they're already in position. Let's bet on who's right?" the gunny said.

"Bet what?"

"I don't know. You choose."

Liege turned to look at his face. He had his Temperest binos to his eyes as he scanned for more sign. She couldn't tell if he was serious or not, but she decided to take him at his word.

"A case of beer of the winner's choice," she said.

"Done," he replied, never lowering his binos.

Liege was still having a little problem reading her team leader. After seeing him in action, she was confident that his rep as an operator was on point. She wasn't sure if she'd ever worked with someone as capable in warcraft. But, when his warrior hat was off, sometimes he seemed hard and aloof, but other times, he was casual and easy-going. He could be quite charming at times, but he could also be hot-and-cold.

As part of a two-man team, Liege couldn't object to Warden's military capabilities, but she thought she'd rather be teamed with Moose or one of the others. She understood them better, and that kind of connection could be the difference between life and death.

"Well, if we're going to emplace the seisos tonight, we need to get some rest. I'm going to catch some Z's now. Give me two hours, then wake me up and I'll spell you."

With that, Warden leaned back, pulled his cover over his eyes, and looked to immediately have fallen asleep.

Warden seemed to go through life as a coiled spring, but as he drifted off, his body seemed to relax for once. He sort of settled into the crook of the roots that the two had used to form their positions, his leg falling slightly to the side to rest against Liege's leg.

She shook her head, amazed at how quickly he'd gone under, then pulled back up her binos. If he started snoring, she'd kick him awake. Otherwise, it was just her for the moment, and she still had a lot of territory to watch.

Chapter 31

Liege crept forward on her belly, all senses on alert. She had a seiso and an ACS ready to place. The seiso was a simple vibration recorder. In soil such as that around Grape, it could detect footfalls out to about 100 meters. This close to the highway itself, it would be able to detect any vehicle driving past from much farther away.

The Atmospheric Contaminant Sampler had an odd, nautilus-shaped gathering cone. Contact strips were attached inside the swirling chamber, and when suspended particles touched the strips, they stuck and were analyzed. The MEB's battle AIs could extract an amazing amount of intel based on what particles could be collected.

The seiso was passive; the power to record the vibrations came from the vibrations themselves. The ACS, on the other hand, needed internal power. However, it was very, very efficient, needing a mere 3 nanoamperes to run. It was heavily shielded, and if anything was picked up, it should be lost in the clutter of insect and animal life present in the area.

The team needed to emplace the sensors for full coverage of Grape. They didn't have eyes on most of the length of the highway as it made its way through the hills. Recon was the king of surveillance, so the team had more than enough options in their bag of tricks. The problem was not so much in the gathering of the data, but in the reception and then passing it on. Seisos could be hard wired, but even shielded, the fact that there was a wire running through the brush could be a red flag in and of itself. It doesn't take high-tech gear to simply walk back along a wire to see where it came from.

To recover the data, the team would either have to physically pick it up or trigger a data dump. Picking it back up meant the team would be exposed, but a data dump was at a significant risk of being picked up by PIP counter-surveillance.

Liege reached out, gripped the dirt, and pulled herself forward. It had taken the four of them three hours to cover the first klick, but the last 200 meters had been at two hours and counting.

She heard a low mumble, and she froze, arms halfway out again. She strained to make out what she'd heard. At first, there was nothing, and she started to relax until a clear, "So what're you going to do?" reached her through the darkness.

Liege carefully brought her arms back and pulled her Ruger out of her thigh holster. She slipped the Ruger under her chest, using her body as a shield.

Liege couldn't make out what whoever was there was going to do, but the first person said, "I don't know. That's a big step. Have you thought about the consequences?"

What's a big step? Liege wondered. *Getting married? Going to school? Deserting?*

She saw movement, and two shadows stepped into view. They kept walking slowly in her direction.

"Yeah. I told you, though. I haven't made up my mind, so you keep quiet about it," the second soldier said.

Under her chest, she reached with her thumb to flip the safety lever. Her Ruger was a fine piece of hardware. It fired a 2mm dart at hypersonic speeds. Best of all, it was relatively quiet. The mag coils could be detected by surveillance, but only as a momentary flash of energy. If these two discovered her, she'd take them out. They didn't know she was there, and she should be able to zero them before they could react. Of course, when they didn't show up whenever they were due back, there would be a search, and the PIP command would know someone was out there. The team's mission would turn from passive to active.

"Hey, hold up, man. I've got to take a piss," the second man said.

Oh, fucking great.

The shadow stopped a couple of meters from her, and a moment later, she heard the stream of urine hit the leaves. The sound started strong and stayed strong longer than Liege would have thought it physically possible before it finally petered out.

The shadow turned. If they had night vision devices, she would be caught dead to rights. There was no reaction, though, as the two men started walking again.

NVDs were extremely common. Even civilians could buy them easily. Liege didn't have her monocle on at the moment as she didn't want any collected light to reflect off her cheekbone, but these two soldiers wouldn't have that same concern. So she was surprised that neither of them seemed to have NVDs deployed.

The two kept casually walking down the side of the road, one stepping less than two meters from Liege's head. She was just inside the line of foliage, but it really wasn't dense enough to give her full cover. The two soldiers didn't stop their conversation, however, as they walked past. Even if they didn't see her, Liege was surprised they couldn't hear the pounding of her heart; it was beating so hard.

She waited a good five minutes after they'd passed before she pulled herself up that last meter. She re-holstered her Ruger, then pulled out the seiso and the ACS. Both were easy to set up. In less than a minute, she was scooching back into the bushes lining Grape.

Due to her delay, she was the last one back to the rally point.

"Did that guy piss on you?" Warden asked as she crept in.

"No, but it was close."

"I was about to tap them," Moose whispered.

"And I never even saw them. Moose told me," Fidor said, almost sounding disappointed.

"Well, that was fun," Warden said. "But we've got a long way back, and Dannyboy's probably about ready to shit his trou wondering where we are."

Liege had to smile as Fidor led the way out of the RP. Dannyboy was great, but more than a little high-strung. With half of the team on this little mission and without comms, he'd be beside himself until they got back.

Which wouldn't be for another three hours at least. Liege shrugged and followed Fidor as they carefully made their way through the trees.

Chapter 32

Liege's gut was beginning to get that familiar clenching feeling. She was only three days into her FIP, so it was a little early. The Fecal Inhibitor Protocol, better known the "butt-plugger," was used when passing a bowel movement would be "inconvenient." With the recon culture of leave no traces, that meant that recon Marines were perhaps the biggest customers of the little bottles of syrup.

Liege was not totally on board with the protocol. As a medical professional, she knew that the more a person's body was screwed with, the more chance there was that there would be consequences downstream. The much feared Brick, for example, had never existed until after regeneration became possible.

From a practical point of view, sure, the butt-plugger worked to eliminate elimination, at least the solid kind, but in another three or four days (probably three for her, if her gut was any indication), she would let loose with all of what was building up inside of her. When that happened, a person could be indisposed for a good 15 or 20 minutes.

She gave her belly a little pat, then lifted her binos again. Several more armored vehicles had arrived at the checkpoint, including a Tonya tank. This was vital information, she thought, but still, Warden hadn't initiated forwarding any of the intel they were gathering.

Liege gave Warden a quick glance. He was taking notes in his journal, which was all well and good, but whatever he was writing wouldn't do the MEB any good unless they could see it.

Sometimes, Liege thought the recon community went overboard. Sure, recon was the elite of the Corps, on par with the Navy SEALS. But sometimes, she felt they took the high-speed, low-drag culture too far. Here she was, using an old-fashioned optical Zeiss when Zeiss also made the best, highest-tech electronic binos in the world. Liege could look at that Tonya, hit the analytics, and then with one blink of the eye, send all of that info to the MEB where they could make use of it. The emission of a shielded upload like that would be very hard to pick up.

She and Warden had discussed the subject a few hours ago. His position, which reflected the recon party line, was that if something important needed to be passed up, then they would use whatever means they had at their disposal to get the intel up the chain. However, with the Navy overhead, the fact that three more Patties and a Tonya had joined the party would have already been known. The team was there to observe what the *Sunlight City* might miss and to be ready to take any action as necessary should the PIP forces advance.

Liege understood that. But she also felt wasted at the moment. They weren't *doing* anything.

She was getting to know Warden better, though. With just the two of them in their hide, they were stuck with each other for conversation. Quietly, and slowly, they each told parts of their stories.

Warden Johansson had been a member of the Youth Brigade back on Ostermein, so he and Liege had that in common. The Youth Brigade tried to portray itself as a conservative, patriotic group of young people, but in reality, it wasn't any different than the gangs in Liege's favela—just bigger and better funded. Like Liege, he'd joined the Marines to break free of the pattern, and like her, he'd accidentally found a home in the service.

What surprised Liege the most, though, was that, despite his hard-ass reputation, and despite his sometimes awkward social manners, he was actually personable when he wasn't trying to be the super-leader of Marines. Liege had finally called him out on that, and he'd ruefully smiled and told her he was trying to put into practice what he'd read in *Better Leaders, Better Federation*, one of the self-help books currently making the rounds. Warden was a certified hero, but he'd told Liege his last sergeant major, with whom he didn't get along, had accused him of relying on his combat record to advance in the Corps, and that he'd better learn leadership if he ever wanted to get past gunnery sergeant.

Liege thought that sergeant major had to be a jealous jerk. Warden had the leadership qualities, even if he didn't quite realize that about himself yet. She sure didn't have any problems following him despite having a few misgivings early on.

She'd even felt comfortable enough to let him know what had happened at the Golden Mountain Resort and her aborted marriage. She was rarely so open. Only Leticia and Rex, her temporary husband, had known the whole story until then, and, she had to admit, it was a pretty good story. Some of it was lost forever in an alcohol-induced haze, but what she did remember was pretty epic.

In turn, Warden told her about his two-year marriage and fathering a son with his ex. The boy was ten now, going to school and playing beatball. Warden was both proud of the boy, but also worried about him acting out. Liege could tell that Warden blamed himself for the latter, for not being there all the time.

Getting people to open up to her was nothing new. People had done that all her life. It was a little rarer when she opened up to others, at least with anything consequential.

Liege pulled out her last bag of Sprockets, popped two into her mouth, then nudged Warden with her foot, holding out the bag. Geedunk was a big no-no out in the field, but one that was usually ignored. Warden reached over, and, breaking time-honored Sprockets protocol, looked inside so he could pull out two of the venerated green ones. He simply smiled as Liege stuck out her tongue at him.

"All hands, all hands, Threat Condition Alpha. I repeat, Threat Condition Alpha. There has been a Class 1 Event. Stand by for further instructions," suddenly came over their earbuds.

Liege dropped the bag of Sprockets and raised her binos, glassing the checkpoint below. Nothing looked out of the ordinary.

"What's going on?" she asked Warden despite knowing that he was just as in the dark as she was.

For the MEB to pass that on AC, all circuits, meant something big had happened, and the command didn't care if opposing forces picked up the broadcast. The PIP forces would know that something had been passed, even if they (hopefully) didn't know just what it was. The AC was the most efficient and quickest way for everyone in the MEB to get the message.

Liege looked 30 meters to her right. Moose was looking back at her from under his and Fidor's tarnkappe, his shoulders shrugged and hands out in the universal what's-going-on sign. She returned the same gesture.

"All hands, all hands. The *FS Sunlight City* has suffered damage from an outside source. She is withdrawing from orbit until a full assessment has been made. We believe the damage was done by a PIP diplomatic shuttle that was arriving to conduct negotiations. All Federation forces are now in Threat Condition Alpha. We put the probability of offensive action by PIP forces at 82%. Stand by for further instructions."

"The *Sunlight City*? What the hell?" Warden said.

It was inconceivable that a Federation cruiser could be damaged by a diplomatic shuttle, of all things. The *Sunlight City* might have been old, but still, she was a Navy cruiser. This was too hard to fathom.

Liege and Warden turned towards each other at the same time. There were a little over five thousand Marines in the MEB. There were over 50,000 soldiers in the PIP Army. The Marines had the edge in weaponry and experience, but without the *Sunset City* watching over them, that might not be enough.

"I think the shit's about to come downhill," Warden said.

Liege simply nodded, then brought up her binos. Down below, PIP soldiers were just now scurrying around in motion, like ants in an anthill that had been kicked open.

"Yeah, I think you're right, Stein. I think you're right."

Chapter 33

"Organic surveillance has been compromised. Seventy-three percent of Class Six assets are no longer functioning," the operator passed over the CLN.

"Organic surveillance" meant the MEB's armada of nano, micro, and full-sized hummingbirds, dragonflies, and high-altitude drones. Nano-drones were hard to spot, but if an enemy had large reservoirs of power, they could simply sweep the airspace, knocking the tiny drones out of the air like so many no-see-ums. The high-altitude drones were slightly easier to locate, but much harder to knock out of the sky.

The mere fact that they were now in direct comms with the MEB was a pretty good indication that things were getting serious.

As if the attack on the Sunlight City wasn't indication enough, Liege reminded herself.

MEB had launched a chatterbox, which was in low synchronous orbit over the AO. Using that, they could relay through the Cognitive Light Net back down to units. The CLN was perhaps the second-most secure form of active comms, right after meson, but meson comms were far too expensive and logistically convoluted for small unit use. If—when—the PIP forces knocked the chatterbox out of orbit, the Marines would revert to normal tactical comms, but until then, the CLN gave them a slightly stronger security blanket.

No longer in the dark, the team was now faced with a sobering reality. The *Sunlight City* had been heavily damaged by a suicider. The diplomatic shuttle had been cleared for landing, and its explosive cargo had somehow passed by the ship's scans. It had detonated inside the hangar with tremendous effect, killing over 100 sailors, damaging the fire control and shielding systems, and knocking the bubble-drive navigator off-line. Without the bubble-drive navigator, the ship could still enter bubble-space, but there would be no way to know just where she would emerge back into real-space. The ship, accompanied by the smaller *FS Bongo* for security, had retreated from the planet, and her crew was feverishly trying to repair what they could. They estimated it might take 35 hours, which was also about the earliest the Marines could expect reinforcement from the Navy's Second Fleet. Meanwhile, the PIP forces were in motion, and no one thought they had 35 hours to spare. The inevitable clash would occur long before that.

"The best we can tell, and I'm sorry we can't give you better intel, is that there are two divisions advancing down Route Grape. We estimate their ETA at your pos in seven hours.

"We need both Granite-Three and Granite-Four to take action to deny passage through Grape at your pos. We need the road knocked out, but don't initiate anything until the main elements are at Licorice. You will have air support at that time."

That made sense to Liege. "Licorice" was the Marine designation of the PIP checkpoint at the waystation below them. If the team—both teams; they would be working in tandem with the captain's Team 1 coming in from the east side of Grape—closed off the highway too early, the advancing PIP forces would simply angle off Grape and go around the range of hills. The Marines needed to stop the column, turn it into a clusterfuck, and force the enemy to "un-cluster" it before changing direction and going cross-country to get around the hills. Infantry wouldn't be stopped, but the armor, which was the bigger threat in their AO, could be delayed half-a-day at least.

Of course, "closing off" Grape, which was a major highway, was easier said than done. The teams had some pretty serious assets, but this was a big task for a single recon platoon. They would have to have lots of help from the Wasps and arty. The MEB had seven Wasps: five that were attached and another two the CO of the *Sunlight City* had detached before retreating. They wouldn't be particularly effective in damaging the roadbed, but they could take out a shitload of armor. Arty, though, even if the south side of the pass was at the very limit of the tube's range, had a few munitions which could be helpful.

"We will update you as we know more. Keep comms to a minimum, but we want half-hour progress reports."

Liege looked at Warden, who rolled his eyes. "Keep comms to a minimum" and "half-hour progress reports" were pretty much diametrically opposing commands.

"Good luck"

"Roger that, the captain answered from somewhere to the west of Grape. "Granite-Three, out."

Liege sat there for a moment, gathering her thoughts. This was a heavy mission, she knew. And despite her confidence in her platoon, 15 recon Marines and one gung-ho Navy corpsman would be hard-pressed to hold back two divisions of enemy armor.

"Well, Doc, I guess it's go-time," Warden said.

Chapter 34

A Tonya rumbled past, creaking and squeaking as it went. Liege hugged the dirt as the behemoth shook the ground.

The tank was made by Gentry, the source of cheap munitions and equipment for a good chunk of humanity. That didn't make the Tonya any less of a threat. It hadn't been in production for over 30 years in its various forms for nothing. It couldn't stand up to the best the Federation (or any of another six or seven militaries) had to offer, but against ground troops or less-advanced armor, it could more than hold its own.

Liege clutched the Kelpie in her hand, ready to use it if she was spotted, but knowing she only had a 30% chance of getting a kill with it if it came to that. Recon was the elite of the Corps, and they had lots of cool toys to play with, but they were only human, and without PICS or other strength-augmenting means, they could only carry so much into battle. And their mission was to gather intel first and foremost, but even when it came to offensive ops, their missions tended to the more clandestine, so what they carried was designed with that in mind. A recon team was not set up to take on armor.

Still, they had to be able to protect themselves, so they had Kelpies to use against armor and powered combat suits. The Kelpie was a slimmed-down version of the venerable Banshee. The range was shorter, the warhead less powerful, but it was significantly smaller and lighter to carry. It should be able to take out any combat suited soldiers, but against a battle tank, things got iffy.

The Tonya never hesitated, though, and kept rolling down Grape. Liege didn't need to recover the siesos to know that there had been a steady stream of vehicles moving down the highway. The PIP forces were setting up another position on the south side of where the highway came out of the hills. She guessed that someone on the other side had finally realized that they had to keep the route open.

Liege raised her head from the ground and spotted Moose ten meters in front of her. He looked back, caught her eye, and gave her a thumbs-up. Liege warily got to her feet, and along with Warden and Fidor, started forward again. They'd been able to parallel the road from a good 40 meters in, but as the canyon narrowed, they were getting pushed closer and closer to the road itself. They were losing their cover, and as they placed their charges, they would be totally exposed.

Thinking of being exposed, she looked back, but she couldn't see the other four Marines. They were going to be placing the cratering charges where the highway crossed the small creek about 200 meters from the pass, but they were out of her sight. That was good, though. If she couldn't see them, then hopefully no soldiers could see them either.

The rocky face that made up the Seagull kept edging closer to the highway, funneling them closer as well. They would soon be out of cover entirely.

Just to her front, Moose stopped and took a knee. He pointed up. Liege flipped down her monocle, and let her gaze travel up the rock wall. Sixty meters up, at the top, she saw movement.

Shit. I guess they're not so stupid after all, she thought.

Liege had been somewhat surprised that they hadn't run into any ground troops. With their divisions on the way, it was extremely obvious to her that where Grape crossed the range was a natural chokepoint. Yes, they were putting positions at either end of it, but they had to know that Marine teams were in the area. This was rather old military science.

But they had put at least a team on top of Seagull where it abutted the road. Liege could see three from her vantage point, and there could be more up there. Her monocle's night vision capability wasn't great in the passive mode, but she could still see enough. One soldier was crouched beside a crew-served weapon of some kind, and he was glassing down the road. Liege had spent the last few days observing the Seagull as well, but from the east. This was the first time she'd seen it from this side. But she knew what was on top. She knew the soldier would be able to see Dannyboy when the staff sergeant led his team out onto the roadbed.

Warden was motioning Liege and Moose to where he was up against the side of the hill.

"How many are up there?" he asked quietly when they got there.

"I could only see one," Moose said.

"I saw three. And they have to have full visuals on the bridge," Liege added.

"Shit! Well, we had to have expected something like this," Warden said.

He craned his head to look up, leaning out from the wall, then looked back at the other three.

"I don't think they can see us down here this close to the wall. I'm going to halt Dannyboy, and we're going to continue on with our mission."

"What? With them right up there?" Liege asked.

"If they can't see us, then they can't do much about it, right? So no reason to change our plans, at least as it pertains to the pass."

"And after that?" Moose asked.

"After that, I think we need to do some hunting."

Liege didn't need her NVDs to see the smile take over Moose's face as he heard that.

Warden went active comms and told Dannyboy to hold up his team. Then, the four of them edged forward, hugging the rock face. As they got closer to the road itself, while those on top might not be able to see them, anyone coming down the road couldn't miss them. Liege strained her ears to catch any sounds of an approaching vehicle.

The gods of chance were with them, though. The four stepped onto the roadbed with no vehicles in sight.

For almost 40 meters, the rock face ended at the edge of the road on one side, and with only a small stream and a less-shear face rising up from the other side. From the base of their wall to where the other side started getting steeper was less than 30 meters. If they could bring down the higher rock face, they knew they could block the highway.

Liege knew something about collapsing walls, and she knew how effective they could be as a weapon of war.

Taking down a solid rock face was not as easy as it sounds, but recon was built for sabotage, and they were well trained. The effort would be a two-step process. The first would be to place molecular compressing charges along the bottom of the excavated edge of the rock face, right alongside the edge of the road. The second step would be to place explosive charges at the sides of the face where it curved back from the road. The compressor charges would make the molecular structure of the wall collapse in on itself in several broad swathes, maybe five to seven meters deep. With the collapse of the molecular space, huge chunks of the rock would essentially disappear, causing a collapse of support.

A split second later, the explosive charges to the side would detonate, penetrating the rock and expanding it. With a "pull" from the bottom and a "push" from the sides, the entire face of the wall should shear off and collapse onto the highway. The Seagull might not be comparatively large as hills or mountains went, but it was plenty big enough to do the job.

With Fidor providing security, Liege emplaced the compressor charges while Warden and Moose set the side charges. Just after setting the second charge, a small rock came tumbling down the cliff to hit the road and bounce across. Liege froze, but nothing else followed, so she finished with her final two charges. She'd have liked to have had three more, given the length of the face, but that was all she had. Dannyboy had taken two more that he'd use on his mission.

She was making her way back off the road when the sky lit up to the north in a brilliant flash. A fireball had appeared, 20 or 30 klicks away, but still bright enough to light the area. It quickly faded, surrendering back to the darkness. Not everyone was waiting for the imminent clash. For some, combat was already joined. Liege hoped that the flash of light represented a Federation win, not a Wasp being shot down.

As the four of them gathered, all three looked to Warden for guidance.

"Look. We know what the top of the Seagull looks like. Our friends up there, they're on the beak," he said, naming the lower of the two ledges. "I think it's time we went up the lower trail. I think we can get to the head and gain not only the high ground, but the element of surprise. We've still got four hours, so we've got some time, but not enough to waste it down here. We ready to take it to them?"

"Damned right," Liege said, joining the other three, the low volume of her voice not reflecting her enthusiasm.

"OK, then, here's what we're going to do. . ."

Chapter 35

Ninety minutes later, and breathing hard from both the exertion and the relative lack of oxygen, Liege lay prone on the top of the Seagull's head, looking down at the five soldiers on the beak, about 70 meters away. They had taken longer than they had thought it would take. At first, while they knew where the lower trail came out on top of the Seagull, they couldn't find the entrance down on the canyon floor. Second, the trail switched back and forth more times than they had figured. In the distance, dawn was already reaching the plains, and dust was visible, signaling the approach of the two PIP divisions.

From their hides back on the far hillside, it looked like it was smooth rock from the head to the beak of the Seagull, but the head itself had blocked part of the view. What they hadn't seen before was a line of thick brush that had gained a foothold at the base of the head at the juncture where the ledge that made up the beak jutted out. The five soldiers might only be 70 meters away, but the four team members couldn't reach them quickly if need be.

"Which is why we need to be on point the first time," Warden reminded in a whisper. "Do we all have our targets?"

"Left guy, the fat one," Liege said.

"Mr. No Helmet, on the crew-served," Fidor said.

"The NCO," Moose said, eagerness evident in his voice.

"And I've got the other two. Check your weapons. I want this to be in unison."

Liege turned her M91 over to check the safety and round selection. She'd decided on a three round burst. The 91 was merely the carbine version of the M99. She was comfortable with the longer weapon, so unlike many recon Marines, she'd stuck with the 91 as the shorter variant of the 99. Moose was carrying a New

Budapest F-2. The weapon was decidedly ugly, but it packed a powerful punch.

"Just like you," Liege regularly told her friend.

Both Warden and Fidor carried the M114, a bullpup .3002 squirt gun popularized by the SEALS. It was short, thanks to the bullpup configuration, and it could put out a lot of jacketless rounds quickly, but Liege thought it a little hard to control. Her 8mm darts might not pack the same shock value, but she had thousands of rounds to their hundreds.

"OK, on three," Warden said.

Liege brought her M91 to bear, then centered her crosshairs on the heaviest soldier's back.

"One. . .two. . .three!"

Liege squeezed the trigger just before Moose's F-2 sounded beside her ear. With the dart-thrower's low recoil, the three darts impacted within a few centimeters of each other, shredding the soldier's uniform in the middle of his back. He dropped bonelessly to the deck.

She shifted her aim, but all five of the soldiers were down or going down. Mr. No Helmet lurched forward, and when he hit the ground, he bounced once, then slid over the edge of the drop-off.

"Shit!" Fidor said, his accent making it sound like "seet."

Liege knew the body wouldn't stop until it hit the ground level. It should land among the bushes, but there was a chance that it would be visible to anyone travelling down Grape.

"Hold your fire," Warden said. "See any movement?"

Liege clicked her monocle to 3X and checked her victim for movement, but he was motionless, one leg bent back underneath his large body—and it suddenly hit her. She'd just killed a person, probably for the first time. She'd fired her weapon in anger before, but she knew that it took about 10,000 rounds fired for each enemy killed. She'd always just assumed that her rounds going downrange were part of the environment, no more consequential than mosquito. But this time, there was no doubt. She was a Navy corpsman, dedicated to saving lives, but she'd just snuffed out the life of another human being.

Liege lowered her M91 in surprise. She felt, well, not much, and she knew she should feel something: elation, sadness, whatever, but something. She was hyped, for sure, but that was the adrenaline of the fight still coursing through her.

Maybe I'll feel something later, she told herself.

"Fidor, Moose, go check them. We'll cover you," Warden said.

The two Marines nodded, then slid down the rocky scree to the bottom.

"Nice shooting, Doc," Warden said matter-of-factly.

Liege stole a glance at him. She couldn't detect any underlying tone to his words. She knew Warden had been in the shit before, that he'd killed more than a few enemies, so maybe to him, this was just another day at the job.

"Hey, it's all wet here," Moose passed. "And muddy."

The two were only 10 or 15 meters directly below them, so Liege could hear their voice through the air and over the comms at the same time. Moose and Fidor were pushing through the heavy brush at the bottom, struggling to get through some mud.

"On solid rock, who would have thought?" Warden said. "Dirt must have gathered, then windborne seeds got established, but water? I wonder if it's runoff or if there's some sort of spring. It's got to be—"

A shot rang out, and Fidor spun around, hand going to the side of his head. Without thinking, Liege fired off two three-round bursts at a mud-covered figure who had jumped up, a UKI-52 in his grip. The man fell to one knee, tried to rise, then collapsed. Moose was struggling with another figure when Warden fired, and suddenly, Moose was grappling with a corpse.

"Holy Saint Gregory," Moose said. "I never saw them."

"Check the area. Stomp your big number 48's on every centimeter of those plants," Warden ordered. "Fidor, you OK?"

"Son of a bitch got my ear," Fidor said, looking up to give the two a bloody thumb's-up.

"Are you OK while Moose checks the rest of the slough there?"

"Yeah, I've got him covered," he said.

At least that was what Liege thought he'd said. After getting shot in the ear, his accent took a turn for the worse. But he raised his weapon and watched Moose stomp through the plants.

"I think it was only those two. It looks like they were catching some Z's. I guess they rolled over into the mud to hide after we opened up, then when we came down, they tried to take us out," Moose reported.

"Big mistake," Fidor said, his voice steely hard.

"OK, cover us. We're coming down."

Liege and Warden, weapons at the ready, half-ran, half-slid down the slope. Liege landed in five centimeters of water over another ten of mud. It sucked at her feet as she struggled through the two-meter-wide ribbon of vegetation. Breaking through, she immediately went to check on Fidor.

He was right. The PIP soldier had shot him right through the antitragus, taking most of it and the lobule off. The entire lower section of his ear was gone.

Fidor was more angry than anything else. He didn't seem to realize that a centimeter or two to the right, and his head would have been pulverized. There really wasn't much Liege could do except to stop the bleeding and inhibit infections. She gave him a quick Series 4 injection, foamed the wound with disinfectant, and sprayed it with Quick Stop. He'd need to get it treated later, but for now, he was good to go.

The four went up to the PIP position. All four of the soldiers there were dead. The one who'd gone over the cliff was probably dead as well. Liege purposely ignored the substantial body of her kill, taking in just about everything else except the corpse.

She stepped behind the crew-served machinegun, looking over the barrel. Down below, the weapon had perfect fields of fire over the bridge. If Dannyboy had taken his team out to it, they'd have been dead meat.

"What now?" Moose asked Warden.

"Now we cover Dannyboy, of course," Warden said before opening up comms to get the bridge charges laid.

Liege sat with her back to the soldier she'd killed and completely put the other one, the one back at the bushes, out of her mind. Out past the bridge, past the hilltop that blocked their view of the PIP checkpoint, a dark line had appeared some ten or twelve klicks out. The four of them may have just taken out seven soldiers, but there were two divisions of their friends approaching, and they wouldn't be as cooperative in getting zeroed.

Chapter 36

Liege watched Dannyboy's team emplace their charges. The bridge itself shouldn't be too difficult. It was about 15 meters long, 20 meters wide, and hung two or three meters over the creek. The gap over the creek wasn't that wide, and if the oncoming enemy had bridging equipment, they could probably span the creek within ten minutes. The hard part was the area around the bridge, which is why Dannboy's team, with Gidge, their school-trained EOD Maine, had this mission rather than the more straightforward cliff. To make it more difficult to get the bridging equipment to the edge of the downed bridge, the team was going to crater the road, but back from the bridge. It wouldn't make sense to do it too close where the rubble would flow down and accidently fill the gap.

A fifteen-meter gap would be nothing to a Marine Davis or Pangolin. Both vehicles had limited hover capabilities, and they could essentially jump it. But jumping such a huge beast took lots of energy and extra equipment and added significantly to the cost. The Tonyas and Patties were designed with economy in mind, and neither vehicle had hover capabilities. They could traverse some pretty serious terrain, but the gap over the creek would be too much for them. They could sacrifice two Patties, however, simply driving over the edge and into the creek, one after the other, to form a makeshift bridge over which other vehicles could drive.

"How long for the captain?" Moose asked.

"He thinks another 70 or so minutes," Warden answered.

Another eight Marines wouldn't turn the tide of an upcoming fight, but still, Liege would be happy to see them coming down the far side of Grape. She'd thought that they would have already married up, but terrain had worked against them. Seventy minutes was still a long time, however, and, at a minimum, the lead PIP elements should have reached Licorice by then.

Liege looked over to the approach to the hills, trying to figure out how close that lead element was, when something caught her ear. It took her a second to categorize it.

"We've got company coming," she said.

A Tonya was a hydrogen-powered tank, and her engines were almost silent. However, there were so many moving parts in the big vehicle, parts that were not always of the highest cost and quality, so after time, they creaked and squeaked against each other as the tank rumbled along.

They'd just been in a firefight five minutes ago, and that had to have been noted by the PIP forces, but they'd figured they had at least 15 minutes before a reaction force from Licorice could arrive on the scene, and maybe not even reaching them by then. Personnel had been stripped from the checkpoint to head south, and they might simply stay in place until the first element of the divisions arrived. What the team hadn't considered was that there had been anyone close enough to the south to react.

Stupid mistake.

Liege ran to the other side of the beak, but for the same reason the dead soldiers couldn't see them when they were emplacing the charges, she couldn't see the actual road bed.

"What do you got, Doc?" Warden asked.

"One, maybe two Tonyas. A couple of Pattties. I can't see them."

"Dannyboy, get out of there. You've got company coming. We'll blow what you've got."

Dannyboy looked up to them and waved an arm. Within a few heartbeats, three Marines were sprinting for safety, but Dannyboy stayed.

"I said get out of there, Dannyboy!"

"Twenty seconds," Dannyboy passed back. "I'll have the last charge emplaced."

"Doc, where are they? Are they in the blast zone?" Warden shouted to Liege.

"I. . .it's hard to tell. The sounds are echoing," she said as the first fingers of panic threatened to take hold of her. She leaned out over the edge, trying to see anything.

"I think they might—" she started, only to be interrupted by a blast below.

She immediately looked to the bridge just in time to see Dannyboy disappear in an explosion of fire.

"Get back now, Doc!" Warden shouted.

Her feet were moving before she realized what she'd heard, and within a second or two, the entire outcropping shook underneath her, knocking her to the ground. Still prone, she looked back. The edge of the beak still looked whole, but a huge cloud of dust was rising from the gorge.

"Gidge, blow the bridge," Warden passed over the comms.

Liege stood up, hoping that the round that had killed Dannyboy hadn't dislodged the charges. A second later, the bridge erupted into smoke as pieces of it flew high into the air. She edged forward, testing the footing, until she could see straight down below her.

Before Warden had detonated their charges, their view of the road immediately below them had been blocked by a bulge in the outcropping. That bulge had now been sliced off, and tons of rocks had fallen. Beneath her, in the rubble, the dust was heavy, but she could just make out what had to be the back end of a Tonya sticking out through the rubble. A Patty was on its battered side. As she watched, a hatch opened, and a lone figure crawled and flopped out to lie still on the rocks.

Further to the south, where the rubble ended, another Patty was on the road, slightly dented, but upright. Soldiers were pouring out of the back, eyes and weapons pointed up. Liege quickly stepped back out of the line of sight.

"The gorge is blocked," she shouted to the others. "It looks like a Tonya and a Patty are down, but another Patty survived, and the soldiers inside are debarking."

"Going active on comms," Warden announced.

Liege heard him contacting the MEB with a SITREP, then adding a request for air support on the approaching column. Liege felt a welcome wave of relief at that. It was time they were not out there all on their own.

"That's a negative on the air, Granite-Four," came back after only 20 seconds, erasing that feeling of relief. "Assets are needed elsewhere."

"Are you kidding me?" Warden asked, proper comms procedure out the window in his incredulity. "We've got two full divisions coming down on our asses. What are we supposed to do now?"

"Granite-Four, delay the column to the best of your ability."

"What kind of order is that? 'Delay to the best of your ability?'" Warden asked aloud before keying the comms and passing, "You do realize that Granite-Four is a recon team, without heavy offensive capabilities, right?"

There was a ten-second delay, then in a quieter voice as if the Marine at the other end of the comms didn't want to be heard by those around him, "Granite-Four, I hear you. But we've got four divisions heading our way from the east, and the MEB Six is retaining all air assets to protect the capital. You blocked the highway, so whatever else you might do is your and Granite-Three's call. Maybe you delayed them enough; I don't know, so anything you can do to delay them longer will help. I'll see what I can do to free up an air strike, but I can't promise you anything. God be with you. Lightening-Three-Six, out."

Chapter 37

Warden's four-man section ran down the upper trail full tilt, heading to the valley floor. The upper trail ran alongside the high ground, down along Popeye, the smaller hill between Seagull and Licorice, then down the access road from the abandoned home on Popeye to the valley floor. Fifteen minutes later, they burst through the final 20 meters to join Gidge, Teri, and Hank, who'd simply moved along Grape. Warden called a hasty halt as he passed the plan.

"We've got no time," he said, breathing heavily as he caught his breath. "The captain can't get here for another 40, so he's stopping up on the high ground where First Team can give us covering fire. It's not optimum, but it's all we've got."

"Hank, you can fire that thing? For sure?" he asked.

"Ain't nothing, Stein," Hank said. "We had 'em in the militia."

Hank had spent three years in the Panut militia before enlisting in the Marines, and he'd probably thought he'd never have to revert to the older equipment again.

"Me and Teri, we've got it licky-dicky. You just keep dem pipsters offa our asses."

"Team Two, we've got overwatch," the captain's voice came over the comms. "We count nine combatants, an up-armored Lucy, and what looks to be an Adai technical. We're sending you the positions in a moment."

"How about the column?" Warden asked.

"It looks like it's getting underway again. The lead element is at 6.4 klicks."

"Roger. We're commencing in one mike," Warden said.

"OK, you heard him. I was hoping the column would delay longer, but it is what it is."

After the hill and the bridge went up, the entire column, both divisions, had accordioned to a stop. That was poor tactics, a sign that whoever was in charge out there was overly cautious. The lead element, at the very least, should have sped into the assault, linking with the small remaining force at Licorice. Licorice was still out of range for the Marine's arty, and if air hit them, the hills on either side of the checkpoint would offer a small degree of protection. Stopping and bunching up on a highway rendered them sitting ducks—which would matter if the MEB released an air strike. It was poor warfighting, but the Marines had hoped they would delay longer before moving out again.

"We need to move, and move quickly. We've got to be taking them out before they realize we're coming. I'm hoping they're looking to the north to watch their relief, and not back to the south. So let's go stick it in their asses, OK?"

He looked around, but no one said anything. It was a pretty shitty operations order. But there just wasn't any time for anything else. Sometimes, a leader just had to point his Marines in the right direction and then rely on personal training to kick in.

"OK, then, semper fi, do or die!" he said, turning to jog down the side of Grape.

Licorice was only 400 meters ahead. As soon as they cleared the stand of oak and popular, they'd be in clear view of the checkpoint, by then only 200 meters in front of them.

Moose caught up with Liege, and he raised an eyebrow, a shit-eating grin taking over his face. Liege blew him a kiss, M91 at the ready.

Liege was afraid, but surprisingly, that was not her chief emotion. She was excited, her nerves on edge. Intellectually, she knew that she could die within the next few minutes, but running alongside the six Marines in her team, she almost felt invincible.

In the Hollybolly flick *The Invincibles*, during the scene depicting the Battle of Stiklestad, the Norwegian farmer-soldiers poured over the hills, waving their swords and pikes, shouting out the now famous *"Fram! Fram! Bonder!"* as they fell upon King Olaf's professional army. The flick had won two Oscars, largely due to stirring scenes like that. This was real life, though, not a

Hollybolly flick, but Liege felt the same stirring as her team burst through the trees.

Two soldiers were in a fighting position alongside the road, but, as Warden had hoped, both were watching north to the approaching divisions. As they turned to see who was coming, the little wooden shack seemed to come apart as fire from First Team plunged into it.

At the sound of firing, the soldiers ahead of them spun around, surprise evident on their faces. One soldier darted for the technical as rounds pinged off the vehicle. He hugged the side of the technical for cover until Fidor, at a full sprint, zeroed the guy. And that was about all Liege had time to notice before she was engaging.

She cracked off two three-round bursts at a running figure but missed. She and Moose had decided to take positions at either side of a wall, all that was standing from what used to be a decent-sized home or shop. Liege rushed for her position, surprising a soldier who was scrambling for cover. He was an instant slower in recognizing her than she had he, and that was enough. Three rounds stitched him from groin to throat. The soldier had on some ancient, but effective armor, but her throat shot dropped him.

She pushed up against the wall, caught her breath, and looked around. She had several bodies in sight, but no live targets. On the other end of the wall, Moose slammed back-first into it, making the entire thing shudder.

"Some fun now, huh?" he said.

Liege looked around the edge of the wall. Hank and Teri were mounting the Koft 79mm gun. This was the do-or-die moment. The approaching column had to have seen that something was happening at the checkpoint, and they were well within range of the Tonya's main 90mm gun. If they engaged and hit the Koft, the plan, what little of it existed, would be effectively over.

Hank slapped himself in the gun operator's seat and powered the beast up. Liege could see the displays come to life.

Whoever had set in the gun had done a very nice job. A dirt berm had been erected to the front of the gun, putting the main body into defilade. A cover had been placed over the gun, both for concealment as well as protection from airbursts. And as the gun powered up, the tell-tale grasshopper-green glow of counter-beam projectors revealed that the gun had some protection from energy weapons.

Liege tore her eyes away from the Koft, checking the area. The firing had stopped. No Marines had been hit, and it looked like ten soldiers, one more than Team 1 had counted, were down. Liege would have to check them later to see who could be saved—if there was a later.

"The first vehicle is a Tonya," the captain passed from above them. "I'm ranging it at six-one-two-zero from your position."

"Roger that, Captain," Hank said. "Engaging. . .now!"

The big gun belched out a burst of smoke, and Liege tried to look downrange. She saw a flash of light, but her view of the lead vehicles was blocked.

"Hit!" the captain said, the excitement in his voice battling to get out. "Target destroyed."

The big gun belched again, and once more the captain called out a hit, this time on a Patty. Again and again, Hank fired, racking up six hits out of eight fired.

"The idiots only had the one Tonya in the lead element," Moose called out, "and now, with only Patties, they can't reach us. It's a turkey shoot."

Patties were decent-enough armored vehicles, and their 30mm chainguns were effective, but they only had a max range of 3500 meters. While mobile arty and missile launchers could reach them, only the Tonya from the PIP's armor assets had the range to reach the Koft. And with that one Tonya in the lead element knocked out, Moose was right; it was a turkey shoot.

But they have an awful lot of turkeys, Liege reminded herself.

The captain was keeping up a running account of Hank's effect on the column. The lead element was at least ten klicks ahead of the main body, and with the attack on the lead, the main body had stopped in its tracks. The lead element consisted of one Tonya and ten Patties. The tank and five of the Patties had been knocked out of action.

Six Patties as Hank scored yet another hit.

Soldiers were conducting combat debarks as the vehicles got in each other's way. They sprinted to the sides and took cover. Another Patty reversed direction and started back to the north.

"Doc, this one's alive," Fidor shouted out.

Liege turned to where the Marine was standing over the body of a PIP soldier.

"I've got this," Moose said. "Go take a look."

The Koft fired again, and the captain identified another hit as Liege ran to Fidor. There wasn't any incoming, but she wasn't about to just casually saunter over there.

The soldier was alive—barely. He'd been shot low in the back, the round completely severing his spine and blowing out most of his groin in the front. He was breathing erratically, his eyes closed. Liege ran a quick scan, which pretty much validated what she'd seen with her naked eyes.

She gave him a Series 4, then hesitated. She only had 10 ziplocks. The soldier would probably survive if he got into stasis, but Liege had limited resources, and her fellow Marines were her priority. Still, with Dannyboy gone, that left seven of them, including her. Doc Pierce, up the hill with First Team, should have ten more ziplocks with him.

As a member of the team, Liege had killed three of the PIP soldiers today, but as a medical professional, she had to give everyone, friend and enemy alike, the accepted standard of care.

Liege pulled out a ziplock. The soldier came to for a moment, then looked around in panic as he saw the two standing over him.

"Don't worry," Liege said, putting a hand on his shoulder. "You've taken a pretty serious wound, but after regen, you'll be fine. I've got to put you into stasis first, though."

She started to pull the ziplock around the soldier, but he resisted, trying to keep the bag from covering him.

"Fidor, a little help here?"

Together, they basically stuffed the man inside. He clawed at the bag as she activated it, then within moments, fell first into unconsciousness, then into stasis. Once he was completely under, Liege asked Fidor to help her drag the soldier out of the way.

Leaving him against some rubble, she'd done what she could do. He'd have to be treated now by either Federation or PIP forces, whichever side won the battle.

"We've got approximately 50 infantry deployed," the captain continued with his play-by-play.

Liege looked up, but she didn't have a good angle from which to see what had happened. She could see the smoke rising from the destroyed vehicles, but she couldn't make out the infantry.

"Everyone OK? No one hurt?" Warden asked.

Everyone checked in fine. Liege would have never guessed that they could have taken Licorice without a casualty, but the speed of the assault, coupled with the support from First Team, must have been enough.

Still, the soldiers had to have known their brethren to the south had been hit. Who did they think hit them? Whoever was giving orders to them had to be incompetent.

"Mighty nice shooting, Hank," Warden continued. "How many more rounds do you have?"

"I've got nine HEAT[18] and four HE. After that, I might as well be farting at them," he said.

"That might be even more deadly," Moose said, unable to resist.

Hank and the Koft had proven to be a deadly combination. He'd used the old canon to take out 11 armored vehicles. A modern Marine would barely sniff his disdain for the Koft, thinking they might as well be using bows and arrows. But with a good emplacement, aided by very poor enemy tactics, the gun had proven itself to be quite effective.

"We've got movement," the captain said. "Looks like the infantry's up next."

Warden spun around, bringing his glasses up.

"Can't see shit. The terrain's too low."

As the highway approached the hills, the area just to the north of the checkpoint was low, and the mountain creek spread out into a marsh. This was horrible armor terrain, which was why the

---

[18] HEAT: High Explosive Anti-Tank

armor was in columns on the highway. To the south of the hills, the plains were higher, and armor could deploy in the broad formations that gave armor-heads wet-dreams, but to the north, it was really better infantry country.

"Can you give us a view?" Warden asked the captain.

"Wait one."

Within 30 seconds, each Marine in the team had a visual of the area to the north. The burning tank and Patties were clearly visible, but the infantry to the east of Grape were not. A moment later, avatars popped up, showing the locations of the advancing soldiers.

"I'm going to hit them with an HE round," Hank said.

The big gun blasted out a round, followed a few moments later by a muffled explosion. A smaller-than-expected geyser of black mud reached up into the air.

"That's a negative effect on target."

"It's the marsh," Hank shouted, bypassing the comms. "I can't get a good pattern. The mud swallows everything up."

"Can you get an airburst?" Warden shouted back.

"Not with these. They don't have the capability. I told you, this is really old tech."

"Lightening-Three, this is Granite-Three. We've temporarily stopped the armor column at 8734-3396. We've got infantry approaching our position in the marsh abutting Licorice. Requesting air support, Nine-Line[19] to follow—"

"That's a negative, Granite-Three. No support mission will be authorized."

There was a soft click as the captain left the platoon net—undoubtedly to get into it with the FSC.[20] Liege looked to Moose who rolled his eyes. The captain might have missed Warden's confrontation with the FSC earlier.

"Should I fire again?" Hank asked.

"No. No use in wasting your ammo," Warden said.

---

[19] Nine-Line: A set brief designed to call for air support.
[20] FSC: Fire Support Coordinator

"OK, we've got infantry coming in. I'm guessing we've got two hours at most to prepare. Let's see what we can do to give them a warm reception."

Chapter 38

It was closer to three hours before the leading line of the PIP infantry came within range. The team was as ready as they could be, with hasty barricades erected and a few mines laid out in front of them. All the time, the oppressing presence of well over 100 armored vehicles hovered over them. The divisions' armor hadn't advanced yet, but no one really thought that they would stay out of the fight. Once the Koft was knocked out, they would come streaming down Grape, guns ablazing.

The captain, in a foul mood after fighting with the FSC, had gotten into a huge argument with Warden. The captain had wanted to come down and join Second Team, but Warden had stressed he would do more good up above them.

The unspoken message in that was that none of the seven were going to get out of this alive, and it would be foolish to sacrifice anyone else.

The excitement of the battle that had ramped Liege up before was gone. Now, she felt sad more than anything else. Her thoughts kept drifting to her Avó and Leticia. They'd miss her, she knew. She just hoped they weren't kept in the dark on what was going to happen, that they'd be able to get closure.

She was also more than a little angry. She didn't understand why the general wouldn't authorize an airstrike. She didn't understand why they had to stay and fight. She didn't understand why the PIP commander waited three hours to force his way through the pass when he could have been half-way to flanking the line of hills by now.

And she was angry that her friends—and she—had to die.

Not once, though, did her thoughts consider any other alternative. She'd made a contract a long time ago, with the Federation, with the Navy, with the Marines. More importantly, she had a contract with Moose, Warden, Fidor, Hank, Teri, and Gidge. They were her team, and she'd share whatever fate befell them.

Hank and Teri had managed to traverse the Koft so that it was aimed at the PIP infantry's approach. Hank had the barrel almost parallel with the ground, and he thought he could hit the rocks as the infantry came out of the marsh, hurtling pieces of shrapnel out in a deadly cloud.

"Light them up when you can," Warden told him. "We'll act on your cue."

"Roger that," Hank said.

He never got the chance. Screaming out of the sky, a missile plummeted.

"Hank, get out!" Warden shouted, but it was too late.

The missile left a sweeping trail as it curved around and slammed into the Koft. Liege ducked as pieces of the gun peppered the wall behind which she crouched.

As the Koft—along with Hank and Teri—exploded, the infantry rose up and started to fire and maneuver up the rocky slope to the checkpoint.

"Incoming," the captain said, his voice back to his usual calm and collected manner. "Mortars. Impact, 55 seconds."

"Looks like they're finally using some tactics," Moose said sourly.

If the infantry had attacked alone, Moose had thought they could hold out. But with a combined arms attack, Liege knew they had no chance. They could inflict as much damage on the bastards as they could, though, before they fell.

The line of infantry was about 500 meters away, well within range. Liege began to fire, and she was sure she'd seen some soldiers drop. It became evident that the fire teams, squads, or whatever they called their smallest units were moving in a set order, which made it easy to shift fire and pop them as soon as they got up to rush.

And then the first salvo of mortars landed, most against the side of the east hill. Only one or two hit the bottom of the valley, and none close to any of the Marines.

Ten, fifteen of the enemy fell to their fire, but they kept advancing, now starting to fire themselves. Rounds started pinging around Liege.

Two soldiers on the enemy's far right flank plopped down with a crew-served weapon.

"You've got an energy gun on you," someone from above passed. "And we don't have a shot."

"Gidge, the 88," Warden shouted.

"Where? Where is it?"

"Down to our two o'clock," Liege shouted back as she tried to engage the crew.

They were in pretty good defilade, and while she thought she had hit the beam projector, her darts didn't have any effect on it.

The air between the two positions shimmered with ionization as the weapon discharged its first shot. Liege thought she felt her hairs rise from a side lobe, but she knew that could be her imagination. Firing, though, had revealed the team's position to Gidge.

"Got it," Gidge said as he stepped out from his fighting position.

He had his M88 off his back, and with a thunk, the grenade launcher fired.

"Downrange!" he shouted, turning to run back to cover.

Another series of mortars landed, this time corrected to hit them. The second round struck just before Gidge could get down, and the explosion picked him up and flung him 15 meters.

Without thinking about it, Liege ran for him. A round hit her low on her back, but her bones kept it from penetrating. She slid to a stop on her knees beside him, and she immediately knew there was nothing she could do. Gidge had almostbeen cut in two, his head barely attached to his neck. Arterial blood flowed instead of pulsed.

She turned and dove for Gidge's fighting position, ready to carry on the fight. She glanced at the beam projector but couldn't see anything left of the position. Evidently, Gidge had been on target.

"The armor is inbound," the captain passed.

Liege's view down Route Grape was blocked, but it didn't matter. What mattered were the 30 or so infantry who had taken to ground and were now firing on them.

"Lightening-Three, the armor is on the move. SITREP to follow," the captain passed on the command net, which he'd kept slaved to the platoon net.

The members of the platoon could listen in, but not transmit unless actively switching to the net. Liege listened with half an ear as she popped shot after shot at the soldiers. Understandably, they were taking cover, waiting for the arrival of the armor, and Liege didn't think she'd hit anyone. The enemy infantry's mission would now be to keep the Marines pinned and unable to respond to the armor.

Liege darted out from her cover, grabbed Gidge's M88, and dove back. She'd fam-fired[21] the blooper before, but she wasn't an expert. The magazine had five more grenades. Liege put three of them downrange, hitting the general area where the soldiers were taking cover, but once again, she didn't know if she'd hit anyone.

"We need an immediate air strike, Nine-Line to follow," the captain went on.

"No change in circumstances," the FSC interrupted. "No air assets will be released."

"Fucking assholes," Moose said over the P2P. "What the hell do we got Wasps for if we can't use 'em?"

"Didn't you hear? They have to protect the capital," Liege said, a sour taste in her mouth. "And how the hell did Intel just happen to miss four freaking divisions that are coming at them now? It doesn't make sense."

"If we don't get air, Granite-Four will be overrun," the captain passed, his voice hard.

Liege knew that was true, but it was difficult for her to hear her captain say that. He was supposed to give them hope, wasn't he? She snarled, rose over the lip of the broken-down wall, and fired another three-round burst before dropping back into cover.

"Understood. But there will be no air support."

---

[21] Fam-fire: Familiarization fire, a chance to fire a weapon a few times merely to become familiar with it.

There was a very pregnant pause, then as cool as can be, the captain said, "I'm requesting a C12 with the six."

Moose looked back at her, his eyes wide with surprise. He gave her a thumbs-up.

Clause 12 was the right of any Marine, no matter the situation, to request a meeting with his or her commander. In the middle of a battle, a commander could defer the "mast," as the term was known. But back at the MEB headquarters, there wasn't yet any fighting, and for the general to refuse the mast could look bad upon him later.

"Wait one for the six," the FSC passed after only a few moments.

In less than a minute, the net crackled with, "Granite-Three, this is Lightening-Six. You have your mast. So go."

"I've reported that we've got two divisions' worth of armor advancing down Route Grape, and the lead elements are now four klicks from Licorice."

Almost on cue, a round from an advancing Tonya exploded against the side of one of the still-standing buildings. It didn't have much effect on anyone in the team, but it served to keep their heads down.

"Granite-Four has three KIA, and the remaining five Marines. . ."

Four Marines and a sailor, Liege thought

". . .cannot stand up to them. We need air, and we need it now if we are going to stop the column. I've got a Nine-Line ready to transmit. On the record, are you going to accept it or reject it?"

"Oh, too hot to handle!" Moose passed back to her. "The skipper's duking it out for us."

A surge of hope ran through Liege. The captain, probably in a career-ending move, had trapped the general. If the general refused, he'd be on record as having done so, and that could reflect later on him as he came up for promotion. Then again, it might not, but would he risk it?

Liege noticed that not one of the team was putting rounds downrange. They were all hanging onto every transmission. Another tank round exploded, this one deep into the checkpoint.

"Reginald—it's Reginald, right?" the general asked in a supremely artificial buddy-buddy voice. "I wish there was something I could do."

"There is, sir. Authorize the strike."

"Reggie, it's not that easy. We've got four divisions closing in on us here at the capital, and our mission is to defend it. We can't even isolate their positions, so all assets have to pull back here to react when we do locate them."

"We know where our divisions are, sir. Four klicks out."

"Look, I know God-damned well where those divisions are," the general snapped, losing his I'm-your-friend tone. "But I've got more important people to save here. Look, sometimes, we have to sacrifice Marines for the greater good, and this is one of those times. I'm sorry about that, but as a commander, I have to make those decisions."

The hope Liege had felt started to evaporate.

"And I'd sacrifice a hundred Marines if it meant I could succeed in my mission. Captain Vichet, your team is lost, so accept it. You knew that when you didn't join them for the fight, right? I'm not blaming you, because you made a command decision. You tell your team to fight to the last, to delay the armor, and I want you to watch and report back. Colonel Huang needs to know what's heading this way. Then you take the rest of your platoon and exfiltrate back here the best you can."

"If you want to delay the armor, one strike would block the highway, sir, for hours."

"Damn it, Vichet, I've given you your orders, and I don't have time to mollycoddle you. You are relieved of command, and I'm pressing charges. I'll deal with you when all of this is over."

The general cut the connection on the other side.

"Son of a bitch. So we're fucking expendable," Fidor passed on the platoon net.

"Sorry you had to hear that. I just wanted to keep you in the loop," the captain told them.

"And we appreciate that," Warden passed. "But he's right. We *are* expendable."

"Not to me, Stein, not to me," the captain said.

Not to me, either, Liege thought. *I don't feel expendable.*

A line of mortars walked their way across Licorice. Liege barely felt the piece of shrapnel that pinged on her butt, her bones hardening to protect her.

"Granite-Three, this is Oriole-fFve. Sorry, my comms are spotty, but I caught you have a Nine-lLne?"

That caught Liege's attention. Oriole-Five was one of the Wasps.

"Uh, roger, we had. But Lightening-Six shot it down," the captain passed.

"Granite-Three, once again, my comms are wonky. I just heard you pass you had a Nine-Line, but all after that was cut off. I say again, I didn't hear anything you said after that. Please pass your Nine-Line now. I am overhead looking for approaching enemy forces, and I can be at your pos in two mikes."

"Oriole-five, this is Lightening-Three-Alpha-Oscar," a voice came over the net.

Lightening's G-3AO would be the air officer located within the MEB headquarters, Liege knew.

"You are not authorized any additional missions. Granite-three's Nine-line has been denied."

"Granite-Three, I think Lightening keeps trying to contact me, but I can't hear a thing. Nothing. If you have a Nine-Line, I suggest you send it. I'm now 90 seconds from your pos."

Send it! Liege silently implored the captain.

The pilot could hear the MEB, she knew. She was giving herself cover to come save their asses, not that it would do any good. They'd know once they examined her instruments that nothing had been wrong with her comms.

There was another pause, then the captain made his decision.

"Roger that, Nine-Line to follow."

His Nine-Line brief might not have been complete given the time crunch. He cut it down to basically "shoot the bad guys on the road." Fifteen seconds after he sent it, a Wasp came screeching over the hills to make its first run over Route Grape. Her guns were already blazing and she flew low, strafing the PIP armor.

"Yee-haw! Get some," somebody yelled over the net.

Liege watched the pilot crank up her Wasp, a steady stream of orange falling like piss to splash onto the road. She couldn't see the armor itself, but clouds of black smoke reached up into the sky. Liege wanted to stand, shout, and pump her fist in the air, the infantry just 200 meters away notwithstanding.

The Wasp broke high into the sky, her anti-air flares popping out behind her. She conducted a huge loop, coming back around for another pass.

Liege was vaguely aware of MEB raising hell on the net, ordering the pilot to break off, but she didn't bother to listen.

The big, beautiful bird came swooping down for another strike. Her 30mm guns spit out death and destruction.

"She's fucking them up but good," Moose said from where he had his head around the corner of his wall so he could watch.

For the first time in almost four hours, Liege thought she might actually survive. She swore she'd find the pilot when all this was over and buy her a drink—ten drinks.

The Wasp broke off again, reaching for the sky, when it seemed to shudder just the tiniest bit. Liege watched as the smooth arc was interrupted. It looked like the Wasp was falling to the side. When in controlled flight, the Wasp was deadly grace. Oriole-five was wounded, though, and she started to fall awkwardly back to the ground.

"Kick ass, recon," was the last transmission before the Wasp hit the ground 20 klicks away.

Cheers sounded from the PIP infantry. Both sides had quit firing as the Wasp made its run. One run from the Wasp would have wiped out the soldiers, and with it downed, they had regained the upper hand.

With another snarl, Liege stood up and fired on auto down into the soldiers, hitting at least one of them as the guy cheered. He dropped like a rock, but that seemed to remind those around him that nothing was settled. Several opened fire at her, and the fight was back on.

"There has to be 80 vehicles knocked out," the captain passed. "Some tried to make a break for it, off the road, and now everything's blocked. There's no way they're clearing that for at least a couple of hours.

"I've got Doc Pierce and Bumhead moving forward to see if we can't get some better plunging fire on the infantry down there."

Liege looked up the hill. She wasn't 100% positive where the captain was, but while he had great lines of sight down Grape, with the PIP infantry just 200 meters away, the hill blocked his view on them. If Pierce and Bumhead could bring them under fire, they could pick them off one by one.

A large blast sounded from less than 150 meters away.

"I see they found the directional," Moose said. "Maybe that'll slow them down."

The team had emplaced their four C13 Directional Personnel Mines 100-150 meters out from the edge of their position. Each directional could put out 300 stainless steel ball bearings. With a narrow setting, that was a curtain of destruction, as a soldier evidently just found out. If the Marines were lucky, the directional had taken out more than one of them.

Liege didn't like her position. She just couldn't see enough. She looked to Moose to consider if she should get back with him. Moose was on one knee, firing on auto, when he suddenly lurched forward, his face in the dirt. He stayed that way, butt in the air, for a moment until he slid flat.

"Moose!" Liege shouted as she sprinted to him.

Two rounds hit her, and the second one knocked her off her feet, but her bones did their job. She'd be bruised tomorrow—if she had a tomorrow—but the rounds hadn't penetrated.

She turned her friend over. Arterial blood was pouring from his neck, spurting bright red arcs up and splashing on Liege's chest. He'd been leaning forward to fire, and the PIP round had caught him right over his collar, cutting down through his right carotid and into his chest cavity. He'd bleed out in about 90 seconds.

Another round hit her shoulder, knocking her back on her ass. She dragged Moose closer to the wall.

She couldn't hesitate. Reaching into Moose's neck, she tried to squeeze the severed edge of the carotid that was closer to his heart. It slipped two or three times before she was able to get a hold of it. With her left hand, she reached into her kit and pulled out a hemostat, clamping it into place next to her fingers.

The carotid was not the only blood vessel that had been destroyed. Blood was still pouring from him. Liege broke open the AM pack, spreading the foam through as much of his mangled neck as she could. She knew the round had torn up his lung as well, but she had to prioritize her efforts.

With the AM pack administered, she slapped on a number 6 pressure patch.

It's not going to work, she thought.

There was too much damage. But short of cutting him open and getting at his lung, there wasn't much else she could do. The volume of fire from the PIP forces was picking up, and she doubted they'd give her the time for field surgery.

"Fidor, shift right," Warden passed. "You're being flanked!"

Liege knew she had to get Moose into stasis and quick. But he'd lost lots of blood—too much. Stasis with this much blood loss raised the chance of a catastrophic systemic collapse, one in which resurrection might not even be possible. If she could get a Hemocap and a saline into him first, he'd stand a much better chance of survival.

She broke out both packs, piggybacking the Memocaps into the saline, and then thumbed the AV snake free. She activated the snake and watched it worm its way into his cephalic vein. Once it was seated, she lifted the bag with her left hand to let gravity take over.

"Doc, I'm hit!" Fidor shouted out from 30 meters away.

"Where?" she passed on her P2P.

"Right through the foot," he said, calmed by the mere fact of using comms instead of screaming.

"Is it spurting?"

"No, my boot is keeping it tight. But it hurts like shit!"

"OK, keep fighting. I'll get there when I can."

"Doc, how's Moose?" Warden asked.

"Bad, but I'm stabilizing him. Four minutes, five minutes, tops, and I can ziplock him."

"I don't think we've got that long. Can you move him?"

Liege looked down at Moose. He was twice her size, and although she'd bulked up over the years, between his size and the need to keep him still until she could put him in stasis, she didn't think moving him as a possibility.

"Here they come," Warden said. "We've got to move back. Can you move him?"

"No. You go back. I'll stay."

"Fuck that," Fidor said. "I'm coming."

"No! You go!" Liege shouted as Fidor started to sprint to her.

He only made it half-way before an energy beam hit him, his body locking up before it fell stiffly to the ground. The "stiff dive" was the sign that he'd been hit with a disrupter, and his nervous system had been scrambled. There was almost no chance of resurrection from that.

"Fidor," Liege said quietly, the only emotion she allowed herself for the moment.

"Liege! You've got to move back," Warden said.

Three soldiers rushed into view. Liege had laid her M91 just out of reach, a rookie mistake. She pulled the Ruger out of her holster, firing at the three just as they noticed her. Amazingly, all three went down, the first before they started to react, the last getting off a shot that hit Liege dead on the chest.

She gasped for air. Whatever she'd been hit with packed a kick.

"I'm staying here with Moose," she told Warden, barely managing to get the words out.

She looked at the IV pack. She needed another minute for it to empty, then yet another to get Moose ziplocked.

Three rounds hit her side, one after the other, and fire exploded in her left kidney. She went down, her right hand out to stop her fall. One way to defeat the Marines' reactionary armor was to hit the same spot in succession. When the bones embedded in the fabric of the skins hardened, it was only for a moment. As they swung back to normal, the armor inserts were vulnerable for a few seconds at that spot. Hitting at the same spot again before it could recover could defeat the armor. And that's what the PIP soldier had done. At least one round had pierced her skins and bones and had penetrated her left side.

Trying to keep Moose's IV pack high with her left hand, she reached under her body with her right hand and fired her Ruger across her front. She didn't really aim, but at five meters, the soldier who'd just shot her took at least one round low in his belly. He folded over into a fetal position, moaning.

"Are you coming?" Warden asked.

Liege could hear the distinctive chatter of his M114 as he kept fighting.

"I can't. I'm hit."

"Oh, hell, I didn't want to run, either." Warden said.

An energy beam of some sort hit her. Her mind went bright white for a moment, her consciousness gone before the real Liege rushed back into her body. Her skins didn't offer much in the way of protection against energy weapons, but she was still alive, so it must have been a near miss.

Near miss or not, her arms weren't working right. She dropped the IV pack. She couldn't hold it up anymore, so it would have to do. She fumbled out the ziplock just as something exploded near her. Hot knives dug into her neck, but what horrified Liege was the ziplock. It now had at least three rents. It was now useless.

She fumbled out another, but her arms were rubber.

A body landed beside her, and Liege scrambled to pick up her Ruger.

"Need help?" Warden asked as he fired off another burst from his M114.

"I can't get this on him," she said.

Together, the two managed to slide the ziplock over Moose's big body, and with relief, Liege activated it. The lights cycled green.

"Can you walk?"

"I think so," she answered.

"Let's get into Gidge's position. You know, away from here."

Liege's body was failing her, but her mind was back. Warden wanted to get away from Moose so there would be less chance of the PIP soldiers damaging the ziplock while trying to kill the two of them.

"You've got it," she told him.

She stood, then doubled over and screamed as the pain in her side overwhelmed her. Warden put an arm under her right arm and around her back and supported her as they stumbled away from Moose. Liege somehow managed to not only shoot at a soldier with her Ruger, but hit him. She felt a surge of satisfaction as the soldier dropped.

She tried to make her legs move quicker, but they weren't cooperating. She made one last huge effort to reach Gidge's fighting position when the world exploded around her. She was vaguely aware of falling, then of Warden falling on her, when darkness took over.

Chapter 39

Something was tugging at her medkit. Indignation struck her. No one messed with that.

She tried to sit up, but her body wasn't cooperating.

"Moose," she croaked out.

Her kit was for Moose.

She felt her kit being taken away, and she struggled to open her eyes.

Oh, God, it hurts, she realized as waves of pain washed over her.

A PIP soldier had her kit in his hands. He rummaged through it, then pulled out her ziplocks.

"I count seven in here," he said. "You know how to use them, right?"

"Yes, I do," said another voice. "They're not hard."

"But you're really a vet, not a people doc," the soldier with her kit said.

"Medicine is medicine, and as I said, the stasis kits are not difficult to operate."

"OK, if you say so. God knows we need them. I don't know if Suffy's going to pull through, so you gotta save him."

"Don't forget the one on the big Marine. That makes eight of them," another voice said.

Big Marine? Moose! she thought as she tried to figure out what was going on.

She was a prisoner, obviously. *Where were Warden and Moose?*

"No, I told you, once activated, they can't just be taken and used again. They're one-time use only," the vet said.

"We can try," the soldier replied before looking back down at Liege.

"Hey, she's awake," he said, nudging her with his foot.

Liege stifled the scream that tried to escape past her lips.

"So what do we do with them?"

"Zero them," the unseen soldier replied.

"OK," the first soldier said with a shrug as he dropped her medkit and reached to unsling his UKI.

There wasn't any more fear left in Liege. She looked up at her executioner with steady eyes. When she'd gone unconscious, she'd thought she'd already been killed in the battle, so this was just the conclusion of the process. She knew she should yell out, she should try and run, but she just didn't have it in her anymore.

"No!" the vet said. "You can't kill her like that."

The soldier turned to look back, a condescending smile on his face and said, "You heard the second corporal, Doc. Orders are orders."

"And I'm a sub-lieutenant, Private. I outrank him."

The soldier looked confused, then turned to look past Liege to where the second corporal had to be.

"But you're not a real sub-lieutenant," the other soldier said. "You're just a doc."

"Do you see the star on my collar? Does that look real to you?"

"Only one star, Doc. You've got one of those medical thingies on your other collar."

"A caduceus, Second Corporal. But my one star still out-ranks you."

Liege turned her head to see the other soldier, sitting on the remnants of a wall. He looked like anyone she'd see back home, just another guy. There wasn't anything remarkable about him, if you discounted the little fact that it seemed like he had the call on whether she lived or died.

"Touché, mon sub-lieutenant. But pray tell, why should we let this feddie live? These turds killed a lot of us, friends of mine."

"Well, I'd say because we aren't animals, and we follow the UAM[22] Retained Persons Convention. I'd say because who do you think put the brevet major in stasis, saving his life? One of us? I'd

---

[22] UAM: United Assembly of Man, the over-arching organization of humanity.

say because if anyone harms one of the prisoners, I'll bring them up on charges, so if you're going to kill them, you'd better kill me."

"Jason," the first soldier said to the second corporal, "you can't kill the doc. He's gotta save Suffy, right?" He paused for a second as it seemed what else the medical officer had said just registered. "You're saying she saved the brevet major?"

"Who else?"

"Oh, man. I don't think we should kill any of them," the soldier said. "Right, Jason? I mean, we're the good guys here."

Second Corporal Jason got off the wall, walked over to Liege and squatted low, his face centimeters from Liege's face.

He looked her in the eyes for a moment, then whispered, "Lucky girl."

Standing up, he said, "I don't give a shit one way or the other. I'm not going to waste my time here, so, Sub-Lieutenant Horse Doctor, they're all yours."

Over the low wall, a line of vehicles made their way down Route Grape, shaking the ground under Liege.

Chapter 40

"That's about all I can do for you here," Sub-lieutenant Frencle di Murray said as he cut the loose end of the bandage off. "You're going to need surgery soon."

"I need a Series 4," Liege said, then added, "I'm not blaming you for that, though."

Contrary to the Retained Persons Convention, Liege's med kit had been confiscated. That bothered her more than was logical. They'd been a gnat's hair away from being executed, and they would have been had the good doctor not intervened, so why was she still bitching about the kit?

She looked over to where Warden was laid out beside Moose. Moose's ziplock indicator panel still showed a steady green. Warden, despite the fact that Moose had been much worse hurt, was in more danger. Liege would have put him in stasis had she still had the ziplocks, but that was now out of the question. With an interested di Murray assisting, Liege had field-dressed Warden's face, stabilizing his shattered jaw, and inserting a tube scavenged from a destroyed vehicle to keep his airway clear. The airway was vital. He was swelling up, and without the tube, Liege knew he'd already be dead.

She wasn't doing well herself, either. Before she'd let di Murray work on her, she'd put seven of the PIP soldiers into stasis, even "Suffy," with the soldier who'd been about to kill her watching her every move. The young soldier had hugged her when the lights on the ziploc went green, and apologized for well, wanting to zero her. She'd helped treat five other soldiers before a truck picked up the PIP WIA and evacuated them.

Di Murray had examined her, cleaned the entry wound on her side and the gash along the side of her ear where a round had creased her skull, and gave her a broad-spectrum antibiotic. Liege knew she needed more. She was pretty sure she had a concussion, but she was positive that she had internal bleeding. Her belly was distended, and she was running a fever that her native nanos could not contain. Without a simple Series 4, she doubted she had ten hours left, even if di Murray kept promising to get the three recon team members back to a hospital.

He kept telling her that even as a vet, if he just had access to proper equipment, he could treat both Warden and her, but he'd been scooped up in the flash draft, given a uniform, and sent out to war without much in the way of real equipment.

As a Marine, Liege's sworn mission was to escape if captured. Both PIP divisions had filed through the pass and were advancing on the capital. While supply vehicles were rushing back and forth between the staging area some 100 meters north and the main body, there were fewer than 10 soldiers, one being a veterinarian, at Licorice itself. If she'd been even at 50%, she was pretty sure she could escape. But with her fading condition, and with Warden and Moose there, she didn't think that was going to happen.

She took a seat, then slowly leaned back to relieve pressure on her belly. Di Murray nattered on about his practice, how he'd enjoyed working from his specially-outfitted hover, and how he loved cows. Yes, cows.

Liege didn't give a flying hoot about cows. It had only been recently that she could bear the idea of eating real beef, and that was only from cloned tissue, not living, walking, farting animals. His van sounded interesting, though. She wondered why the PIP Army hadn't just had him bring that along with him. It would have been far better than what he had now.

Liege's mind started to wander, her thoughts fading. She realized she was about to slip past consciousness. This was the third time in 10 hours she thought that she was going to die, and three times was too many. Her emotions couldn't take the stress.

A crack of a rifle sounded from over by the old TravelMart.

Stupid soldiers, she thought. *No weapons discipline.*

When a burst of rounds reached her, she sat up. She recognized the reports.

Frencle di Murray stopped his story, looking confused. He stood up, looked about, then dove for his UKI.

"No, Frencle!" Liege shouted, somehow getting to her feet and diving at the doctor, taking him to the ground. "Stop! Stop!"

"Doc, break free! I've got him," Pierce Blumenthal shouted from behind her.

"No, he's OK!" she shouted as di Murray suddenly stopped struggling. "He saved us!"

She slowly turned around. Pierce was lowering his weapon. Behind him, three more very familiar faces appeared.

"You want to blow this joint, Doc?" the skipper asked.

Liege stood up, still blocking their line of fire to the sub-lieutenant.

And for the second time in seven hours, everything went dark around her.

TARAWA

Chapter 41

"I swear, Liege, I'm about go crazy!"

"Sorry, Warden, but that was our agreement. I get *Cloud Nine*, and you get *Rassiter*."

Liege smiled as she turned up the volume. The two had requested to be roommates, and their daily bickering about the channel on the wall screen had become part of the norm. Each could watch something else on their PAs, but it was more fun to bug each other.

Sometimes, it was hard to believe how close it had been. Moose had never been in any real danger. Being in stasis had worked as it was designed. He hadn't even gone through full regen. The cardiobots had worked on his neck and lungs, inserting a mesh around his carotid. He had received only a regimen of local regen, and he returned to full status only five weeks later.

Warden hadn't been much worse. He'd suffered systemic failures, and he'd spent two weeks in full regen before being assigned to inpatient rehab. He kept insisting that this was a vacation. He'd been in full regen twice before, so this was nothing. He was scheduled to be released to an outpatient status in the Wounded Warrior Battalion the following week.

It was Liege, the one who'd been conscious and working on the others, who'd come close to buying the farm, and if Pierce and the rest of First team hadn't reached her in time, she probably would have died. Her fellow corpsman had slapped her into stasis, and she'd stayed like that until reaching Tarawa.

One kidney had been totally shredded, along with her bladder. The bleeding and urine had cut off blood flow. The round itself, along with what it had drawn into her, had infected her intestines, most of her liver, and her spine. The fact that not only had she been conscious, but functional as well, was still a topic of argument among the medical staff at the hospital.

She'd been in regen for a full month getting new organs, only joining Warden in their hospital room two weeks ago. The regen tech had assured her that she'd have a complete recovery after another five months of rehab.

She turned up the volume on the wall screen. If Warden was going to be gone in another week, she was bound and determined to ride him hard until then.

Warden made a dramatically loud sigh and turned on his side. Liege acted like she hadn't noticed him still watching the screen, though, as Katie-Kath told her mother she was dropping out of the university to become a nun.

He bitches, but he loves it.

She paused the show, though, when Captain Vichet walked in. He was attending meetings at HQ for a week and stopped by every day to check up on them.

"How are you two doing?" he asked, adding, "Oh, *Cloud Nine*," when he saw the paused image. "Do you want to know what Katie-Kath does?"

"No!" the two roommates shouted in unison.

Liege had thought that when the skipper disobeyed orders and came down the hill to rescue the three of them, especially after he'd been relieved of command, he'd face a court martial at a minimum. It hadn't quite worked out that way. In fact, it was General Lamonica who was facing charges. He'd probably be demoted and resign rather than face brig time, which Liege thought sucked, but that was the Corps.

Liege didn't find any of this out until she came out of her regen coma, but it turned out there had never been four divisions approaching the capital from the south. It had been a very elaborate and technically amazing feat of spoofing. Approximately 200 PIP soldiers had somehow spoofed not only the loyalists, but a Marine MEB. With the *Sunset City* out of the loop, no one seemed to realize that until the *FS Cypressville* arrived in orbit.

The two divisions Team 2 had faced were the main effort, and they'd reached the outskirts of the capital before the *Cypressville* had arrived and stopped the advance. Another hour or two, and the forces would have been into the city, two divisions facing a single MEB, and too closely entangled for the *Big Cypress* to unleash her full capabilities. Without Team 2, and more importantly, without one Captain Tracile Reyes, who Liege knew as Oriole-five, parts of the city could have fallen before the Navy ship arrived. The MEB would most likely still have prevailed, but at a much, much higher cost in civilian and Marine lives.

The general was not facing charges for ordering Team 2 into a suicide mission; that happens in wartime. But he had not only failed to realize the actual threat, he'd specifically denied the air mission that would have stopped a real, known enemy force.

The fact that the skipper had pulled a C12 on him and had him on record saved his own ass. He'd been reinstated and was back with the platoon on Gobi.

Liege would have loved to confront the general in a court martial, but that was not going to happen. If she couldn't have that, though, the shit he was in was good enough for her.

And she was happy that Captain Reyes had been nominated for a Federation Nova. Pilots didn't get them very often in the infantry-oriented Marines, but Liege thought the award would be well deserved.

The skipper had told her that most of her team would be receiving high-level awards, too. She was OK with that, but the Navy Cross she'd already been awarded was sometimes a little heavier than she'd like, and it was going to get worse.

A surviving drone had captured most of the *Battle of Yancy Station*, as it was now called; Yancy Station being the name of the little rest stop before it had been abandoned in the fighting. Part of that recording had been an image of her firing her Ruger with one hand while holding Moose's IV pack with the other. The image had gone viral, and the Naval Hospital had been inundated with requests for interviews. Liege was protected for the moment, but as a head-shed public affairs major told her only this morning, she'd probably have to face them sometime.

"Fox, you know Gunny Stanerov, right?" the skipper asked.

"Stanerov? Pug? Sure."

"Well, he's inbound. Taking over Team 2."

"Good man," Warden said.

Liege had gotten to know Warden much better, and she knew that hurt him. He was still the Team 2 leader, at least in his mind. But he wouldn't get back to full status for another four or five months, and the Marine Corps had to march on. Warden wouldn't be put out to pasture, though. He'd get something else.

She rolled up the napkin still on her tray from lunch and launched it at Warden, hitting him on the head.

"Good, now you can stop calling Tal and grilling him about the training schedule."

Staff Sergeant Xavier Story, "Tal," had been brought over from Third Platoon to temporarily take over Team 2. With only Moose back on full duty, though, it was an entirely new team.

Warden rolled the napkin back up and threw it back at Liege, missing her head and almost hitting the captain.

"Geeze, glad I'm not relying on you to cover me," she said with a laugh.

And sure enough, a smile reappeared on Warden's face.

"Hello, Dave! Hello Lester!" a familiar voice sounded from out in the ward.

"Run, skipper, if you value your sanity!" Warden said.

"Oh, she's not that bad," Liege said, "especially when she's bringing ginger bars."

Gladiola swept into their room, a force of nature that could not be denied, Liege's Avó swept up in her wake.

"Liegey, darling, how are you today. And Warden, you are looking chipper," she said, coming over to kiss Liege on the cheek.

She placed a vac-pack on the table between the two beds, which Warden immediately snatched. He opened it, took out a ginger bar, and offered the pack to the skipper.

Liege's Avó made his way to her and wormed himself in to give her a peck on the cheek as well.

Liege was extremely pleased to see her Avó doing so well—not just physically, but mentally as well. He was still undergoing treatment, but his appointments were monthly now. His mind seemed as sharp as Liege remembered it before he'd started his slide.

As a man of a certain age, he'd been more than popular with the women of that same age—and on both sides of the scale for quite a long ways. Once he'd started getting better, he'd taken advantage of his popularity with what was essentially serial dating, often with overlapping women. But the effervescent Gladiola had finally nailed her Avó down—and he seemed fine with it. More than that, he seemed happy, and that warmed Liege's heart.

"Avó, Gladiola, this is Captain Vichet, our platoon leader. He was the one who rescued us on new Manitoba."

"Oh, Captain, it's so good to meet you. And thank you so much for what you did, giving us back our Liegey and Warden."

She took him by the hand and physically pulled him in so she could kiss both his cheeks.

"I. . .uh, we should thank Liege and Warden for what they did, ma'am," he said.

"Oh, don't posh me, Captain. I've been around, I have, and I know about false modesty, an affliction that I don't have, I assure you."

Liege had to laugh. Gladiola had it right. Married to a colonel that she'd buried, then a Federation administrator who she'd also buried, she was a rather well-off contractor in her own right. Modesty was not one of her attributes.

"Our Liegey, though, we're so proud of her."

The skipper looked over to Warden and mouthed, "Lie-*gee*?" Warden just laughed.

"And Warden, too. Such a nice boy, maybe a good match for Liegey?"

Liege rolled her eyes. Gladiola always knew best, and she was bound to let others realize that as well. It was impossible to take offense with her, though. And she made her Avó happy.

"Uh, Captain, I've got an idea that I've been thinking about," her Avó said. "I've been telling the gunny here about it, but I think I should talk to you."

"Avó! The captain doesn't want to hear about your flying drill bit," Liege scolded.

"Nonsense, Liege. He's a Marine, and this could be a great weapon," he said, taking the now captive skipper by the arm and pulling him aside. "And I keep telling you, it's not a 'flying drill bit.'"

Captain Vichet was a good sport, listening attentively for 20 minutes while her Avó went into his ideas. He hung around for another 15 minutes before making his regrets. Gladiola and her Avó stayed for another 45 before they left.

Liege gratefully lowered the head of her bed. She loved the two dearly, but they could be a bit exhausting, and she wasn't anywhere near full strength.

Warden held up the vac-pack, offering her the last ginger bar. She flicked her hand, letting him know it was his. He eagerly grabbed it and stuffed the entire bar into his mouth.

"Well, now that that's over for the day, I guess we went well into your time," she told Warden, reaching for the screen control. "I'll change it to *Rassiter*."

"Uh, well, *Cloud Nine* is almost over. If you want, you can leave it there until the end of the episode."

"Really?" Liege asked. "I mean, an agreement's an agreement. I can come back to *Cloud Nine* later, when you're in therapy."

"No, no. I don't mind. *Cloud Nine* is fine."

Liege tried to hide her smile as she booted *Cloud Nine* back up. Both of them settled back into their racks to find out just what Katie-Kath was going to do about her mother.

Epilogue

Twelve years later. . .

Command Master Chief Hospital Corpsman Liege Neves waited impatiently beside the statue of General Lysander. She was in her Navy Service Dress Blues with full medals. And she had more than her fair share of them, right at the top of the display being her Navy Cross with gold star in lieu of a second award.

She'd been recommended for the Federation Nova for her actions on new Manitoba 11, no, 12 years earlier, but it had been downgraded to a Navy Cross—as if the word "downgraded" was even appropriate for the Navy Cross. At first, she'd been disappointed, but being the only servicemember on active duty with two Navy Crosses wasn't too shabby.

And now, as the Senior Enlisted Medical Advisor to the Marine Corps, Liege had reached the pinnacle of her career. With two-and-a-half more years in the billet, she still didn't know what she'd do next. She'd be eligible for one of the major Navy command master chief billets, and she'd probably get one, but after an entire career with the Marines, she wasn't sure she was ready to make the switch and go blue.

Even her Service Dress Blues seemed awkward to her. All her other uniforms were Marine Corps, but corpsmen did not wear the Marine Dress Blues. In formal situations, they wore their Navy uniform.

Liege was aware of a number of enlisted Marines and even a few corpsmen hovering behind her, vultures waiting at a kill. But they gave her room. No one was going to crowd the command master chief.

Finally, the first brand new butter bar started down the path to the statue. Traditionally, the new second lieutenants made the pilgrimage to the statue to render his or her respects. And the enlisted gathered, crocodiles waiting for the wildebeest to cross the river.

The first lieutenant was not her target, so even if his eyes lit up as he saw who was standing there waiting, she deftly stepped aside, refusing to meet his eyes. A Marine behind her quickly stepped up to intercept him.

There! she thought as she spotted her target.

She stepped into the butter bar's path, came to attention, and rendered her best salute.

"Good morning, ma'am!" she almost shouted out.

The second lieutenant came to a halt two paces in front of her, came to attention, and solemnly returned the salute.

"Congratulations, ma'am!"

"Thank you, Command Master Chief."

The lieutenant reached into the tiny pocket of her Dress Blues and removed a silver dollar. Not an electronic credit, but as what most new looeys bought for their first salute, a real, physical coin—in this case a United Federation Marine Corps 325th Anniversary Commemorative Silver Dollar, Liege noticed with a quick glance. She pocketed it without examining it closely.

Command master chief and second lieutenant stared at each other for a few moments before Liege reached out and pulled the lieutenant into a bone-crushing hug.

"Oh, Leti, I'm so proud of you!" Liege said, burying her face onto her sister's shoulder.

The two stayed that way for a good 20 seconds as other new lieutenants made their way to the statue and their first salutes. Liege released Leticia, but their medals got entangled, and they had to slowly disengage themselves. Leticia didn't have Liege's impressive display, but with a BC1 and two BC2s, she'd done pretty well so far for herself.

"OK, go give your regards to the general," Liege told her.

She watched proudly as her little sis marched up to the statue and saluted. A few Marines rushed up to salute her as well, hoping they were her first, only to walk away disappointed when she only saluted them back in return.

Leticia walked back to her, and the two sisters hugged again.

"And how's the househusband?" Liege asked.

"Oh, you know."

"Uh, the 'househusband' can hear you," Vic said from where he was standing, camming the two for posterity.

Four-year-old Lorna and two-year-old Max were hanging from him, ready to run to her.

"Oh, you know. He's doing househusband things." She lowered her voice and said, "And last night, wow, those things were pretty amazing."

"Leti!" Liege said in mock astonishment, punching her shoulder.

"I can still hear you."

Leticia turned to her children, knelt, and held out her arms. Both kids, who'd been strictly told that they had to leave mommy alone until after all the ceremonies, left their daddy and ran on little legs across the grass to hug her. Leticia swept them both up and Vic followed in a more leisurely pace. He gave her a kiss on the cheek as he reached them.

"Househusband things?" he asked innocently, then turning away from his wife, said, "Liege, we're glad you could make it."

"I wouldn't have missed it for the world," Liege said, even if it had been a close thing.

She'd been stuck on Earth for the last three weeks, testifying before council committee after committee. She was proud of her billet, but that was one aspect that she really didn't like. She'd had to tell the commandant himself that she was going to the commissioning, come hell or high water. He'd arranged for her to miss the next testimony, but she'd have to return once more to wrap things up.

"I'm hungry," Lorna said from where she was perched on Leticia's hip.

Vic took her and said, "We're going to eat soon. Avó and Auntie Gladiola are getting the table now, so if you can wait just a little longer, sweetie?"

"Speaking of which, maybe we'd better get going?" he told his wife and sister-in-law.

Vic had matured into a fine husband and father. With his family wealth, he didn't have to work, even when Leticia was corporal and sergeant, so the "househusband" label that Liege liked to tease him with was not that far off. Most of all, he was good for Leticia, and for that, Liege was eternally grateful.

Leticia had Vic. Avó had Gladiola. Liege wondered what her future held.

As if reading her thoughts, Leticia asked, "So, you're still on for February?"

"Yeah, the 20th."

"I've already put in for leave," Leticia said. "Only five days, though."

Leticia was assigned to 1/13, out on New Palestine, and new second looeys were not expected to take leave throughout their first assignment. But as they both knew, family came first.

"That is, if you still want to slum with us enlisted scum. I was thinking of asking Sergeant Major Papp if she wanted to fill in for you."

"What? That's not going to happen!"

"I don't know, you being an officer and all now," Liege said as she took Max's hand and they all started to walk to the parking lot.

"OK, for my first official order as a second lieutenant in the United Federation Marine Corps, I order you to keep me as your bridesmaid."

"Well, when you put it that way, aye-aye, ma'am!"

Leticia leaned over to give her another quick hug as they walked.

"Hard to imagine, my sister, the command master chief hospital corpsman for the Marines, and Warden, the Second Marine Division sergeant major, getting hitched."

Liege just smiled. It was hard getting her mind wrapped around it as well. But when Warden proposed, seemingly out of the blue, she suddenly realized that they'd been working up to it for a long time, and it was the right thing to do.

It still scared the shit out of her.

Liege looked to where Vic had taken a knee to talk to his young children, catching him saying, ". . .and the tavern's called the Globe and Laurel. It's very famous. And mommy's lieutenant class, they put up a box on the wall for their future. We'll go see it. Isn't that nice?"

"Do they have strawberry sandwiches?" Lorna asked. "I like strawberry sandwiches."

"I know you do, sweetie, and we'll see what we can do."

Liege took a deep breath, as if she could smell Tarawa, smell Marine headquarters. Around her, new lieutenants were slowly scattering, families in tow. They were the new Corps, at least from as far as officers went. These men and women would lead the Corps in the future, long after she had retired. And Leticia was one of the new crop of leaders. Liege wasn't done yet, but she was getting closer to when the uniform came off.

But not yet.

She gave Max's hand a squeeze. Her sister had been an under-educated daughter of the favelas, and now she was a second lieutenant in the Marines and had a loving family. Her Avó's mind had been gone, leaving him an empty shell, and now he was his old self and was married to a wonderful, if eccentric woman.

And Liege, she had joined the Navy to save her family. She had succeeded in that. But it hadn't been the sacrifice she'd first considered it to be. It hadn't been merely a stepping stone to learn a trade. It had become her very being. She was a Navy Corpsman, and that filled her with pride. And now, she was about to start a new chapter in her life as one-half of a married couple.

Me, married! The ultimate party girl getting hitched!

Only, the party girl had been an illusion that was left behind long ago, and Liege didn't miss her.

A huge smile broke out over her face. Life didn't get any better than this.

Thanks for reading *Corpsman*. I hope you enjoyed it. As always, I welcome a review on Amazon, Goodreads, or any other outlet.

If you would like updates on new books releases, news, or special offers, please consider signing up for my mailing list. Your email will not be sold, rented, or in any other way disseminated. If you are interested, please sign up at the link below:

http://eepurl.com/bnFSHH

Other Books by Jonathan Brazee

Women of the United Federation Marines
Gladiator
Sniper
Corpsman

The Return of the Marines Trilogy
The Few
The Proud
The Marines

The Al Anbar Chronicles: First Marine Expeditionary Force--Iraq
Prisoner of Fallujah
Combat Corpsman
Sniper

The United Federation Marine Corps
Recruit
Sergeant
Lieutenant
Captain
Major
Lieutenant Colonel
Colonel
Commandant

Rebel
(Set in the UFMC universe.)

Werewolf of Marines
Werewolf of Marines: Semper Lycanus
Werewolf of Marines: Patria Lycanus
Werewolf of Marines: Pax Lycanus

To The Shores of Tripoli

Wererat

Darwin's Quest: The Search for the Ultimate Survivor

Venus: A Paleolithic Short Story

Non-Fiction

Exercise for a Longer Life

Author Website
http://www.jonathanbrazee.com

Printed in Great Britain
by Amazon

32546949R00131